MY BROTHER'S KEEPER

MY BROTHER'S KEEPER

Keith Gilman

severn
House

This first world edition published 2011
in Great Britain and in the USA by
SEVERN HOUSE PUBLISHERS LTD of
9–15 High Street, Sutton, Surrey, England, SM1 1DF.

British Library Cataloguing in Publication Data

Gilman, Keith.
  My brother's keeper.
  1. Ex-police officers–Fiction. 2. Private investigators–
  Fiction. 3. Organized crime–Pennsylvania–Philadelphia–
  Fiction. 4. Murder–Investigation–Fiction. 5. Detective
  and mystery stories.
  I. Title
  813.6-dc22

ISBN-13: 978-0-7278-8102-1 (cased)

All Severn House titles are printed on acid-free paper.

Severn House Publishers support The Forest Stewardship Council [FSC],
the leading international forest certification organisation. All our titles that
are printed on Greenpeace-approved FSC-certified paper carry the FSC logo.

FSC
MIX
Paper from
responsible sources
www.fsc.org   FSC® C018575

Typeset by Palimpsest Book Production Ltd.,
Falkirk, Stirlingshire, Scotland.
Printed and bound in Great Britain by
MPG Books Ltd., Bodmin, Cornwall.

Last Exit Before Toll

PROLOGUE

The cops called it Judy Garland Park. It was less than a square city block of stunted trees and trampled grass and withered rose bushes strangling in a bed of noxious weeds. The old ladies from the neighborhood had once taken great pride in caring for their precious roses, waiting for them to bloom a rich red in spring, their aroma saturating the air and acting like an aphrodisiac on anyone who caught their scent. No one seemed able to resist. Young and old alike, male and female, all succumbed to their power. It was only natural. It was the power of love. It was the power of sex.

Susie Randall could be seen there all the time with her watering can and clippers, pruning the drooping vines and repairing the trellis that circled the small garden. Rumor had it that Grace Kelly used to go there and paint, setting her easel near the stone wall and pushing her hair back against the wind, the brush in her delicate hand barely touching the canvas. And there were others, the famous and the infamous.

It sat on a wedge of ground between 22nd and Lombard, walking distance from Center City. And even on a cold night, the darkness of Judy Garland Park seemed to come alive with the movement of shadows between the trees and sound, whispering voices and moans and an occasional scream. There were parks just like it all over the city. Philadelphia seemed to have a love affair with its parks, as if it needed some place to escape from all that asphalt and concrete. Even if it was only for an hour, a place to go for lunch, somewhere to sit alone and read a book or just think; a place you could be yourself, where you could forget the person you pretended to be all day and be someone totally different.

But no one was ever really alone there. The park had eyes and ears. And no one stayed there very long. It was much too dangerous.

*   *   *

Not long after Susie Randall's rose bushes withered and died and Grace Kelly's paintings found their way into the dusty attic of time, Judy Garland Park had become a haven for the sexually adventurous of Philadelphia, the sexually ambivalent, the sexually curious, the sexually perverse and the sexually confused. Men trawled the tattered lawns and shaded corners looking for other men. There were straight men and gay men and everything in between, men dressed as women, women who had once been men. The transvestite population seemed to take refuge there – men looking for something to make them feel whole, make them feel special, make them feel loved, men searching for their true selves, men willing to do anything just to feel good. And it all seemed to culminate in one long orgasm.

But it wasn't enough. It would never be enough. And with sex came violence. It wasn't long before the first body turned up.

It was the body of a man in his early thirties with a full head of hair and a rugged, wind-blown face, well dressed in a wool coat, scarf and gloves and a pair of stiff leather shoes. No one needed to ask where he'd come from. He didn't live in the neighborhood. That was obvious. He'd followed Lombard Avenue from downtown. He could have had a car nearby but probably not. Maybe he'd followed somebody. Maybe he'd seen a man and what he thought was a woman, walking arm in arm toward the park. He'd decided to follow, keeping a good distance back and hiding behind the stone wall where those decrepit vines still clung though they hadn't produced a flower in years.

The police had conducted interviews and heard the same story. They'd all seen him. At this stage of the game, he'd seemed content to just watch. And that was OK because most of the regulars at Judy Garland Park preferred an audience. It was one more thing to heighten their pleasure, knowing someone was looking and playing it to the hilt. Not such a difficult game to understand, breaking down sexual barriers, starting down that slippery slope. Breaking barriers was what some people did best. It often started with a tendency toward voyeurism. It wasn't that kind of luring the papers had been talking about; it wasn't that blatant. It was more like spying, like a haughty old spinster poking her nose through the lace curtain at the window, peering at a pair of young lovers kissing in a car.

He wouldn't have been the only one testing the waters of Judy Garland Park. There were others. They'd drive by, their eyes wide with anticipation, giving a casual wave or a nod from the comfort of their car. They'd see something out of the corner of their eye. It would look like a woman, heavy with make-up, strong legs under a clinging red cocktail dress, a little awkward on high heels, a lot of blonde hair. He would think how cold she must be with all that exposed skin, using it as an excuse to pull over and say hello.

Night after night it was the same routine, the cruising up and down Lombard Avenue, an elaborate game of watching and longing, a dance choreographed to send a message: *I'm not what you think. I'm different than I look. I'm just like you.* They would summon the nerve to cross over the threshold of Judy Garland Park, a place that appeared charming, even innocent by day but brooding with a bizarre attraction at night. The sun would set behind the skyline of Philadelphia and the transformation would be in full swing, like some masquerade ball where no one really knows who is who.

None of the witnesses the police had spoken to had had any contact with him. They'd begun seeing him one evening on Lombard as if he'd been walking home from work. Occasionally he'd stop and feign some conversation on his cell phone, light a cigarette while his wandering eyes seemed to be surveying the terrain. The last time anybody remembered seeing him he was strolling into the shadows with the woman in the tight red dress and spiked heels. What happened after that, the cops could only speculate.

They kept referring to him as the victim. And he was a victim, of his own impulsiveness if nothing else. And if he was a victim, then the killer was a victim as well.

By police standards, he wouldn't be a typical murderer. He didn't kill out of greed or jealousy or revenge. This would have been his first kill and it was probably planned. Not organized in every detail but something he'd been thinking about, dreaming about, going over in his mind until the opportunity presented itself; an act of murder he'd carried out in multiple scenarios in his imagination. The only pattern to his crimes being that the act of murder and the act of sex had become interwoven in his nightly visions.

He'd be in a sort of disguise when the spirit of Judy Garland Park took possession of him. It was to be his unveiling. The humiliation and paranoia he'd once felt had disappeared. The ridicule could no longer touch him. It had all fallen away, molted like the skin of a snake. Now, he was able to defend himself. He was justified. He would draw blood no matter whose and afterward he'd call it up in his memory and it would give him strength. He'd relive it in all its potency and it would sustain him. It would be something real, something he'd be able to see and smell and even taste.

He had escorted his victim into the shadows, lured him there with whispers, with a body that was lean and hard but yielding, with a mane of blonde hair, a long flowing wig smelling of musk and smoke, with accoutrements and adornments, rings and earrings, piercings that seemed to stitch together the skin on his strong, feminine face. He was entirely hairless, his arms and legs and his head beneath the wig shaved clean. And when the moonlight caught his eyes, black and hypnotic and wild, there was death in them and his victim would suddenly know it was too late, that he'd made a terrible mistake.

From what the cops had pieced together, from the position of the body and its condition, they'd been standing against the stone wall. There had been shoe prints in the soft ground. They'd been close. There had been an exchange of fibers. They'd found hairs from the blonde wig and sequins from the red dress. There had been an exchange of saliva. They'd kissed and in their excitement they'd reeled back against the damp stone.

The cops had taken pictures and soil samples and measured the blood splatter and, if they hadn't known better, they would have presumed there'd been a struggle. But that wasn't the case. Pleasure had preceded the crime, mutual pleasure certainly, the killer initiating a sexual encounter that essentially trapped his victim. The pain that followed would come during a final moment of terror meant to coincide with his victim's ultimate sexual release, a deep, throbbing pain accompanied by an enormous amount of blood and a slow death, coming like a dream, like a demanding, insistent sleep.

The killer had fallen to his knees before his victim. He wasn't in a hurry at that point. He wanted this man to succumb to a pleasure only he could provide. He needed him to give in to it. He wanted him aroused, engorged with warm blood. He wanted him under his control, consumed with the passion, a slave to it, unable to live without it and ready to die for it.

The body had been discovered later that morning in the cold darkness of Judy Garland Park. At first glance he could have been one of the many homeless of Philadelphia. But as the sun rose slowly in the east and the growing light chased the walking dead from the park, the lingering face of death became unmistakable. The medical examiner had listed the cause of death as massive hemorrhaging. The instrument of death was a box cutter, a brand-new razor blade as sharp as a surgeon's scalpel. The dilated veins had been cut with precision along with the stretched tendons and elongated muscle. The victim had undoubtedly been taken by surprise, considering the location and the intimacy of the wounds. He'd been castrated.

The howling could be heard blocks away but no one had thought to call the police. They thought maybe a dog had been hit by a car.

ONE

He'd heard the scream before. He was sure of it. Not just in the dream but somewhere else, somewhere in the past, a past already flooded with anonymous screams.

Bathed in sweat, he tore at the sodden sheets, his sleeping hours consumed by the same recurrent dream. He was digging, a hole in the ground opening beneath him. He looked down at his soiled hands, the skin blistered and sore, his arms on fire as the sharp metal point of the shovel touched upon something in the darkness. He'd groan aloud in his sleep, the sweat burning his eyes as he peeled away layers of dirt and rock. There was something down there. Or was it someone?

And even in sleep, he stood over the freshly dug grave and listened, thinking he heard movement, thinking this wasn't a dream at all.

And then the scream would reach him, shrill and animal-like, calling out to him in a wailing echo that trailed off and went silent, night after night, the eyes of a child staring at him out of the darkness, out of the earth, always those same pleading eyes meeting his, her mouth sealed shut as if her lips had melted together under a layer of wax.

He recognized the face but it had been so long since he'd seen her. He'd hoped he would have forgotten. It seemed now that the chapter of his life that had defined him as a cop and her as one of the nameless victims had been suddenly reopened, the wound still not healed. But she did have a name. It was Catherine Waites and she'd been nine years old. And just lately, he'd begun thinking of her again, becoming obsessed with the dreadful event that had brought them together and the terrible confusion that followed.

The district attorney had called it a miscarriage of justice. Lou believed that also but for very different reasons. And even after his dismissal from the Philadelphia Police Department and the long separation from his family and the inevitable divorce, he still believed it. But now he wasn't remembering it right, not seeing it as it had actually occurred. His thoughts had become tangled in false memory and it was slowly suffocating him.

He recalled the face of Catherine Waites in vivid detail: the diminutive features, the slim freckled nose and dull green eyes like dusty emeralds, the reddish-blonde hair the color of honey. And yet she would sometimes drift away from him, a fading, elusive image that would escape from his mind's eye and hang just out of reach like some dim, night-time shadow.

Shaken from sleep, lying awake in his bed or more often on the couch, he tried to remember the details of that night so long ago but he couldn't seem to remember the scream. Because there wasn't one or it was a silent scream, if that's even possible. Maybe it was better that way, better to forget, better that he roll over and wish it all away.

*   *   *

He'd awakened cold and stunned in the night heat of a Philadelphia summer, with the air like vapor, smelling of something old, something stagnant like dirty water in the street. He'd bolted upright, the face still flashing before him, the dream replaced by the overwhelming silence of his mother's house, where he'd come back to live only a year ago, where he'd hoped the dreams would finally stop. But he'd been wrong. They hadn't stopped. They'd followed him home like a faithful dog, waiting at the edge of the bed for him to drift off.

He'd sit there in the dark, asking himself if he'd really heard the scream at all. Though it had sounded so real, how could he have heard it? What he remembered most about that night was the quiet, the overwhelming stillness that preceded his discovery of Catherine Waites pinned to the ground, a thick hand pressed ruthlessly over her lips, preventing her from uttering a sound. He was seeing it so often now, hearing it almost every night: an uninterrupted scream that would sometimes take on a musical quality, one long note that seemed to go on and on, the ringing in his ears continuing even after the screaming stopped. He would cover his face and close his eyes and if he had to go on hearing it, he thought, he would go crazy.

But even with his eyes closed, the fear he'd seen in the girl's eyes was still there. And every day that fear became all the more real as if it was a thing unto itself, a living thing that could take on any shape it desired. And that fear lived in him as well. And though he wasn't the victim, it became more than he could bear. For in the dream, the face of the child was transformed into the face of his own daughter, her eyes turned to him, beckoning him to save her, to either be saved or helped to die, knowing her life could never be the same.

And then the guilt would come, in waves like a typhoon over an unprotected beach, coming during those waking moments when he'd asked himself how self-pity came to replace the iron will he'd once admired most in himself, remembering a time when he'd worn the uniform of the Philadelphia Police Department with pride, when he'd pin a badge to his chest and fit a gun into the holster on his hip and wouldn't dare feel sorry for himself. It was possible, he feared, that his will had been permanently broken and that Lou Klein, the man, and Lou Klein, the cop, had become two very separate people, one estranged from the other.

There had been other dreams as well: dreams of falling, dropping out of the sky from some unimaginable height, unable to catch his breath as the ground came up to meet him. And dreams where he was running, his feet heavy and unwilling to obey the command of his whispering voice to move faster, faster. Running for his life, he thought now. He'd been dragging himself along a dark city sidewalk, clinging to a chain-link fence that seemed always to have him boxed in. He recognized the place. The basketball courts at Eighth and Locust, where he'd played in the Police League on Sunday nights. Though, thinking about it now, it could have been any playground in the city.

It could have been Parkside, where he'd played as a kid with his friends from Wynnefield. It could have been on Diamond, where in his last year as a cop he'd seen thirteen-year-old Sheila Foster take her last breath, bleeding out from a stray bullet while she watched her older brother dunk the ball for her cheering girlfriends.

He thought it strange that as the dreamer he was a witness to these events and not a participant, though he often awoke gasping for air, his heart pounding like a drum. These dreams weren't so hard to figure out. He'd always preferred to objectify his emotions, crumple them up like a scrap of paper and toss them into the garbage where they belonged. There were so many things he was running from, so much of his past closing in on him, the past and present on a collision course.

And now that he'd stopped running there was only the screaming child left to his dreams, though her face would no longer be that of a child, not after all these years. It would be a young woman's, maybe nineteen years old, the same age as his daughter, her hair a dirty blonde or frosted silver, her eyes opaque against the lightness of her hair. But it was that scream, real or imagined, that was a constant reminder of the incident that changed his life, ending his career as a cop. A call for help that pushed him over the edge.

The truth of the matter was that he'd saved a girl's life. There was always that. With four or five blows from a retractable steel baton he'd reduced a sexual predator into a drooling cripple. But something had happened in him as well, some change. Lou Klein had gone from being a policeman, a father and a husband, to someone else. What or who that someone else was, he still wasn't sure.

It had begun as a routine call in a quiet residential neighborhood on the outskirts of the city. Somebody had called 911 and said they'd heard a scream, maybe the scream Lou had heard in his dreams. He'd never know. He'd been close by and he'd responded as most cops would, regardless of the fact that it had already been a very long day and he was exhausted and the insomnia that gripped him now had begun to take hold even then. He'd responded because he had to, because his conscience told him to, though he hadn't been dispatched. It wasn't his call. He could have turned down the volume on his police radio, parked behind some abandoned building and let his eyes drift shut until the end of his shift.

He had even thought about it for a second. Why not? he asked himself. After the way he'd been treated by the department, passed over for promotion, the worst assignments, pressure from above. They'd been trying to push him out for a long time and they'd made his life miserable in the process. So why go the extra mile? Why do anything at all if he didn't have to?

But he did answer the call and even as he'd searched for the address in the dark and double-parked his police car on the street, he'd had a premonition. This was the type of call that came back to haunt you, the wrong place at the wrong time, the type of call where cops got hurt. It was a feeling that stuck with him, a feeling he couldn't put his finger on, a vague apprehension that seemed to crawl around in the back of his head telling him that this day would end badly. And end badly it had.

He'd climbed the front steps of a small brick colonial and knocked lightly on the door. The shades were drawn down over the front windows. He tipped up the lid of the mailbox and reached inside, hoping to find an envelope with a name on it. There was nothing. He did find the front door slightly ajar and he entered cautiously, fingering the padded grip of his duty weapon and then unsnapping the retention strap on the holster.

This shouldn't be happening, he thought. Not here. If someone had screamed, it was probably a cheerleader rooting for the local high-school football team. Anything else just didn't make sense.

Northeast Philly was a section of the city where many of the cops chose to live, a place of extended families where grandmothers could still walk to the Mayfair market and grandfathers sat at the Frankford Diner passing around pictures of their grandchildren. Pictures they kept on the front of their refrigerators: their children's children in various stages of development, smiling toothless smiles, bar mitzvah pictures and graduation pictures, all held together by an assortment of magnets they'd brought up with them from Florida, plastic-coated magnets advertising the local plumber, a landscaper, a funeral home.

As he made his way through the house, through an outdated kitchen to the back door, he was already talking himself out of it, hoping the only thing he'd find was an old alley cat rummaging through an open garbage can. On the back porch there were open garbage cans and he had seen a cat peering at him from the shadows. The yard was surrounded by high green bushes in a perfect square. And in the grass, not far from the set of steep wooden steps, he'd seen her.

In a fleeting instant all his fears seemed drawn together into a great black hole. There was a moment of hesitation followed by a realization that he no longer had the luxury of delay. He forced his mind to focus. He had no time to think. For Catherine Waites, with whom he would be inexorably linked from that point forward, time was running out as she lay on her back, stunned as a fawn in a lion's jaw.

How many times had he relived it? As many times as she must have in the years following? He doubted it. All he saw at first was the broad back of a man, a monster with no neck and a bald, dimpled head and legs like tree trunks that seemed to blot out the girl's body. His hand was over her mouth, leaving only those wide glassy eyes looking for somewhere to go, looking at the darkening sky as if it could bear witness to the crimes against her, looking to the sagging porch and to the bushes and to the fence behind the bushes and then to him.

If his presence had elicited some faint glimmer of hope in those eyes, she didn't show it. Nor had she given him away. If he'd contemplated what he was about to do, he might have taken some other course of action. He couldn't remember how many times he'd hit the man. He'd approached silently from behind and struck without warning, aiming for the back of the man's head, shiny with sweat. The doctors at the hospital said it was a miracle the man was even alive. But Lou hadn't seen him as a man. He was more like an insect beneath his shoe, a parasite, and if there were such a thing as miracles, Lou thought, that thing would have died right then and there.

His name was Stegman and when they wheeled him into the courthouse, paralyzed from the waist down, and the charges against him were dropped by the state because of alleged police brutality, Lou knew he could no longer participate in the broken system of justice he'd been a part his whole life. His badge and gun had already been taken from him but that had been a mere formality, a symbolic gesture that meant nothing to him then and even less now. He'd been emptied, his soul still lost in that backyard. And if any part of him had survived it had been lost in that courtroom. He'd kept a partial pension but the chapter of his life as a Philadelphia police officer was over.

TWO

Cars flew down Remington Road, avoiding the traffic on Haverford Avenue. They did it every morning, trying to beat the rush into the city. Jimmy Patterson and the other residents of Remington Road, people who had lived on that street their whole lives, who'd inherited homes from their parents and were raising their own kids on that very same street, were sick of calling the police and asking why there were so many cars going down their street, a narrow winding road in a residential neighborhood. They were sick of the cops' condescending attitude, telling them there was nothing they could do and that no laws were being broken. They'd hang up the phone in disgust and look out their front windows at the cars zipping by, coming dangerously close to the line of parked cars on both

sides of the street. They'd look nervously at their children waiting
for the bus.

The procession of bumper-to-bumper traffic moved along like
a long passenger train snaking from one stop to the next. The
school bus would come slowly down the street and cars would
squeeze past it, ignoring the flashing red lights and the blinking
stop sign and the group of irate young mothers huddled together
on the cracked slate sidewalk who would hold their coats tightly
across their breasts and shake their fists in the air. Then they'd
throw their cigarettes down and watch them bounce off the
weathered pavement and fall into the trickle of water backing up
in the gutter, the sewer grate blocked by a pile of wet brown
leaves. They'd wave to their children as the bus drove away,
trying to get a last glimpse of them, all hats and gloves behind
the fogged windows.

It wasn't just happening on Remington Road. It was happening
in every neighborhood in Philadelphia.

Jimmy had come out that morning and discovered his car had
been sideswiped, a long, thin scratch across the driver's side
door. He'd have to report it to the police if he planned on filing
a claim with the insurance company. By the time the cops arrived
he'd be two hours late for work and rush hour would be over
and there would be no sense in complaining about the speeding
cars because they'd be long gone.

The cop that eventually showed up was a baby-faced rookie.
Jimmy could see where he'd cut himself shaving that morning
and he could smell the fresh oil on his brand-new gun. The cop
looked around from behind a pair of mirrored shades at the
suddenly empty street, wondering what all the fuss was about.
He stared reflectively at the bare metal showing through the dark
green paint, running his fingertips over it, the kind of scratch
done with a key. It would have made a noise like fingernails on
a blackboard. Not an accident, he imagined. He held a clipboard
in his hand and began jotting down numbers on a report with a
ballpoint.

'You sure it's not vandalism?' the cop had inevitably asked.
'There are a lot of kids in this neighborhood. You know how kids
can be.'

'Lotsa kids around here,' Jimmy agreed. 'But they know better than to be scratchin' the paint on my car. They know what'd happen to 'em.'

Jimmy waved at Lou Klein, who was jogging slowly up the opposite side of the street.

Lou was running every morning now. He'd quit smoking and had decided he didn't want to be one of those ex-cops who blew out a valve at fifty after signing over the remnants of a police pension to an ex-wife who had never liked him very much.

He figured he had a few more good years left and chasing the bad guys around town kept him young, though his decision to become a private detective still haunted him. He didn't have much of a choice, it seemed. It had been thrust upon him, evolving from city cop to private eye like so many other cops before him. But for Lou it had been personal, and not a day went by that he didn't weigh it out, the pros and the cons, the risks and the rewards. And the regrets. There were plenty of those.

It had started with a woman, the wife of an old friend, his partner back in the glory days when they rode the Nineteenth Precinct together. She had a daughter that was giving her trouble and she needed help. His friend was dead but there had been promises made, promises that Lou had intended to keep. He'd tried his best to fulfill those promises but he'd fallen short and the specter of failure seemed to hang over him. Maybe that's why he stayed in the game. He still had something to prove.

There were days when it ate him alive. It was the kind of regret he could taste. It came out of his pores as he ran, a sour sweat dripping down his face. Some things you just needed to learn to live with. Even the whiskey hadn't been able to wash it away. That's what happened when you dredged up the past, he'd told himself. Nothing good ever came of it.

It was days like this one, churning his tired legs up Remington Road, that he wondered if he could still do the job, if he wasn't just wasting his time, clinging to some misguided sense of purpose. He'd known guys that had hung on too long, tried to go it alone as private detectives and had lost it all, more than just their self-respect. They'd turned into caustic old men. And for what? They'd tried to prove something to themselves and ended up losing their pensions, their families and sometimes even their lives.

The morning sun wasn't doing much to warm his back and the crisp November wind stung his face. The summer had come and gone like a flower and with the sun becoming scarce he was already turning pale. His mouth was dry. November mornings in Philadelphia would never change, Lou thought: ice-cold mornings, frost-covered cars, black ice and everybody holding their breath, waiting for the afternoon warm-up when the sun would peek through the clouds for a scant few hours.

Jimmy Patterson had been a cop right there alongside Lou and Joey Giordano at the Nineteenth Precinct, back in the days when Rizzo was chief and the cops could do whatever the hell they wanted. Once Goode became mayor and that whole MOVE thing put the spotlight on Philly, a lot of guys bailed out, took early retirement just to avoid taking the heat for someone else's mistakes.

It was about that time Jimmy had busted his knee dragging a four-hundred-pound guy in a wheelchair down three flights of stairs in a working apartment fire. Now he was subsidizing his meager disability pension by selling cars at the Honda dealership and working a security gig at Haverford College. Lou had responded to the same fire. He'd been on the third floor, kicking in doors and clearing rooms, when the smoke got to him. Two firemen with air packs had dragged him out by his shirt. They'd dropped him in the front yard as if he was a stray cat they'd pulled from a tree and stuck an oxygen mask on his face before going back inside the burning building. He should have taken his disability right then and there, walked out the door behind his old pal, Jimmy Patterson. If he'd had a crystal ball, if he'd been able to see what was coming, he would have done just that.

On Lou's first day out running, he'd seen Jimmy coming down the front steps of a brick twin on Remington and recognized him immediately. They'd been more than just casual acquaintances. There had been some history between them, ancient history now. A rumor had once gotten back to Jimmy that Lou had been chasing Franny Patterson around with his tongue hanging out, as if maybe he'd forgotten she was Jimmy Patterson's little sister.

It wasn't just a rumor, though he wouldn't have been the first cop to get his hopes up about Franny Patterson – false hopes for the most part. It came to a head in front of the Penn Wynne Firehouse in one of those legendary confrontations where no one was sober enough to remember who threw the first punch or who threw the last. They were both still standing at the end and to this day neither of them had ever admitted defeat.

Now, Lou would see Jimmy every morning dressed up nice for work in a sport jacket, a collared shirt, pressed pants and a pair of polished Dockers. He'd slow down a little, trudging up that long hill, and Jimmy would say something to him and Lou would say something back. It had become a ritual.

Lou was running three miles regardless of the weather and Remington Road was the last leg, taking him back toward the office in time for a quick shower and then breakfast at the Regal. He was breathing heavily as he drew closer to Jimmy Patterson, who was waving his arms and pointing at the scratch on the car and then up the road in the direction he'd assumed the striking vehicle had come. The cop kept writing, ignoring Jimmy and Lou, seemingly annoyed that his new job was turning out to be nothing but a lot of paperwork and that he had twenty more years of it ahead of him.

'It's a goddamn hit-and-run. That's what it is. And you better write it up that way,' Jimmy yelled. 'Hey, Lou, you better watch you don't give yourself a heart attack.'

Lou put a hand over his chest and wiped the sweat from his forehead. He wore a blue sweatshirt and sweat pants and a pair of black leather sneakers laced up over his ankles. He stopped in front of them, his legs still moving, running in place.

'You better watch you don't get yourself arrested.'

'It would take three more guys like this one to lock me up.'

'Why don't you give your brother a call? He's still a cop, isn't he?'

'You see what I mean? It's no wonder Philly's a shithole.'

Lou heard the screech of rubber on the road. Jimmy heard it, too. If the cop heard it, he didn't show it. Maybe he was too engrossed in his report to turn around. A white Mustang convertible was negotiating the curve at the top of the hill. There was a girl driving. She looked in her early twenties with a lot of blonde hair, spinning the wheel with two fingers and talking on the phone. The music was blaring and her dark, oversized sunglasses had fallen down on her face. The car was moving too fast. The windshield was a reflection of glaring white light. Jimmy backed up onto the sidewalk and Lou followed.

The next sound they heard was the crash. The Mustang rear-ended the police car with enough force to move it three feet forward. The front bumper of the police car clipped the cop at the knees and sent him to the ground. There was glass all over the road.

The blonde behind the wheel hadn't been wearing her seatbelt and she'd kissed the windshield with her nose and mouth and was slumped down in the seat, bleeding into her lap. The windshield hadn't shattered but a spider's web of cracked glass had formed where the girl's head had made contact. Lou looked over at the cop who was pulling himself slowly to his feet, keeping his right leg awkwardly straight, his mirrored shades hanging on by one ear. Jimmy ran over to the Mustang. The steel crunched as he ripped open the driver's door, the music still blasting from the stereo. He reached inside and took the girl by the shoulders and gently eased her back in the seat.

Her face looked like it had been cracked in half. Her forehead was split down the middle and her nose was obviously broken. The blood ran freely from both nostrils, pooling in her open mouth. Her head was beginning to swell from her hairline to her eyebrows.

Lou was trying to help the young cop who was bracing himself against the side of his police car and hopping toward the door. He shook Lou off and reached inside for the microphone, muttering in a high-pitched whine like a child who had just pissed his pants. He was trying to give his location but he was unsure exactly where he was. Lou had seen grown men piss themselves before. They were either very scared or dead.

Jimmy was holding the blonde upright in the seat, watching air bubbles pop through the blood in her mouth. She was making that kind of gurgling sound, a sort of snoring that was often followed by no breathing at all. Lou thought she might have had a couple of broken ribs to go with the crushed face, maybe even a punctured lung.

Across the street, an old lady in a light blue housecoat had come out of her front door and stood watching from her porch, peering through the bare branches of an old maple tree, the few remaining leaves fluttering precariously in the cold morning breeze, determined to hang on for one more day. She leaned on the wooden rail to get a better view and the handset of a portable telephone slipped from the pocket of her housecoat. She probably would have called the police if she hadn't seen the police car in the middle of the street. Why bother, she thought, the cops were already there.

Jimmy kept the palm of his hand against the girl's forehead. He didn't want to move her. That much he remembered. She was starting to go into seizure. Her head and shoulders had begun to shake and her eyes fluttered and rolled back into their sockets, showing a cloudy white sclera, speckled with blood. A drop of blood trickled from her left ear and ran down the side of her face. It was a bad sign.

'I think her eggs are scrambled, Lou.'

'Hang on,' Lou whispered, 'just hang on,' repeating it silently to himself, not sure if he was talking to Jimmy or the girl.

They heard the sirens and in the next minute a police car roared around the corner with an ambulance right behind it. The cop with the bruised knee tried to look poised and uninjured. He'd managed to adjust his sunglasses, which now sat lopsided on the bridge of his nose. Another police car came around the corner, an unmarked blue Ford with a white shirt behind the wheel. Patrolmen wore blue.

The unmarked navigated around the wreck and came to a screeching halt. The door flew open and Lieutenant Kevin Mitchell swung out his two feet, put them flat on the ground and pushed himself up from the vehicle with a low groan as if he had a bad back or a nagging case of heartburn. He took one look at Lou and shook his head in disgust, the smirk showing at the corners of his mouth.

'As soon as I heard this come out, you know whose face popped into my mind? Lou Klein. Don't ask me why. Maybe because of the location or maybe because I'd spent almost thirty years with the Philadelphia Police Department and knew what kind of cluster fuck I'd find when I got here.'

'It's good to see you too, Mitch.'

A gust of wind caught the wave of coarse gray hair that flowed over the flat top of his head, exposing a broad, tightly-knit forehead, shiny with sweat. He squinted in the sunlight, his eyebrows knitted together, forming a continuous ridge over his steel-blue eyes. The color of his eyes seemed to match the color of his hair and the black pinpoint irises shown in stark contrast. If he was cold he didn't show it.

The skin on his face looked freshly shaven. Mitch always looked freshly shaven, as if he was one of those cops that kept an electric shaver planted deep in a desk drawer and took advantage of every idle moment to whip it out and run it a few times around his hanging cheeks and nub of a jaw. He probably liked the way it sounded, the electric buzz, and he liked the way it felt, the vibrating steel blades massaging his thick skin.

'Put yourself in my shoes, Lou. I got the radio on the desk and I hear, "vehicle into a police car," as if a police car was some kind of fixed object. It couldn't have been a vehicle into a tree or a pole or even a hydrant. But into a *police car*, like we can't even get out of our own goddamn way anymore.'

'Take it easy, Mitch. You have an injured officer over there and a badly hurt girl.'

'He don't look injured.'

'He's doing a good job at hiding it.'

'She gonna make it?'

Mitch pointed with his chin at the ambulance crew loading the girl onto the stretcher and then loading the stretcher into the back of the ambulance. The paramedic already had her hooked up to a monitor and was preparing an IV.

'Honestly, Mitch? It doesn't look good.'

'If she dies the *Inquirer* will have a field day. They've been crucifying us lately.'

'Why's that?'

'Homicides are up. Manpower is down. Every thug in the city is running around with a gun in his pants.'

'Since when are you guys to blame for that?'

'Since when did it matter?'

Jimmy Patterson was wiping the blood off his hands with a paper towel as he walked slowly toward Lou and Mitch. His eyes

seemed to have glazed over and the color had drained from
his face.

'You all right, Jimmy?' Lou asked. 'You look like you could
use a drink.'

'I'm fine,' Jimmy answered. 'Funny how it all comes back to
you. After so many years in the business you just know what
to do.'

'What kind of business is that?' Mitch asked.

Jimmy looked at Mitch as if he'd just noticed him standing
there, as if Mitch had interrupted a private conversation, poked
his nose in where it wasn't wanted. And if he hadn't had a badge
pinned to his chest and a gun on his hip, Jimmy might have
taken a swing at him. It was the kind of look that cops used to
intimidate people, only nobody was intimidated by cops anymore.

'The cop business,' Jimmy barked, 'the business of helping
people.'

Mitch grabbed hold of his duty belt with both hands and hiked
his pants up a little higher over his protruding belly. The gun in
his holster had an undisturbed layer of dust on it about half an
inch thick. He started to get back in his car and paused.

'Try to stay out of trouble, would ya, Lou?'

Mitch slammed the car door shut before Lou could answer
and sped away.

'How the hell did you tolerate that guy for all those years?
He was one of the reasons I wanted out.'

'He's not as bad as he looks.'

'I guess that's a matter of opinion.' Jimmy was looking down
at the towel in his hands, smeared with fresh blood. 'Can I ask
you something, Lou?'

'Yeah, sure, Jimmy.'

'How does someone go about hiring you, like, for a job?'

'What kind of job did you have in mind?'

'It's Franny. She hasn't been herself lately. She's worried. I
mean, really worried. I don't know what it's about. Something's
up and she won't tell me what it is. I think it has something to
do with her husband.'

'Since when does Jimmy Patterson ask for help, especially when
it comes to his family, and especially from a private detective?'

'It's a different world out there, Lou. Maybe I'm different. I don't know. And you don't know this husband of hers. Franny married money, big money. Don't get me wrong, I'm not afraid of him. I could take him without battin' an eye. But if he wanted to, he could get the muscle to push back and I don't want to put Franny in the middle.'

'If he wanted to?'

'Yeah, if he wanted to.'

'Who is this guy?'

'His name's Haggerty. Brian Haggerty. Ya heard of him?'

'I've heard the name.'

'He talks all high and mighty, always polite, the college boy charm. But he don't fool me. I know Franny falls for that shit. But I'm telling you, Lou, the guy's nothing special, grew up on the same streets we did. He's no different than me or you.'

'OK.'

'His old man was a big shot in the city but that was a long time ago and you know how we are around here, Lou. We got short memories.'

'More like selective memory. We remember what we want to remember.'

'Whatever.'

'You just relax, Jimmy, and don't go doing something crazy.'

Jimmy patted Lou on the back.

'Same old Lou: a nice guy. Catch more bees with honey, right, Lou?'

As they were standing there facing each other, the sun had crept higher in the sky behind them and the temperature had risen by a few degrees. The tow truck had the white Mustang hooked up and ready to haul away. The driver was still sweeping broken glass off the street. The police car looked drivable but they wouldn't move it until the highway safety unit got there and took a few pictures and drew a few diagrams and wrote up the accident report so as to relieve the Philadelphia Police Department of any liability.

Suddenly Lou and Jimmy found themselves alone on the street.

'The family's still got money, Lou, but the old lady, Brian's mother, seems to control most of it. Eleanor Haggerty. She's a real piece of work. Hates Franny. Thinks she's not good enough for her son.'

'Not uncommon for mothers to disapprove of their son's choice in women.'

'Yeah, but this goes a lot deeper.'

'Is that what Franny says?'

'Franny's staying with me for now and she's not saying much. You'd have to see them together to know what I mean. I never liked it, Lou. But you know, no one could tell Franny what to do.'

'What do you want me to do?'

'How about I bring her up to your office later this afternoon? I think she'll talk to you. She was always able to talk to you. I'm asking as a friend, Lou. Just talk to her.'

'Yeah, OK, Jimmy.'

Jimmy was smiling now, with the sun on his face and the street in front of his house quieter than it had ever been. The cops had placed barricades at both ends of Remington Road and nothing was coming up or going down. The old lady across the street had seen enough and went back into her house, slamming the door behind her, either because the neighborhood was going down the drain and she'd seen enough or because the show was over and she hadn't gotten her money's worth.

'Do you ever get sick of it, Lou? I mean, listening to people's problems, hearing the same shit over and over again. Don't you ever feel like telling them all to go to hell?'

'Sometimes.'

'Sometimes? Is that all you have to say? Does anything ever bother you?'

'Just 'cause I don't show it, doesn't mean I don't feel it. If I let everything get to me, I wouldn't be any good to anyone, would I?'

'I guess not.'

'There is one thing that does bother me, though.'

'What's that?'

'People who talk like they know it all but never spent a day in anyone else's shoes. You know what I mean. We've seen things, Jimmy, and done things most people only see on television, things they wouldn't dream of doing themselves because, down deep, they're afraid. They depend on people like you and me and I'd like to slap them sometimes when they presume to know what we know, in here.'

Lou put his hand out and tapped Jimmy in the chest just over where his heart would be.

'I usually slap them before it gets to that point.'

'I'm keeping an open mind on Haggerty. If the guy senses hostility he might get suspicious. Gets harder to catch him in something. Or he gets defensive and it's harder to negotiate.'

'Negotiate?'

'As in divorce. As in settlement. I've dealt with these types before. They'll do anything to avoid a scandal and they don't like parting with their money.'

'You think it'll come to that, Lou? Franny'll be crushed.'

'I don't know.'

'What if he wants to play hardball?'

'Then we play.'

'Play how?'

Lou wiped a drop of sweat from his forehead with his shirtsleeve.

'I'll give you an example. I did a favor for a couple of guys last year, took me three hours. I'd been taking my lunches, the liquid variety, in Craig's Tavern in Drexel Hill and one day I met these three Mexican landscapers who could barely speak English. I didn't know how the hell they made it to Philly and I didn't care. Anyway, they hadn't been paid for a job and all they wanted was their money but they didn't know how to go about getting it.'

'So whad'ya do?'

'They bought me six or seven beers and drove me to this big stone mansion on Lexington Avenue. I rang the doorbell and asked the shithead who opened the door if he hired a couple Mexicans to cut his lawn and trim the pubic hairs on his asshole.'

'What did he say to that?'

'He ordered me off his property and threatened to call the cops. But by that time, I had to piss like a fucking racehorse. So I turned my back to him, unzipped my fly and started pissing on his freshly trimmed junipers.'

'Did you get the money?'

'What do you think?'

THREE

ou had rented a second-floor office on Lancaster Avenue in Bryn Mawr. If there was a high-rent district left anywhere in Philadelphia, Bryn Mawr was it. At least that's what the zip code would tell prospective clients, the wealthy and the spoiled from the suburbs who didn't know shit about the city anymore except what they saw through the streaked-glass windows of their high-rise office buildings. They'd see Bryn Mawr and think Lou Klein was the type of private dick who knew the difference between his ass and a hole in the ground.

It was two rooms over a Chinese laundry, up a dark, constricted staircase that smelled like urine and ammonia. Even in the high-rent district, the homeless needed a place to crash and it wasn't their fault if the accommodation failed to provide adequate facilities. Lou had signed the lease earlier in the month while sitting at a table in Starbucks with the landlord, a retired teacher from the Philadelphia School District with a bad comb-over and a twitching left eye. He'd dropped two sets of keys on the table in front of Lou and bought him a latte and a dried-out piece of yellow sponge cake. He'd failed to mention that Lou wouldn't need the keys since he'd stopped repairing the broken lock on the stairwell door a long time ago.

The next morning Lou had gone over early with a bucket and a mop and a few old T-shirts he used as rags and a toolbox full of rusty screwdrivers, a wrench, a hammer and a tape measure. He stopped at the Home Depot on the way over for a pack of sandpaper and a can of paint. The color on the label said Eggshell.

The screen door had let out a squeal as he yanked it open and the guy asleep on the stairs pried his eyes open and rolled over with a congested groan. They had stared at each other for a long second, Lou noticing the pint bottle of cheap bourbon poking out of a crumpled brown bag on the stair. Lou had stepped back and propped the door open with a brick that appeared to be there for that exact purpose. He'd slid the brick into place with his foot hoping a little cold air would motivate the guy to check out early. He'd looked a little too comfortable and Lou had assumed he was a regular.

It smelled like an open sewer in there. Lou had put the bucket and the toolbox down in the foyer with a thud and reached around on the inside wall for a light switch. He'd found the switch and been surprised when a dim bulb clicked on at the top of the stairs.

The guy had been wearing a green and black Philadelphia Eagles knit hat pulled down low over his forehead. His clouded red eyes had slowly opened. He'd used his green army field jacket as a blanket, a bare knee poking out through a tear in his jeans. A pair of socks that might have been white at one time bunched up around his calves. His work boots were stained with black tar. He had a scraggly gray beard and a red nose etched with thin blue blood vessels. He'd sat up and put on the jacket and reached for the bottle, tightening the cap and sliding it into his pocket. He'd grabbed hold of the banister and pulled himself slowly to his feet.

'Have a nice day,' Lou had said to him, trying not to breathe as he walked away. The guy hadn't responded but as he'd stumbled toward the door he'd pivoted loosely on one leg and took a wild punch at Lou's face. Lou had dodged the punch easily. He'd expected it, learning from experience that drunks often woke up swinging. Lou decided not to hold it against him and had simply grabbed him by the arm and pointed him toward the corner.

The guy had turned a toothless grin back toward Lou and disappeared into the alley behind the building. Just then the fans had kicked on at the laundry with a roar like a jet engine. Lou had mopped the stairs and wiped down the walls, and when he'd been satisfied that the stains he couldn't remove were permanent he'd put down a welcome mat and spilled the dirty water from the bucket into the street.

Lou got back to the office after his run and his meeting with Jimmy Patterson and quickly peeled out of his running clothes. He stuffed them into a green garbage bag and when the bag was full he'd drop it off with the little Chinese lady downstairs. By the next morning it would be waiting for him in front of his door, the clothes washed and folded. She was the kind of girl next door he'd always dreamed of – did his laundry, didn't ask for money and couldn't speak a word of English.

The office bathroom was the size of a small closet. There was a toilet, a pedestal sink, and a shower he'd installed himself. He'd cut into an adjoining wall to do it and tapped into a hot-water pipe from the laundry below. There would never be a shortage of hot water and it would never cost him a dime.

He turned on the shower and let it run until the tiny room filled with steam. He stared at his naked body through a growing layer of condensation on the mirror. He might have lost a few pounds but not many. The weight was getting redistributed and that was about all he could hope for. He stuck out his chest and sucked in his gut and tried to picture himself as a twenty-eight-year-old beat cop, walking the streets of West Philadelphia for the first time and trying to live up to his father's reputation. His father had been a legend at the department, big shoes to fill. Lou let the air out of his lungs; his chest deflated and his belly sagged a little and the mirror became further obscured by the rising steam. He stepped under the hot water, letting it pound his shoulders and roll down his back.

He threw on the same suit of clothes from the day before: a navy blue sport coat over a light blue button-down and a pair of khakis with a brown belt. He'd never been one to shave every day and today was no exception, leaving a rough, day-old shadow across his face. He slipped into a pair of brown shoes and drove over to the Regal Deli, where he'd meet Joey Giordano for breakfast.

The Regal Deli was an institution. There weren't many places like it still standing and there didn't seem to be anyone left in the neighborhood that could remember a time when the Regal wasn't there. The ceiling inside was tin, laden with six layers of peeling paint the color and texture of dried avocado. In front of the counter was a line of chrome stools with a chrome foot rail across the stained linoleum floor. The chrome had been polished and new vinyl glued to each seat, but they were the original stools, the same stools that Philly cops had been warming their asses on since before they gave them cars to drive around. They still let out a human-like shriek when someone spun away from the counter.

Lou walked through the front door and Joey Giordano rotated slowly away from a stack of pancakes dripping with maple syrup.

'Where the hell have you been?'

'Talking to a client.'

'Yeah, right.'

Heshy Rigalski's voice boomed from behind the counter, where he was making a pot of fresh coffee and dumping the remnants of the old pot down the drain. He stood in front of a large steel sink. He turned the water on full force and it sounded as if a pipe had burst in the basement. His balding head was dripping with sweat and the white apron tied around his waist had turned a dingy gray. His Russian accent was still thick, even after forty years behind the counter at the Regal Deli.

'You are late.'

'Nice of you to notice, Hesh.'

'I mean late with the money, Officer. You have balance due. You eat here every day and I don't see no money. "Put it on tab," you say.'

'You'll get it, Hesh. Stop worrying. Have I ever stiffed you?'

'I do worry. Your father, he eats here every day, like you. He pays. Every time.'

'My father was a good man, Hesh, and a good cop. But he's dead. So for now you're stuck with me.'

'Stuck?'

'Yeah, stuck. It's an expression, Hesh, like you can't get rid of me, like I'm sticky with glue, never go away, difficult to peel off. You get it?'

'I got it. Like fly on flypaper. Flap wings but don't go nowhere.'

'You got it, Hesh.'

Lou cracked a hesitant smile and turned toward a set of swinging double doors where his daughter, Maggie, had emerged from the kitchen in a black apron and white shirt, a yellow pencil tucked behind her ear. She sped past them, grabbing a couple menus off the counter. An elderly couple had taken a booth in the back and Maggie approached them with a smile. She handed them the menus and they sat, squinting at the small lettering and glancing at each other over the top of the molded plastic as if they were still in love after a lifetime of late breakfasts at the Regal Deli. Maggie poured them each a cup of decaf coffee and turned, saving the tail end of her smile for her father.

Heshy filled a cup of coffee for Lou and set it on the counter in front of him. Maggie slid behind the counter, smoothing back her hair and retying her ponytail. With her hair off her face and flat against her head, Lou thought she looked like her mother back in the day, back when they'd first met, when he believed he'd found a woman who wasn't afraid of a little hard work, a woman who could deal with the daily struggle of being a cop's wife. Those days were long gone and now as he took a second look at his daughter, he realized how startling the resemblance actually was. But it was a physical likeness only and as he sipped his coffee, he smiled.

Lou had arranged for her to work at the Regal while she was in school. At first he'd asked Hesh as a favor, but it turned out to be a good arrangement for everybody. Maggie never had to ask Lou for money and she was typically too tired to do anything but work, study and sleep. Heshy had even offered her one of the apartments over the deli, a one-bedroom with an entrance on the side. She'd gotten excited about it and asked her father for his permission, though she was old enough not to need it.

She'd been living with him and he'd hoped they would be comfortable together, back in his mother's house, in the old neighborhood on Meridian Avenue where he'd grown up. The house hadn't changed that much. The neighborhood had but he'd hoped since she'd come back into his life she could have learned to love the place as he had, let it become a part of her. But she'd found out what had happened there, knew of her grandmother's murder, knew how long she'd laid there on the floor in the Philadelphia heat. Maggie had never been able to erase it from her mind. And it wasn't from lack of trying. She slept there and ate there but always her eyes went to the spot on the kitchen floor where her grandmother's body was found and a chill went down her spine.

Maggie set out napkins, knives and forks and paper placemats in front of her customers in the booth. She brought them eggs and toast and refilled their cups. Lou sipped his coffee and turned toward Joey.

'Sorry I'm late.'

'Forget about it. Any trouble?'

'Not really.'

'You don't sound very convincing.'

'Remember I told you I've been seeing Jimmy Patterson on my morning runs? Well, I ran into him again today and he wants me to look into a little problem his sister is having with her husband.'

'His sister, huh?'

'Yeah, Franny Patterson. You remember her. Jimmy's little sister.'

'Sure. I thought we didn't do divorce work. Too sticky, you said.'

'Normally I wouldn't touch it, but I've known Jimmy a long time. And I don't think I have the whole story. He's bringing her by the office this afternoon.'

'Franny Patterson? You used to have something going with her, right?'

'I wouldn't say that.'

'I won't say it if you don't want me to. Come to think of it, Lou, there were a lot of girls that you had something going with. But you never seemed to end up with any of them.'

'I get off to a good start but I don't finish well.'

'Whatever you say.'

They both sipped their coffee. Joey pawed the morning paper, crumpling the corners in his meaty hands.

'You know a guy named Brian Haggerty?'

'I know the name.'

'Yeah, that's what I said.'

'He's probably Billy Haggerty's kid. Everybody's heard of William Haggerty.'

'That's right. I know who you're talking about now. Had a couple of run-ins with him myself.'

'He ran the unions down on the docks, back in the days when that fucking meant something.'

'And it doesn't mean anything now?'

'It's all about money now.'

'It was always all about money, Joey.'

'Yeah, but now big money calls the shots. Back then you could be a union boss and wield a lot of power and not necessarily be filthy rich. You'd get rich, if you played your cards right, like Haggerty did. But it wasn't just about the money. It was about control.'

'You mean control over people.'

'Exactly. What good is money if you can't get any work done?'

'Yeah, but how do you stay in control? Money buys a lot of loyalty.'

Joey folded the paper in half and swatted a fly on the counter. A fluorescent light began to flicker in the ceiling. Heshy got under it and tapped the ceiling with the point of a broom handle. The flickering stopped.

'Guys like Haggerty had personality, Lou. They used intimidation, sure. But they kept to their own. They lived in Irish neighborhoods. They employed Irish people. Haggerty was like a fucking saint to those people. If Franny Patterson's husband has got Billy Haggerty's blood in his veins, he's a son of a bitch.'

'Franny always did have good taste in men.'

'Is that why she dumped you?'

'Maybe she set her sights too high. Franny was always a bit of a social climber, Joey. She wanted status. She craved it, if you ask me. I think that's what finally broke us up. And she needed to be in control. Maybe when she landed Brian Haggerty she bit off more than she could chew.'

'Something tells me Franny Patterson wouldn't have any trouble fitting in with the Haggertys.'

'You didn't know her like I did. She wasn't as confident as you think. She dressed the part but she was covering up.'

'Covering up for what?'

'Insecurities. Her working-class background. Her father was a fireman. Her brothers were cops. No real money in the family, no education. That bothered her. All she had was her looks. And she knew she wouldn't have them forever.'

'You make her sound desperate, Lou.'

'I remember when she worked as a salesgirl at Boscov's. She'd spend her whole paycheck, money she couldn't afford to waste, on expensive clothes. Just to look like something she wasn't.'

'And what was that?'

'Class.'

'Well, if she's married to Brian Haggerty, she's got it now.'

The lunch crowd was starting to filter in. A group of college kids slid their backpacks under a booth and crammed three to a side. A few businessmen in suits and ties followed. Workmen from the construction site down the block pushed two tables together and gathered around it. They tracked in mud on their boots and their faces were flushed and sweaty under the visors of their wrinkled baseball caps.

Lou watched Maggie wait tables. Lunch was her time to make money and she hustled. She was about the same age as the kids wedged into the booth but they seemed like children compared to her, a distinction Lou was noticing for the first time. How fast she'd grown up. And though she had the same athletic build as her mother, the same quiet intensity, the same vivid concentration buried in the dark furrowed ridges above her eyes, it seemed like such a cleaner look on her – more alive, more vital.

His wife had possessed those same qualities. That was before she'd made the transition from a young working mother to a bored suburban housewife, before she'd gotten rid of him and married a real-estate lawyer, the first of two subsequent marriages. Maggie had dreaded the idea of her mother marrying for money and after she watched her mother lose the lawyer and hook up with the family dentist she decided that she preferred life in the city with her father, working at Heshy's and eating diner food. There was something honest about their time together and every day Lou was seeing more of the world through her eyes.

'What part of town they from, Joey?'

'The old man has a big house up in Torresdale but he's been dead a long time now. Went out with a real bang, too.'

'What do you mean?'

'They found him in bed with his son's first wife, very naked and very dead. Both of 'em.'

'Jesus Christ! He was fooling around with his son's wife?'

'Don't sound so shocked. These people might have money but they're no different than some of the scumbags you and I locked up. They just dress nicer.'

'I'm assuming they didn't die of natural causes.'

'The DA called it a murder/suicide and the whole thing went away.'

'What do you think really happened?'

'The same as you would, same as everybody else. That Brian Haggerty did it, probably in the heat of passion. Found them in bed together and started blasting. But he bought someone off and they never proved anything.'

'Did anyone try?'

'They went through the motions but I don't think anyone really cared what the truth was. The whole city was having too much fun fantasizing about it, coming up with their own theories. Brian Haggerty never admitted to anything. Half the city didn't care and the other half didn't blame him for what he did. Don't act so surprised, Lou. You were a cop in this town almost as long as I was.'

'Do you think Franny knows about it?'

'Ask her when you see her.'

'How do you learn this shit, Joey?'

'It's all in the papers, Lou.'

Joey reached for the rolled-up newspaper and touched it gently to each of Lou's shoulders. Lou grabbed the paper from Joey's hand, rolled it a little tighter and jabbed him in the ribs with it. Joey flinched and his elbow toppled the coffee cup, spilling the last remaining liquid onto the counter. The coffee had grown cold anyway.

'Nobody knows Philly like you, Joey.'

Heshy mopped up the spill with a wet rag and wrung it out in the sink.

'A Philly boy through and through.'

Heshy switched on the slicer and started slicing corned beef. The spinning blade whined as it shaved the meat into paper-thin slices. Heshy would catch each slice in his flattened palm and slap it onto a piece of wax paper until the pile grew to about three inches high. Then he'd grab the paper at the corners and drop it onto a scale. He'd fold the paper over and seal it with a strip of tape and scribble something illegible on the package in black marker and toss it into a wide steel refrigerator.

Lou and Joey watched Heshy work, mesmerized by the sound of the machine and the motion of his hands. There were beads of perspiration on Heshy's forehead.

'I wonder if he counts his fingers after he's done?'

'Funny. I was wondering the same thing.'

FOUR

They took separate cars back to the office. Joey parked his white Cadillac in a lot across the street. The lot belonged to a rug shop owned by two Pakistani brothers. Joey couldn't tell them apart and when they'd first moved in Joey flashed his badge a couple times and had them both believing he was still a cop.

Joey had always driven a Cadillac, a Fleetwood and then a Deville, a long sedan with spoke wheels, a cloth roof and leather interior. He had a Cadillac before he joined the department, a white one with red leather interior. His ex-wife, Marie, had gone nuts over it. She was the spoiled rotten daughter of Petey Santi, the baby of the family and used to getting whatever she wanted. Petey ran the seventh ward from his office over the Pellegrino Social Club and Joey had always been on good terms with him. Petey got Joey his first promotion. But since the divorce Joey was sure Petey had it out for him. Joey still walked around the car three times, looked under all four tires and checked the trunk before he got in. And he never parked on the street. Never.

These days Lou couldn't have cared less what he drove. He'd gotten rid of his old black Thunderbird and bought himself a used four-door Honda. He was sick of listening to Heshy and Joey ride him about driving a car older than his daughter. They'd told him it looked like a relic from a fifties drive-in movie. He hadn't really gotten rid of it. Joey rented a garage on 54th Street, just off Lebanon Avenue, behind the old movie house and he'd talked Lou into storing it there. Lou parked it right next to Joey's '78 Coupe Deville, all wrapped up under a brown tarp like a body in the morgue.

But it seemed like the more he drove the Honda, the more he missed the Thunderbird. He missed the way the smooth black surface of the hood reflected the trees in the morning and the sky at night. The street lights were like orbiting moons against the polished metal. He missed the red pinstripe that ran the

length of the car from nose to tail in a gentle arc. He missed the
way the motor rumbled and the way it jumped when he hit
the gas, the power and the way it moved. He missed speeding
along the Schuylkill Expressway, the wheels hugging the road
from the Ben Franklin Bridge right through the Conshohocken
Curve and on to Valley Forge. It made him feel as if he was
driving in a race he could win, that if he kept up his speed
and kept his eyes on the road the car would take him to the
finish line.

He'd also believed, as Joey had, that once upon a time it was
the black Thunderbird that first attracted his wife to him with its
low-to-the-ground speed and sleek body. The brand-new badge
and the department-issued gun were equally hypnotic lures, he'd
supposed. But whatever she'd been looking for, she hadn't found
it in the bucket seat of an old Ford or raising a kid by herself
on a dirty street in West Philly. By the time Lou had it all figured
out, the romance had worn off and she was gone for greener
pastures, green as in the color of money. She'd taken his daughter
with her. The car was all he had left.

The few times he'd seen his ex since the divorce she'd chided
him for still driving it, complaining about taking her daughter
around in a vehicle that was fundamentally unsafe. She derided
his taste in cars, his taste in music, in food and even in women.
Lou had told her that if he ever met a woman that was interested
in going for a long, slow ride in a beat-up sports car, a vintage
Ford that guzzled gas and made much too much noise, whose
warranty had expired long ago, whose heater groaned in the winter
and whose air conditioner blew lukewarm all summer, he might
consider marriage for the second time.

Joey came across the street now, dodging the slow-moving
traffic as if he were on a crowded dance floor. Even behind the
sunglasses drivers could feel his stare, daring them to hit him.
He already had his lawyer on speed dial. He crossed quickly
over two lanes, paused for a moment on the double yellow line
to light a cigarette, and in a few long strides was across two
more lanes of traffic and hopping up onto the high curb.

'You pick a hell of a spot to light up.'

'Maybe if you hadn't quit smoking for like the tenth time,
you'd be more sympathetic.'

'What makes you so sure this won't be the time I quit for good?'

'I'm not. But Lou, you can't live forever.'

Joey took a long drag off the cigarette and blew a stream of blue smoke in Lou's face before pushing the door open with his shoulder and leading the way upstairs. A dim light at the top of the stairs cast long dark shadows behind them as they climbed. The steps creaked under their feet. Joey stopped about halfway up the narrow stairwell, turning his head and listening intently. Lou had heard it too, a light rustling like stocking feet on a thick carpet or a sudden release of air as if someone had been holding their breath.

Joey reached instinctively for the forty-five automatic he kept in a holster on his belt. The gun was the size of a cannon in his hand, a vintage Colt, silver, with a trigger as light as a whisper. If Petey Santi had sent one of his boys over, Joey would send him home with a hole in his stomach the size of the Lehigh Tunnel. He kept it pointed at the floor but his thumb was already on the serrated edge of the hammer and digging into his skin like a shark's tooth as he cocked it back. At the same moment, a woman became visible on the landing.

The static electricity from the forty-watt bulb seemed to draw her dark hair toward the low ceiling, a faint glow forming around her head. She was wearing a long skirt, her legs slightly parted with a bony knee jutting out of a slit in the thin material. A small black purse hung from her arm, her hand pressed against a protruding hip. Her face was masked in shadow.

Lou couldn't take his eyes off her. She looked as if she'd stepped out from under a street light on some desolate corner, a woman alone, waiting in the dark. There was something unreal about her, an apparition in the fog or a mirage in the shifting desert landscape. She seemed to float above them. Lou felt the skin at the back of his neck begin to crawl and a shiver ran down his spine as he glanced quickly over his shoulder, checking behind him, wondering if they'd walked into a trap.

She'd blocked much of the light that seeped down the stairs, leaving the stairwell in almost complete darkness. Just then, with a snap of her finger, a long yellow flame shot up from her hand and ignited the tip of a cigarette dangling carelessly from the corner of her mouth. The flame lit her face for a brief second:

the sharp angular jaw, the dark, flowing hair, the straight nose and green eyes. And then it was only the red glow of the cigarette that remained, accentuating a set of moist full lips. She took a long draw and let the smoke drift from her lips and float toward the light. Lou had caught a glimpse of her face.

'Franny? Franny Patterson, is that you?'

She took another drag off the cigarette. This time she turned her head and blew it out, her lips turned down in disgust.

'My name is Haggerty, Lou. Francis Haggerty. I'm married now. An honest woman. Surely my brother must have told you that much. I seem to be the main topic of conversation with him lately.'

'Where's Jimmy?'

'I left him at home. I told him I didn't need his help or yours. I came to tell you that myself.'

'I don't think Jimmy would be worried if there was nothing to worry about.'

'What did Jimmy tell you?'

'Why don't we continue this conversation in my office? It's a little more comfortable than this cramped hallway.'

'And more private. Right, Lou? You always were a private person. Don't like to air your dirty laundry in public? Is that it?'

'Mine or anyone else's.'

Lou could see her eyes wandering in the darkness, squinting at him through the smoke. She stood like a statue, her hip still cocked to one side, the hand without the cigarette still wedged into the narrow arc of bone where her hip met her waist. Her white shirt was unbuttoned at the neck, exposing sharp protruding collar bones and the steep curve of her breasts. A string of cloudy pearls hung between them. Joey hadn't taken his eyes off her either. He still held the gun in his hand.

'You can put that thing away, Joey.'

Lou unlocked the door and reached for the light inside. He gave the door a little push and let it roll slowly open. Franny eased past him, peering disdainfully around the place and moving directly to the window. She pulled the curtain back slightly and looked out, her two fingers fitted between the folds of sheer material as if she were feeling for a pulse. A thin strip of light fell across the floor. She looked down onto Lancaster Avenue and toward the corner where cars were streaming through the traffic light in both directions.

Lou came up behind her and followed her gaze to the sidewalk below.

An old lady with chalk-white hair as transparent as silk stood at the corner waiting to cross. The rush of wind from the moving cars blew her dress against her knees and seemed as if it might snatch the canvas bag hanging off her arm. Franny had the curtain open just an inch, spying the woman with one eye as the light changed and she trotted across the street, barely making it from one corner to the other before the light changed again and the flow of cars threatened to run her down.

Franny abruptly pulled her hand away and the strip of light disappeared from the floor.

'I'll make coffee.'

Franny kept her back to him, her eyes closed.

'I don't plan on being here that long.'

'I didn't say it was just for you.'

She turned and faced him now, her arms folded across her breasts, her eyes moist and blinking back what Lou thought was a tear ready to trickle down her nose. She ran the back of her hand over her cheek, smudging her make-up.

'I'm sorry, Lou. None of this is your fault and I'm taking it out on you. Jimmy thinks he can treat me like I'm still his little sister and I need his protection.'

'But you are his little sister.'

'And a grown woman who can make her own decisions.'

'If something happened to you and Jimmy could have done something to prevent it and he didn't, he'd be devastated. That's the way he is. You're lucky to have him.'

She sighed. 'You're right, Lou. He's been like a father to me since Dad died and I don't think I ever really appreciated it. I never understood what kind of responsibility that took. And when I got old enough not to need him anymore, the only thing I could think of was getting away. It felt like a weight had been lifted off my chest.

'I don't know, Lou. I wanted to be Little Miss Independent when I should have been thinking of him, trying to be the kind of sister to him that he deserved. I never thought maybe he needed me even more than I needed him.'

Lou took Franny by the arm and led her to the chair by the desk. It had deep worn cushions and the fabric on the arms was frayed and torn. The chair had been in his mother's house, in the front room facing the window. Lou had often seen his mother sitting in that chair, looking out the window, waiting for his father to come home from work, the way the wife of any policeman would.

Lou could still smell his mother on that chair: the lanolin and lilac, the moisturizer she would rub into her hands and elbows, the smell of soap. He couldn't bear to throw it out despite its condition, so he moved it into his office where it made his clients feel at home. He'd sit in it himself, if Joey didn't get to it first and fall asleep with his head back and his mouth open, a cup of coffee in one hand and a smoldering cigarette in the other. One of these days he'd set himself on fire.

Joey had been standing at the sideboard, fixing himself a cup of coffee, trying to remain inconspicuous while Lou talked to Franny. Joey put his nose to a carton of cream from the refrigerator under the table and then put it back without using it. Lou let his hand fall on Joey's shoulder and steered him toward the door, keeping his voice low.

'Listen, Joey. Head up to Jimmy Patterson's place and tell Jimmy that Franny is here with me. Take him out to lunch. Buy him a few drinks. Find out what you can but don't push too hard. He's probably upset.'

'Where do I take him?'

'Try Fortunato's. Show him your impression of Mitch. You know, the one when he just made lieutenant and he jumps out of his car while it's still in gear and he ends up chasing it down the road. Jimmy'll love it. He hates Mitch.'

'Hate is a strong word, Lou. I mean, my ex-wife hates me but I don't go around advertising it.'

'You were having a fling with a stripper. What was her name?'

'Candy Bell.'

'Yeah, right. I don't blame her for hating you.'

'And what's Jimmy's problem with Mitch?'

'Jimmy thinks Mitch is a pompous, self-important, old blowhard of a cop.'

'That's it?'

'That's it.'

'It's a little early in the day for drinks, Lou. What if Jimmy doesn't want to go?'

'Insist. Now get going.'

FIVE

Lou set two cups of steaming coffee on a short table in front of Franny. Her smile was faint, thin ridges framing her mouth, her teeth hidden behind lips that seemed to turn colorless and twisted unconsciously as if she'd bitten into something rotten. He brought over the cream and sugar and rolled his chair out from behind his desk. He sat in front of her, leaning forward with his elbows on his knees. Franny's eyes never left the floor.

'Franny, if this is just a lover's quarrel and there's nothing more to it, I'll butt out. You guys haven't been married that long and I know it takes a while to iron things out. But if it's more than that, I should know.'

'It's a second marriage for both of us, Lou, and we're both carrying around a lot of baggage.'

'What kind of baggage are we talking about?'

'Oh, come on, Lou.' Her body jerked to life as if an electrical current had passed through it. 'I'm sure you know most of it. I mean, you were a cop in this town for twenty years and you've lived around here your whole life. Our fathers worked together on the force. And you've been around the block a few times yourself. So please don't pretend you don't know what I'm talking about. My God, I'm so sick of pretending.'

She lifted the cup of coffee and brought it to her lips but didn't drink. She seemed to want only to warm her hands on the cup. The afternoon sun struggled through the thin blinds in filtered rays that highlighted her streaked face, a few strands of gray in her dark hair. She'd always been beautiful, Lou remembered, and still was, but her face had grown haunted. A shadow had fallen over it. Illuminated now by the yellow light from the window, she looked sallow and a little sick.

Lou walked to the window and pulled the cord on the shade. The office grew perceptibly brighter. He switched on the lamp on his desk. It was a green and white Philadelphia Eagles Tiffany lamp with a pewter base and stem and a bronze eagle perched at the top.

'You an Eagles fan?'

'Everyone in my family are Eagles fans, Lou. It's a family tradition. Seems like one of the few we have left.' She took a sip from the cup and exhaled sharply through her mouth as if it had been a shot of whiskey. 'How about you?'

'I root against them. It's kind of a love/hate relationship.'

'I know the feeling.'

The language of football, Lou thought; in Philadelphia it opened channels of communication as wide as the Delaware and as dirty. It flowed between people who otherwise might have never exchanged a word. But he'd questioned Philly's love affair with football. In his experience, it was driven by an obsession with violence and it brought out the worst in them. It made them loud. It made them aggressive. It got them drunk. It made them want to beat somebody's brains in. Football was certainly a tradition in Philadelphia, just like bar fights and domestic disturbances.

'You were going to tell me about that baggage you've been carrying around.'

'Was I?'

'I thought maybe you wanted to.'

'You're wrong. I assumed you knew it all already, heard it from one of my brothers or from one of your cop friends at Fortunato's.'

'I'd prefer to hear it from you.'

'I told you, Lou. I've been married and divorced once already. Now it looks like it's going to happen again.'

'It's not a crime, Franny. Relationships are a funny thing. Sometimes we don't get it right. I'm divorced.'

'You don't understand, Lou. You don't understand how it makes me feel, how it makes me look. People look at me differently. They start to think something's wrong with me.' She fumbled in her purse for the pack of cigarettes. Her hand came up with a crumpled pack of Newports and a plastic lighter. She tapped one out and lit it with a trembling hand. She might have singed her eyebrows with the dancing flame. 'It's so much easier for men. You remind me of my first husband; he had all the answers.'

'I never said I had all the answers, Franny.'

'But you act like you do. And that smug look. It gets me so angry I'd like to wipe it right off your face.'

'I don't mean to be smug and I'm not judging you, so there's no reason to get defensive. Do you know what I think the truth is? If you didn't think I could help you, you wouldn't be here.'

'How do you know I'm not using you? I have a reputation for using men, you know.'

She sucked hard on the cigarette, letting the smoke drift heavily from her open mouth. Her eyes lowered to black slits and her smile regained its confidence.

'Stop it.'

'You never were any fun.'

'Is that how you avoid the subject, Franny? Bat your eyes and let your skirt ride a little higher on your leg? What happens when that doesn't work?'

'I guess you'll just have to find out.'

She stubbed the cigarette out in the ashtray, tapping it repeatedly against the brown glass and then absently pushing around the cold, gray ash. She rubbed her fingers together as though she were sprinkling salt into a pot of soup on the stove and then examined her painted fingernails and the tobacco stains underneath.

'I'm not the woman you think I am, Lou. I'm sorry.'

'Then who are you?'

'You want to know the truth? I don't know anymore. My husband wants to get rid of me because I can't have children. He became possessed with the idea of producing an heir to the Haggerty throne and since I wasn't up to the task he's decided to trade me in on a newer model. How does that sound? Any more believable a story for you? Probably his mother's idea. How is it that some women can pump out kids like they're nothing and not give two shits about them? And some women, who really want children, can't have them. Why is that?'

'I don't know.'

'You know, I actually thought about a surrogate. Only I don't think Brian is the artificial-insemination type. He'd want to hand-pick the girl and do it himself. I think he might have had a few ready to go. Knowing him, he skipped the application process and went right to the oral interview.'

'I'm sorry, Franny.'

'Please don't say that again, Lou.'

'I don't remember saying it before.'

'Yeah, but I can hear it in your voice. Poor Franny Patterson. In another twenty years I'll be just another miserable old woman, just like Eleanor Haggerty, only she has her money to keep her warm.'

She reached for the purse again and the cigarettes inside but Lou abruptly pulled it away. Franny's fading smile was instantly replaced with an animal fear as she tried to snatch it back. Lou held it out of reach, fending her off with one hand, the other thrust inside the purse feeling for the cigarettes. His hand came out of the purse holding a gun.

It was a thirty-eight, a snub-nose revolver of blued steel with a bull-barrel and a checkered wooden grip. It looked like it had seen better days. It had been meticulously polished and oiled as if someone was trying in vain to hide the wear, the scratches along the frame, the worn metal around the hammer from years of sliding in and out of a leather holster, the thumb-brake snapping shut. Lou snapped it open and spun the cylinder, watched it spin like a roulette wheel, the silver, hollow-point bullets loaded like torpedoes. Lou put his nose to the barrel and smelled gunpowder.

'Cigarettes and guns, Franny? A bad combination. If one doesn't kill you the other certainly will.'

'Put that back!'

Lou dropped the purse on the table. Franny almost caught it in mid-air but it landed with a hard thud. Lou walked toward the window once more, examining the gun in the light. It was a belly gun, the kind of gun someone could stick in your ribs and blow out your insides, the kind of gun cops liked for a backup. But it was also small and light, the kind of gun a woman might use, getting in tight, snuggling against your shoulder and whispering in your ear before she pulled the trigger.

'Why the gun, Franny?'

'None of your damn business.'

'We're back to that, huh?'

'You just don't give up, do you, Lou?'

'You know me better than that.'

'There was a time when I thought I did; thought I knew you pretty well. And no, I didn't think you were the kind of guy to give up. Come to think of it, I believed just about every word you said.'

'That was a long time ago, Franny.'

'Really? I don't think so. You haven't changed a bit, Lou. What would you have me believe? When I don't want to talk about my past, you call me evasive. And when I do bring it up, you make light of it, like it's so much water under the bridge. So which is it? What do I call you when you don't want to talk about the past?'

'Call me a fool for chasing you around all those years, dodging your brothers and thinking I was something more than practice. You can call me whatever you damn well please. And you can have your gun back.'

She took it and for a split second before she stashed it in her purse, Lou got a glimpse at what Franny Patterson looked like with a gun in her hand. It wasn't a pretty sight. There wasn't anything appealing about a woman wielding a thirty-eight special except if she was in her underwear and the gun wasn't loaded and she didn't happen to be your sister or your daughter or your wife. It wasn't that he'd felt threatened. Franny had managed to intimidate most men without a gun in her hand. But guns did have a tendency to go off. And Lou was beginning to feel like he didn't want to be around when Franny found a reason to use it.

'It was my father's gun, you know. Jimmy said it was his off-duty gun.'

'Does he know you have it?'

'Jimmy doesn't think girls and guns mix. He always said I'd either shoot myself or someone would take it away from me.'

'He's probably right. Do you think that gun is going to protect you from Brian Haggerty?'

'He knows I have it and he doesn't seem threatened by it in

the least. He doesn't have a problem with the idea of a woman wanting to protect herself.'

'Most men will tell you just what you want to hear with a gun pointed at their gut.'

'Not all men. Not you. Not my brother.'

Lou lit a cigarette. He lit one for Franny and passed it to her.

'Do you know about Haggerty's first wife? Do you know what happened to her?'

'You must think I'm a very stupid woman, Lou. If Brian keeps anything from me, it's because I allow him to. I give him that because he needs it. He needs to have his little secrets. But they're harmless secrets. They can't hurt me or anyone else. I know about Brian's past. I know about his father and his business. I'm not as much in the dark as you think.'

'The gun proves that.'

'For your information, I'm not scared of Brian either.'

'Then what are you scared of? Jimmy said there's been a lot of tension between you and your mother-in-law, that you've had your share of disagreements. He seemed to imply that she controlled the money in the family and used that to control her son.'

'Brian might be afraid of her but I'm not. She's a cruel, vindictive woman, Lou. The fact that I'm not afraid of her is the very reason she hates me.'

She leaned back in the chair, crossed her legs and blew a couple of smoke rings toward the ceiling. She twirled a loose strand of hair in her finger and her eyes seemed to be somewhere else, looking into the past or into herself. He realized now that what he'd seen in her face had been a facade, her stage face. And what he was seeing now was a child's face, lost in orbit around a world she could no longer control, a family where she never really belonged and now threatened to squeeze her out. Her false confidence dripped with contempt and Lou was beginning to feel sorry for her. For all her beauty and feigned strength she still needed approval, still wanted to be something she wasn't and the thought of not having it scared the hell out of her.

'Jimmy also mentioned that Mrs Haggerty might be on her last legs.'

'Jimmy's got a lot to say. You know how many times Brian

has called to tell me his mother was on her death bed? That she could go anytime? But miraculously she always pulls through. You'd think God would get sick of wasting so many miracles on one person.'

'If it's so bad why don't you get out?'

'And do what? Start working on husband number three? Are you applying for the job? It's not exactly steady work.'

Lou smiled but there was little sympathy in it, just a row of well-capped white teeth to go with a hesitant nod.

Franny got up to leave, pushing the strand of hair she'd been playing with behind one ear. Her purse was locked around her left arm. Her heels clicked furiously on the floor as she stepped off the faded rug and moved toward the door. She stood for a second, her hand on the knob and the smooth muscular line of her calves flexing beneath the dark stockings. She turned and faced him as if she had something more to say, a last word.

'Can I drop you somewhere, Franny? I can take you home. It's no problem.'

'No, thanks. But there is maybe something you can do for me.'

'Name it.'

'First of all, you have to promise to leave Jimmy out of it. You know what he's like, Lou. He thinks he's invincible but he's not.'

'I can't make a promise like that. Tell me what you want and I'll tell you what I'm willing to do.'

'Brian's taken some things from me and he won't give them back. He won't even let me back in the house. He's selfish in the same way his mother is. They both figure if they bought it, I don't deserve to have it. If nothing else, maybe you can get some of my stuff back?'

'What kind of stuff?'

'Clothes, mostly. Some furniture. And jewelry. He's given me a lot of valuable jewelry in the short time we've been together. It's my wedding ring I really want back. I think I deserve at least that.'

'Does Brian have it?'

'He must. He took it back as if it had always belonged to him and I was only borrowing it for a while.' Lou saw the tear that had been hanging around run down her cheek. Her eyes had grown bloodshot and swollen. He wondered if an infinite supply of salt water flowed through the veins of all women, dredging it up on demand from some bottomless sea, an endless desert of shifting sand along with it, replenishing the hour glass they forever turned in their hands. 'I rarely took it off. Almost never. It disappeared from the bureau in my room. I know he's got it, Lou.'

Lou rubbed the knuckles on his left hand, his fingers clenched into a loose fist. The hair on his neck bristled as he listened to her become suddenly plaintive, realizing now that maybe he was being used. What the hell, he thought, being taken advantage of went with the territory. And who better to be taken advantage of than by Franny Patterson? He reached into his breast pocket and passed her a business card with his number on it.

'I'll see what I can do. Call me if there's trouble.'

'If you plan on looking for him, you might not find him at the house. He spends most of his time down at the Arramingo Club. It's on Oregon Avenue. He owns it.'

SIX

Lou followed her down the stairs and out onto the sidewalk. Traffic was building on Lancaster Avenue. Cars were backed up all the way to Penn Street where a gray Mercedes sedan sat with its blinker on, waiting to make the left turn. It was a difficult maneuver at any time of day. Now, it was nearly impossible. It sat there with its orange blinker throbbing, waiting for traffic to clear or for some kind soul to slow down and wave him on. A long line of cars had filed in closely behind. A few drivers punched angrily at their horns, their faces hard and tight in the midday sun. The right lane was barely squeezing by and Lou couldn't help but smile, seeing this drama play itself out at that intersection every day. Franny must have thought he was laughing at her.

He walked her to her car, keeping a few paces behind, allowing her the luxury of ignoring him if that's what she preferred. She'd seemed intent on keeping their meeting a secret, though it wouldn't remain a secret for very long, not if he was going to saddle up a stool at the Arramingo Club and start asking a lot of stupid questions.

The light at the corner changed from green to red and the old man behind the wheel still sat there confused, his hat tilted back on his head, the nose of his Mercedes blocking the freshly painted crosswalk. The drivers behind him became infuriated. With no room to go around, all they could do was wait for him to figure it out: either shoot through the light as soon as it turned green or just after it turned red. Those were his only choices.

The old cop in Lou was tempted to step out into all that congestion and start directing traffic but instead he watched from the sidewalk as Franny jumped into a black Audi and started it up. It purred like a cougar sunning itself on a rock. Franny put on a pair of dark sunglasses. He tried to help her with the door as she swung it open and it almost caught him in the knee. He straightened up and pushed the door gently closed.

She lowered the window without turning her head and Lou leaned in. Her face was a mask behind the sunglasses, smooth and hard and unmoving. She had nothing more to say to him. She turned the volume up on the stereo and slammed the car into gear. Lou jumped back as she peeled out, forcing her way across two lanes of congested traffic in a U-turn that pointed her back down Lancaster Avenue and deeper into the city.

Lou's car was parked up the block in front of the camera shop. His cell phone beeped and he flipped it open. It was a text message from Joey. Joey's text messages were beginning to read like pulp fiction. He knew that Lou wasn't much of a talker on the phone and rather than listen to his sighs of impatience and his long silences, Joey had learned how to text. Lou often wondered how Joey managed the dexterity it required with those stubs he called thumbs. He read as he walked.

Jimmy Patterson had caused a disturbance at Fortunato's and got himself thrown out. He'd flung an empty beer glass at Butchy DeLuca, smashing a mirror behind the bar. The argument started after Jimmy got a full house on the video poker machine and DeLuca refused to pay out. Luckily Jimmy missed or it could have started a war with Joey in the middle. Joey thought he'd missed on purpose, that he just needed to flex his muscles. The point was don't disrespect Jimmy Patterson and don't turn your back on him either. Jimmy had made the same point in half the bars in West Philly. Joey had gotten him out of there and loaded into his Cadillac. He would drop Jimmy off and meet Lou back at Heshy's.

Maggie's shift was over at four and Lou had promised to take her out for Chinese food at the Peking Dragon. It had become their custom, a quiet dinner once a week at their favorite restaurant. He'd taken her there as a child, before the separation and divorce. She'd always been mesmerized by the tropical fish floating aimlessly in hundred-gallon tanks. It was dark in the Peking Dragon and it seemed like the only light came from those aquariums. The fish seemed to glow in the clear water, brilliant yellows lacquered with black, rusty orange over translucent silver and azure blue with spots of white. But their eyes were opaque, black and round and empty as painted glass.

Whether it was the colors or the slow, languid movement of the fish that captured their attention, Lou and Maggie could sip tea and stare at them complacently for hours. Sometimes they'd eat egg rolls or an occasional bowl of soup. Lou had been surprised to find himself hypnotized by the fish as well, matching Maggie's fascination with their motion, constantly flowing, never still. He'd imagine himself swimming in one of those tanks, swimming as if in one of his dreams, the same fluid motion as the fish, his eyes open and unblinking, and yet imprisoned by four walls of thick glass. And from inside that glass cage, he could still see the world beyond, the boundary seemingly transparent and yet solid as stone.

Maggie must have felt like one of those fish, he thought. He remembered feeling the same way when he was her age. He'd dreamed of flying like the hawks that nested high in the trees behind Karakung Creek. He would watch them hunt in Fairmont Park, stalking rabbits and mice behind the bronze statue of Washington, his horse rearing at the sight of all those cars going by on Benjamin Franklin Parkway. But the farthest Lou's feet had ever come off the ground was when he'd climbed the marble pedestal to share the saddle with galloping George. His father had snapped a picture of him sitting on that bronze horse and kept it in his wallet, showing it to his cop buddies every chance he got. It looked as if Lou was trying to nudge the old campaigner out of the way.

He often wondered if the dinners with Maggie had made a difference, those silent dinners, trying to understand the power of raw emotion for a nineteen-year-old, hoping he could touch the nine-year-old girl inside and give her a way now to spend time with her father that wasn't equated with pain. Maybe she'd looked at those fish and thought they'd found peace, surrounded by all that water, safe behind the glass.

He always felt that he'd failed her and that sentiment prevailed even now. Though at least now there was conversation between them. There were no answers, not to the questions she hadn't known how to ask then and was afraid to ask now. Where had her father been for those years after the divorce? Why wasn't he around? What kept him away? How could he forget his only daughter? Maybe the emotion that had persisted all these years was actually fear, a fear that one day they'd lose each other forever. And maybe dinners at the Peking Dragon reminded them both that it was within their power to change all that, give the past new meaning and create a future for themselves.

But it had been a few weeks now since they'd been out, Lou's police pension not allowing for much extravagance. He'd made excuses but Maggie knew that it was about money. They'd come to an unspoken agreement, cutting their restaurant trips from once a week to once a month.

Joey had beaten him back to Heshy's and was already sitting at the counter, nursing a cup of black coffee as Lou came through the door. His worn tweed sport jacket hung on a hook at the end of the counter. Maggie was coming out of the ladies' room, ready for dinner, with her hair freshly brushed and a pair of purple glasses on her face and her best earrings in her ears. Lou held up an index finger, signaling her to wait while he had a few words with Joey. Maggie's upper lip curled as she fell into a booth with an exasperated sigh.

'What the hell went on over there, Joey?'

'Your friend, Jimmy. That's what went on. He's a goddamn

maniac. I thought I was bad. He makes me look like a fucking saint.'

'I find that hard to believe.'

'Jimmy's playing the Joker Poker machine, right? He's maybe into it for ten bucks, no more. Pretty soon he's bumping the thing with his knee, slapping it. He's cursing out loud at a video game, for Christ's sake. Butchy is looking over at me like I'm his caretaker, you know, like he'd never even be in there if I hadn't brought him.'

'I thought he was a regular in there.'

'He was, but Butchy didn't want him coming in anymore. They had it out a couple times before.'

'Couldn't you calm him down?'

'Easier said than done. Next thing you know Jimmy's got a full house and he's standing at the bar pointing at the cards on the screen telling Butchy he owes him thirty bucks. Butchy tells him it don't work like that. Jimmy's getting pissed and Butchy tells him to go fuck himself. That's when he throws the glass.'

'Just like that?'

'Yeah, Lou. Just like that.'

Heshy poured Lou a cup of coffee without being asked. He caught Lou's eye and nodded toward Maggie, who was gritting her teeth and growling into her cell phone. Lou recognized the tone. He could picture Maggie's mother on the other end of the line, the same grimace on her face, trying to control the daughter who'd run away from her a dozen times because she was sick of dealing with the different husbands and the moves and the different houses and the schools, sick of feeling like a piece of furniture. Maggie felt Lou's eyes on her and slumped down inside the cramped booth. She was quiet for about ten seconds and then abruptly snapped the phone closed.

'Did you talk to him at all, Joey, or did you two guys just get drunk?'

'Jimmy don't just get angry when he drinks, he's also got a lot to say.'

'His sister said the same thing.'

'It turns out that Jimmy knew Brian Haggerty's first wife, the one that got herself dead with the old man. She went by the name Valerie Price, but he didn't think that was her real name.

The impression I got was that she was more than just a casual acquaintance.'

'Complicates things, doesn't it?'

'He didn't have one good thing to say about her. He did say she started as a dancer at the Arramingo Club, had quite a reputation.'

'The Arramingo Club again.'

'Yeah. Jimmy said she was gorgeous and she knew it. Wasn't afraid to use it either. But she was reckless. These are Jimmy's words, Lou, not mine. I couldn't help get the feeling he thinks she got what she had coming to her.'

'A thousand years ago they would have burned her at the stake or had a good old-fashioned stoning in the town square. A bullet in the brain is much more expedient.'

'You said it.'

'What else did he say?'

'You ever been to the Arramingo Club? It's a home away from home for some of Philly's finest: cops, politicians, gangsters. They call a truce just long enough to sip their Scotch and stuff a dollar bill into a stripper's thong. Put it on the taxpayer's tab.'

'Never had the pleasure. But that's going to change real soon.'

'According to Jimmy he wasn't the only person getting his fingers wet with Valerie Price and neither was Brian Haggerty. She was a climber, kept her eyes on the prize. She'd latch onto the fattest wallet she could get her hands on. Jimmy seemed to imply that he'd gotten her out of his system pretty quick. Couldn't say the same thing about Haggerty.'

'I've seen it happen to the best of them.'

'He said Haggerty made a fool of himself, chasing her all over town, pulling her out of bars, hotel rooms, parked cars. The jealousy drove him insane. Even Jimmy was surprised when Haggerty married her. Jimmy thought maybe she got knocked up and talked Haggerty into making an honest woman out of her.'

'You sure Jimmy was over her?'

'Famous last words, right?'

Heshy grabbed a fly swatter from over the stove and swung it like a tennis racquet at a big black fly circling over his head. The buzzing sounded like an airplane propeller. He fanned the air a few times until the thing landed on the wall. He snuck up on it and got it with his next swing. It slid down the tile and landed on the floor but it wasn't dead. Its wings fluttered and it spun around in a circle like a dog chasing its tale until Heshy stepped on it and kicked it into the corner.

'Did Jimmy say anything about her murder?'

'What's he going to say? "By the way, you know how every-body thinks Brian Haggerty found his wife in bed with his old man and offed them both? Well, that was me who did that."'

'I was thinking maybe he knows more than he's telling.'

'I wouldn't describe Jimmy Patterson as tight-lipped.'

'I guess not.'

'I think the reason he's pissed off doesn't have anything to do with Valerie Price. It's got to do with his sister.'

'And that leaves us right where we started.'

'Not necessarily. Haggerty had an alibi for those murders, if we're assuming they were murdered.'

'Let's hear it.'

'His alibi was Franny Patterson. She said he'd been with her the whole night.'

Lou let out a long whistle and Maggie looked at him from her booth in the back, making no attempt to hide her annoyance.

'And Jimmy thinks Haggerty forced her into it?'

'Could be. Or maybe he just can't stand the idea that it could have been her idea from the start.'

'You're smarter than you look, Joey. When Maggie and I get back from dinner, I'm checking out the Arramingo Club, hear what Brian Haggerty has to say for himself.'

'You want company?'

'No, thanks. You put in your time already today.'

'One more thing, Lou. What exactly are we doing here? We trying to help one of your old girlfriends out of a tight spot or are we trying to solve a ten-year-old murder?'

Lou raised his coffee cup in a mocking toast and took a good long sip. He called Maggie over with a wave.

'Maybe a little of both, Joey.'

SEVEN

The Peking Dragon had been remodeled, a sandy stucco applied over the worn brick in swirling waves the color of the Arizona desert. The windows were trimmed in dark wood and covered by overhanging awnings, black canvas held up by black iron rods, the amber glow of candlelight emanating from each window. There was a portico that led to a parking lot on the side of the building. Large lanterns hung from the exposed beams of the portico, casting a soft orange light over the sidewalk. The soft, artificial light both inside and out seemed, by design, to resemble a western sunset. The problem was there weren't any desert sunsets in Philadelphia and the Chinatown Lou remembered never looked anything like a Hollywood movie set, at dusk or any other time.

Maggie was excited, though, now that they were off by themselves. She was smiling again and hanging on his arm as girls do with their fathers and it seemed to transport Lou back to an earlier time, as if they were both ten years younger, facing an opportunity to relive a lost decade of their lives, do it all over again, do it right this time.

Maggie hadn't hung on him that way since he'd escorted her to her mother's wedding about a year ago, her second since she'd divorced Lou. He'd played the dutiful father and supportive ex-husband, while painfully aware of the conflict in his daughter's eyes. They'd stood together among a small group of onlookers watching her mother walk down the aisle on the veranda at the Merion Country Club. She'd married a short, black-haired Greek who owned three restaurants and had two ex-wives of his own. Maggie had held his arm as if she'd been seasick, gripping the railing on some cruise ship, afraid to let go and fall from the deck into all that bottomless black water.

They'd stood together and watched her mother pick grains of rice from her new husband's hair like the monkeys they'd seen at the Philadelphia zoo, who sat back to back, taking turns scraping insects from each other's skin.

As soon as they stepped inside the restaurant Maggie immediately had her nose against the long aquarium that separated the entrance from the dining room. She ran her hand gently across the outside of the cool glass. The maitre d' gave her the evil eye from behind a wooden stand. He needed a stool to see over it and he slid his bifocals down on his nose and said something in Chinese to one of the waitresses. He licked his thumb and began turning pages in the notebook on his stand.

Maggie had made the reservations. She'd reserved a table for two using her first name and not her last. She'd gotten into the habit because she didn't ever want to be confused with her mother. She'd explained that her mother was mean to waitresses and she knew what it was like to have to wait on people for a living. That kind of thing got around and she'd seen the look on the waitress's face when her mother had sent something back to the kitchen, refusing to eat a perfectly good piece of steak because it was overcooked and she liked her meat dripping with blood.

Maggie said she'd been embarrassed too many times to use the name Klein at a restaurant where her mother might have frequented in the past. Lou had countered by opening the phone book and showing her a whole page of Kleins. The policy still applied, though, regardless of the fact that her mother's name was no longer Klein and hadn't been for years. Lou stepped up and gave the name.

The maitre d' shifted his glance from the handwritten list in front of him, surveying the few available tables within sight and twirling a pencil in his fingers. He showed them to a corner table, handing them menus and lighting a small candle.

The candle sat inside the glass carving of a swan. The glass looked smooth and cold as ice and yet the sparkling light from the flame danced under the swan's breast and moved in its eyes and outward through its open wings as if it was alive. Its long, narrow neck arced downward while its wings were raised as if it were trying to fly. It seemed frozen to the ground. If it could only lift its head, Lou thought, but its neck looked too thin and the candle too weak to melt the ice that held it down. Its fate was still better than the fish, Lou thought. After all, the swan was made of glass.

'Your waitress will be with you shortly.'

Lou nodded, sat back in his chair and looked at his daughter sitting adjacent to him at the table and already unfolding her napkin and laying it across her lap. A youngish boy in a white shirt but no vest and black bangs falling to his eyebrows poured two glasses of water and set a silver decanter of hot tea between them.

Maggie banged a straw on the table until it popped out of its paper wrapper. She speared it into the glass of water, now dripping with condensation. She put her lips to the tip of the straw, stretching her head and neck out over the table, careful not to spill the glass. She reminded Lou of the swan tripping to the riverbank to drink, bending toward the water with its rolling eyes on the sky.

'You know I worry about you sometimes?'

'I know you do. But I wish you didn't. It's my job to worry about you.'

'I just don't understand why you want to keep doing this cop thing. I mean, the department treated you like shit – at least that's what you said. I thought you were sick of it. There are a lot of other things you could do.'

'Maybe.'

'You say maybe like you're thinking about quitting but you don't mean it.'

'I'm not sure I can do anything else. I wouldn't know what else to do.'

'I know why you do it. You're doing it for your father. You're still trying to fill his shoes. You're trying to be the person he wanted you to be, even now, even though he's dead. I find myself doing the same thing. I do what you tell me to. Because I think it's what you want. But it's not always what I want for myself.'

'I'm not sure that's true, honey. My father didn't want me to be a cop. I told you that. I made that decision on my own. It was the last thing I said to him on the day he was killed. I told you that, too.'

'Well, if he really didn't want you to be a cop, did you think you were making him happy by telling him you decided to be one? You must have. Or maybe what he told you and what he really wanted were two different things. It happens like that sometimes. There's nothing wrong with wanting to follow in your father's footsteps, I just want you to see it for what it is.'

'You know he never actually said those words to me. He never came right out and said he didn't want me to be a cop. It was something I just picked up on from the way he reacted when I asked him about the job, the look he got in his eyes when he talked about the direction his life might have taken if he never put on the badge.'

'But the way he reacted when you finally told him contradicts all that.'

'Maybe so. But I'll never be the man my father was. He was a bona fide hero. He left his mark on this city, helped a lot of people. The city of Philadelphia should erect a statue to that man.' Lou poured some tea into a tiny cup and took a sip. 'Don't get me wrong. There's a lot of truth in what you say.'

'But not enough to make you change.'

'Change from what my father wanted to what you want?'

'No. To what you want.'

'I want to eat.'

Lou ordered beef and Maggie ordered chicken and they shared, reaching across the table with their forks and occasionally clanking them together, stabbing pieces of meat on each other's plates as if they were crossing swords. They'd both put down a bed of white rice and drowned it in soy sauce until it dripped black and runny to the edges of their plates.

'Are you still having nightmares?'

'Sometimes.'

'Nightmares could be a symptom of a deeper problem, you know.'

'Almost twenty years as a street cop in the City of Brotherly Love. That's my problem.'

'And you think by helping Jimmy Patterson you'll make it all go away?'

'Who told you about Jimmy Patterson?'

'Joey.'

'Joey should learn to keep his mouth shut. And it's Franny Patterson, his sister, I'm trying to help.'

'Is she pretty?'

'Very.'

Lou offered to take Maggie to Manning's Creamery for ice cream on the way home. It didn't matter that it was November and that most of the old ice-cream parlors in the city were closed for the season. There would never be a substitute for the role ice cream played in their relationship, sweet and rich with sugar and milk like some exotic drink they'd developed an insatiable addiction to. Maggie had inherited her father's sweet tooth and, regardless of the season, they'd kept half the ice-cream shops in Philadelphia in business.

Lou had accumulated many of the photos from their ice-cream adventures on his dresser over the years, dusty pictures leaning against dusty books and empty bottles of aftershave and a square cedar humidor with a few stale cigars inside. His favorite was a faded snapshot of his daughter as a toddler with chocolate all over her face, smiling a brown smile with her first couple teeth. She was sitting in a high chair with a bib around her neck that read 'I love Daddy,' and a fudgecicle in her hand melting onto the tray, forming a puddle of brown soup. He still looked at it just about every day.

They had Manning's to themselves, the girl behind the counter looking surprised to see customers coming through the door. They ordered hot-fudge sundaes and sat by the window.

'How's school coming along?'

'Fine.'

'Just fine?'

'Yeah, just fine.'

'How are you doing?'

'Good.'

'Straight A's?'

'Just about.'

'Just about?'

'Why do you have to repeat everything I say, like you don't believe me or something?'

'I don't normally have to ask how you're doing. You've always been pretty quick to tell me. When I don't hear anything, I think maybe there's a problem.'

'If you weren't such a cop you wouldn't think that and I wouldn't be afraid to tell you the truth.'

'The truth about what, honey?'

'Promise me you'll let me handle it on my own.'

'I can't promise anything until I know the whole story.'

'I'm having a little trouble with one of my professors.'

Lou waited. He didn't say anything, didn't ask any questions, didn't repeat her words back to her as if he was interrogating a suspect in the basement of the Nineteenth Precinct. He didn't lean over her as if he was playing good cop/bad cop with Joey's size-thirteen shoe up on the chair, the sleeves of his blue polyester shirt rolled up and his hairy arms beginning to sweat. He didn't close in on her with his eyes as if he was coercing a confession from his only child. He bit down on the plastic spoon until he felt it crack between his teeth.

'What kind of trouble?'

'It's my French class. We have a language lab twice a week. We sit at computer terminals with our headphones on, working on pronunciation. This guy walks around the class listening to us. He'll stop if he sees somebody needs help. He always seems to stop behind my desk and I don't need any help. Lately he's been putting his hands on my shoulders like he's giving me a massage. It's creepy. I pull away but he doesn't stop.'

There were a lot of things Lou could have said at that moment, things a father would say, things a cop would say. He knew what she expected him to say. It was more like what she expected him to do.

He tossed the remainder of his ice cream into the garbage on their way to the car. He looked across the lot, at a woman next to a blue Ford Explorer with the quarter panels rusting out and gray smoke rising from the exhaust. She looked about his age, an assortment of kids climbing into the back seat ranging in age from about three to seventeen. She had her hands full keeping them from running around the empty parking lot. One of the younger ones dropped her cone on the ground and started to cry. Lou watched the child scoop the ice cream off the ground, placing it back on the cone and picking out the small round pebbles and sharp little fragments of ground glass.

'Did you tell him to stop?'

'Yes, I told him to stop but he just laughed like he thought I was joking or something.'

'Sounds like the guy's got a problem.'

'I'm actually glad I told you about it, Dad. But listen, don't worry, I can handle it. If I can't, I promise I'll tell you.'

'I want to know what happens the next time you're in his class. Don't let it continue another day. The longer he gets away with it the harder it'll be to deal with. We can always go to the school or even to the cops if we have to.'

'I don't want this guy arrested, Dad. And I don't want him fired either. Let's just see what happens.'

'Wait and see. Good strategy.'

'I'm getting cold. Let's go home.'

The remnants of a dark blue sky still hung overhead, turning blacker by degrees as if a heavy velvet curtain was edging slowly from horizon to horizon. With the night came the kind of cold that reminded Lou that winter was just around the corner. It was the wind that brought the cold with it, carrying it down the streets and to his doorstep, blowing away the remaining warmth of autumn, the fallen leaves on the lawn, the songbirds pushed from their nests and flying blindly toward warmer climates, their direction borne out by the sun. For those people like Lou, who still went for ice cream in November and ran in the early morning and sat on their porch at night with a cigarette and a hot coffee or a shot of whiskey, the cold was a fact of life.

It had always stung him, early in the morning and late at night. Philadelphia was a city surrounded by water, the harbor on one side and the ocean beyond that, with the Delaware and the Schuylkill, heavy with sludge, running into it. And always that ever-present wind carrying the icy moisture off the water and down rows of city streets and through the parks. No one was spared. It was a dampness that had gotten into his bones and never left. He knew what it was like to stand on Broad Street at three in the morning, directing traffic around a fatal accident with some teenager lying in the street with her neck broken after getting ejected through the back window of her daddy's SUV.

He'd shift his weight from one foot to the other, his toes numb against the freezing pavement, sleet tapping against the brim of his hat as he waited for the medical examiner's van to take another corpse away to the morgue.

To Maggie, though, winter was just a lot of cold air that made her hands dry and rough and her lips chapped. At her age, the memories of long winter nights usually involved Christmas trees and opening presents, building snowmen and sledding down Fireman's Hill. Winter was part of a weather report she'd hear on the radio, maybe throw on a sweater under her jacket, a pair of gloves stuffed in her pockets.

She couldn't imagine what the approach of winter meant to the aging policemen of the city, the cold grip it had on their knees, the way it cut through the fabric of their uniform and locked their legs into a sharp, cutting vice. She hadn't begun to associate physical pain with the weather, with the seasons of the year and the time of a person's life. How could she? She hadn't experienced it. She had yet to awaken to that deep ache inside her joints. But her father had. He had the arthritis to prove it and the sore hip where his gun had hung for twenty years and the sprained rotator cuff that acted up when his arm rested on top of the steering wheel.

Lou turned up the heat in the car. He leaned down and felt for it coming through the vent. And he had to admit, it felt good.

EIGHT

The lights on Market Street were flashing yellow as far up as he could see. It would happen when a pole got hit by a speeding car or a bolt of lightning. The system would get shorted out for miles. In Philly a blinking yellow light was the same as a green, drivers making time from one intersection to another, racing from block to block before they all turned back to red. Lou was making time himself and he'd jumped onto Cobbs Creek Parkway before he realized there was a police cruiser behind him. The overhead lights came on and the cop hit the siren and Lou pulled his car to the side of the road and rolled down his window.

He glanced in his rear-view mirror, focusing on the officer pulling himself slowly from the patrol car. The officer used two

hands to fit a hat onto his head and then reached for a microphone snapped to an epaulet on his shoulder. He wore a silver
badge and a nameplate on his blue uniform. If he'd gotten any
medals he wasn't wearing them. Lou thought he'd looked young
at first, a rookie maybe, ready to pull over anything that moved,
anxious to reach his quota of vehicle stops for the night. But as
he sauntered up alongside Lou's car, Lou could see the man was
a veteran, older than he looked from a distance.

Lou noticed his bowed legs, the broad forehead, the beginning
of a belly, the wear on the outside of his shoes, his feet gone
flat a long time ago. He was chewing gum and had a flashlight
in his left hand, tapping it in the palm of his right. Lou already
had his badge out. Maggie stiffened in the seat beside him.

'Still stopping cars, Officer? You get paid the same whether
you stop 'em or not. You go looking for trouble, it'll find you.'

'Bored, I guess.' He took Lou's gold retirement badge and
held the worn leather wallet in his hand. He stared down at it.
It looked like a brass trinket, a prize in a cheap carnival game,
something he might have given to his own daughter to play with
like the collection of junk she kept in one of her mother's old
purses under her bed. 'Louis Klein,' he uttered just above a
whisper. 'You worked the Nineteenth, right?'

'How'd you guess?'

'Worked with Joey Giordano.'

'You could say that.'

'I escorted a prisoner down to Southwest Detectives one time.
This is going way back. He's wanted for something, not sure
exactly what. I barely get him out of the car and your partner
starts beating the shit out of him. The guy's still handcuffed.'

'Yeah, Joey got like that sometimes, a real junkyard dog.
Problem was we couldn't keep him chained up.'

'Yeah, well, I ask him to stop, at least 'til I get the handcuffs
off and finish the paperwork. Anyway, as soon as I sign the
property receipt, Giordano kicks the guy in the balls and stomps
his face onto the parking lot. The guy's nose is broken. His ear
looks like ground beef. He's bleeding all over the place.'

'The man's a dinosaur. But you could get away with shit like
that back then.'

'It's the truth. Nowadays someone would have us on videotape and the DA would be ready to prosecute. Hey, if you see Giordano, make sure to tell him the dude he tuned up that day had just tested positive for Hepatitis C. I was going to tell him then but he didn't give me a chance.'

'I'll be sure to tell him but he's probably immune.'

The officer closed the wallet and handed it back through the window. Lou opened the glove compartment and tossed it in. The officer tilted his hat back on his forehead and started to walk away.

'Officer, hold on a minute.' Lou hopped out and started walking with him. 'I'd like to ask you a favor.'

'Shoot.'

'There was an accident this morning on Remington Road. A girl crashed into the back of a police car. I wonder if you know how she's doing? Looked like she was hurt pretty bad.'

'I don't know but I can find out.'

The officer walked back to his car, slipped on a pair of reading glasses and started punching numbers into a cell phone. He kept the window down and Lou heard a loud, bristling laugh. Lou got a look inside and saw an open bag of pretzels on the passenger seat, a mixture of dust and crumbs on the console, the shotgun in a rack overhead. Not so long ago that would have been Lou sitting inside a patrol car, serving out the tail end of his career. There were times he asked himself if he missed it. The answer was always no.

He'd already wasted too much time dwelling on the years he'd spent pushing a patrol car around the streets of Philadelphia. It served no purpose. He knew that those thoughts could get stuck in his head like a blood clot, damming up his arteries with bad memories. Eventually something would burst.

Ironically, though, his thoughts were rarely about the job itself. His years with the department seemed to run together with only a few discernible moments between his auspicious beginning and fairly tragic end. What he remembered most was his time away from the job, long hours spent at Fortunato's with Danny Butler behind the piano and Butchy DeLuca behind the bar.

Back then Butchy looked like a young Brando, with the white T-shirt and the sleeves rolled high onto his shoulders and the grooved muscles in his arms working the tap. He'd yell out a song and Danny would play it, his eyes half-closed, his body swaying and his fingers moving with a life of their own. Danny's face always glowed. It was spotted with light brown freckles that covered the tops of his cheeks and ran like speckled dust across the bridge of his nose. His teeth had gone gray but his smile had remained wild and childlike as if he was always ready with some old joke or thinking of an old girlfriend who was supposed to have broken his heart. He'd get drunk and play as if he'd never regretted a day in his life.

Danny's hair was a dull, coarse red and didn't seem to fit the shape of his head, jutting out at strange angles with no real pattern. Butchy had said that Danny didn't bother to comb his hair anymore. Danny said it had a mind of its own. One of the waitresses, Daisy Arguello, would always beg him to let her cut it and he'd just keep playing with that same contented smile plastered on his face. He'd make love to Daisy when the mood struck him and Daisy would say that Danny Butler had played her like a baby grand.

They found Danny dead behind the bar one night, the needle still in his arm. Butchy never replaced him. It was quiet in Fortunato's for a long time. The piano sat idle with a layer of dust across the top. Guys using the pay phone in the corner started putting their bottles on top of it and Butchy would get pissed, yelling at them to keep the bottles off the piano. He'd wipe the wet rings from the dark wood with a bar towel and soon after that he got rid of the phone. The piano stayed.

It was around that time Lou had been terminated from the police department and his wife had thrown him out, the two events coalescing in his mind, becoming one colossal weight. If it hadn't been for Fortunato's and Danny Butler's piano and the endless supply of Irish whiskey, he might have gone the way of so many other policemen who'd found themselves on the outside looking in, no longer part of the only family they'd ever known. Some cops decided that swallowing a bullet was better than living with the humiliation.

They'd found more than one dead cop with his service weapon in one hand and his badge in the other.

*   *   *

The officer turned to him through the window, the remnants of his dying laughter still showing through the faint smile on his face.

'Any luck?'

'Girl's in a coma. They got her over at the University of Pennsylvania Hospital. One of those deals where she could sleep forever or wake up tomorrow. They don't know.'

'Best damn doctors in the world and they don't know?'

'That's just their way of saying don't get your hopes up.'

'You wouldn't know the girl's name, would you?'

'Sure. Her name's Catherine Waites. Poor girl's over there by herself. That was the medic I had on the phone. He said they still haven't been able to locate a family member. She's over eighteen but they'd still like to get a hold of her parents. So far, no luck.'

Lou heard the name and it hit him somewhere between his chest and his scrotum, like a punch in the gut. He knew the name, knew it as well as he knew his own. Catherine Waites, the girl from his dreams, the girl from his past, his last call as a Philly cop, the face that had been haunting his every night. He'd listened to the officer say it and even as it reached his ears, he didn't want to believe it.

It had taken a few seconds to sink in and hearing it spoken out loud after all this time, from the mouth of a total stranger, gave it a prescient reality that seemed to pin Lou to the back of his seat and take the wind out of him. His face grew pale and he felt suddenly sick to his stomach. His eyes clouded over, parked there on a city street and talking with this cop who was wondering now if maybe Lou was drunk. He hadn't thought so at first. But now he wasn't so sure.

Lou had climbed back into the driver's seat of his car, thanking the officer. The headlights coming at him in broken streams of white light seemed to burst in his eyes. He was holding onto the steering wheel, trying to stop the spinning in his head. A chill moved through his body. He was trying to control the shaking. Maggie was looking at him as if he was a stranger, his behavior beginning to frighten her.

'What's the problem, Dad?'

'I know her.'

'You know who?'

'Catherine Waites.'

'Who's Catherine Waites?'

'The girl from my dreams, the girl I saved. The girl I saved and then lost everything. My God, I haven't heard that name in so long. She was nine years old at the time.'

'You saw her? It's the same girl?'

'It must be. After all these years. And she was right there and I didn't even recognize her.'

'Where did you see her?'

'There was an accident this morning in front of Jimmy Patterson's. She lost control coming down Remington Road.'

'Are you sure it's her?'

'It's her. And I just stood there and watched. It was Jimmy that helped her, not me.'

'You saved her life once already, didn't you?'

'I wish I can say that I had saved her. Oh, I protected her at the time. But I didn't save her from anything. That guy I crippled, it was her uncle, her pedophile uncle, and it wasn't the first time she'd been molested.' Lou's mouth hung open and a broken laugh escaped. It sounded more like the groan of some wounded animal. 'And it wasn't going to be the last, if you'd seen her mom's latest boyfriend in the courtroom.'

'There's nothing you could have done about that. It wasn't your job to solve people's problems. Don't beat yourself up over it. The way I heard the story you did the right thing. You took a dangerous predator off the street. And if he was made to suffer, so what? He got what he deserved.'

'I hit him four or five times with my nightstick, Maggie, in the back of the head. I could have just reached down and pulled him off her. A swift kick in the ribs would have done the trick. I saw him on top of that little girl and I lost it.'

'They should have pinned a medal on you.'

'Well, instead I was strongly advised by the department to take an early retirement, a polite way of saying get lost. The alternative would have been criminal prosecution. The charges were dropped at the time to avoid a messy lawsuit. I was proud to be a Philadelphia cop. I thought those guys were my friends and suddenly nobody wanted to be associated with me. Arnold Stegman walked.'

'You mean he rolled. You put him in a wheelchair, remember.'
Lou turned his head slowly toward his daughter. He reached his
hand behind her neck, her hair tangling in his fingers. He kissed
her on the top of the head. 'You ever see her again after that?'
  'I heard from her once, a couple years after the incident. She
wrote me a letter, thanking me. She must have been about twelve
or thirteen by then but I remember reading it and thinking that
she still sounded like the same nine-year-old girl. She said that
her mom thanked me too but her mom wasn't very good at
writing letters so she was writing for both of them. You know
what she asked me? She wanted to know if I'd mind being her
dad for a while. She'd said her mom had broken up with Jessie
and wasn't home much anymore. I guess Jessie was the boyfriend
I'd seen in the courtroom. "For a while," she'd said. How do you
become someone's dad for a while?'
  Maggie folded her arms across her chest as if the cold was
beginning to sink in. Lou rolled up the window. They both
watched the squad car pull away, the cop giving a brief wave, a
half-assed salute as he passed.
  'You still have the letter?'
  'I could probably dig it up. Why?'
  'I'd like to see it.'
  'I'll look for it.'
  'Why don't we visit her in the hospital?'
  'I was thinking the same thing.'
  They weren't far from home and they drove the short distance
in silence, Lou lost in his thoughts and Maggie lost in hers, both
thinking about Catherine Waites: if she'd live or die and if they
were the only two people in the world that cared. She was in a
coma, the officer said. Maybe the first good night's sleep
Catherine Waites ever had. And if she never woke up, at least
the pain that seemed to stalk her from childhood would finally
be over. There was physical pain and then there was emotional
pain. Was one worse than the other, Lou wondered? Catherine
Waites could answer that question better than he could. Perhaps
he'd ask her if she ever woke up.

Maggie was thinking the same thing. Lou could sense her
thoughts. There had always been that connection between them.

They'd even made a game into it, trying to guess what the other was thinking.

Catherine Waites had become a sort of conduit for them, a passageway back to a time when everything had changed for both of them, a time when he first discovered that everything he'd believed in was false, that there was nothing for him to return to: no job, no family and no home. And just as Lou's life was in turmoil, so too was his daughter's. It was a time of great confusion and sadness, a time when Maggie spent her nights awake in bed wondering where her father had gone and if he would ever return.

So, while Lou had been answering his last call as a policeman, responding to the screams of a child and saving this girl who a moment before was a stranger to him, his own daughter was on the brink of losing the innocence of her own childhood, losing the permanence that came with a marriage and a family and a home, finding out that it was all just a bus ticket away from a long, empty ride to nowhere, finding out that it was all just an illusion. And finding it out the hard way.

They interlocked their fingers on the seat between them. He wished he could give her back the time she'd lost, restore all those wasted years. He wished he could have collected her tears in a great round barrel, all of them running together like some secluded reservoir brimming with rainwater, and return them to her one fragile cup at a time.

NINE

They turned onto Meridian Avenue. A light sprinkling of snow swirled around the street light at the corner, the first few flakes confirming the arrival of winter. His headlights caught the dusting of white on the cars parked up and down the block. It had only been a few months earlier he'd seen moths circling in the light, their small white wings as light as rice paper and coated with a fine layer of white powder like dust on the tattered sheaf of a forgotten book. They were attracted by the light and danced in the night sky as if they were celebrating their last night on earth. And for most of them it was, the hordes of black bats circling nearby, picking them off one by one, drawn to the movement and to the smell of blood.

Meridian Avenue was quickly becoming another link in a chain of forgotten neighborhoods throughout Philadelphia. Every time Lou pulled up in front of his house he saw the subtle changes; the way people kept up their properties or didn't keep them up. Overbrook, Germantown, Kensington, Logan and a dozen other neighborhoods just like them could all be stricken from the map of the city and nobody would notice. They had become like little cities unto themselves, isolated even from each other. They could be written out of the history books and the only people who would know or care would be the ones still living there, the ones too poor or too stubborn or too stupid to get out.

Even Lou was finding it difficult to care what the hell happened here anymore. What did it matter? All the old neighborhoods were disappearing. They were being transformed into something Lou no longer seemed able to recognize. Sections of the city that were once filled with the hard-working sons and daughters of immigrants were fading from Philadelphia's collective memory. The drug trade had taken its toll and the streets teemed now with a kind of zombie, a generation constantly under the influence. Lou could see it in their eyes, in their nocturnal wanderings. They'd become something less than human, something that saw their fellow men as prey, like some kind of reptile in a primordial swamp. The sole purpose of their existence was to satisfy a hunger.

But why should he care? It ceased to be his struggle long ago. He bore witness to it, sure, but it didn't belong to him. It wasn't his goddamn problem anymore. And there weren't many left around to mourn its passing. And yet he'd returned to this neighborhood, to the same brick row house, to the same crumbling steps and rusted iron railing, his daughter joining him here among the ghosts and shadows of the forbearers she never knew, as if by her presence alone their spirit could fill her. He often thought his parents would have done a better job raising Maggie than he'd done. Maybe that was one of the reasons he'd come back.

It certainly wasn't for the gang of sixteen-year-old boys selling crack on the corner. Rosenberg's grocery store used to be there and if Buddy Rosenberg was still around, he would have put those boys to work and if they didn't want to work he would have sent them home to their mothers in the back of a police car. Buddy hadn't come home from World War II to get scared off by a handful of juvenile delinquents. But now there was a pile of rotting garbage in front of the place and Lou didn't even know where it came from or who put it there. He only knew that the smell of decay wafted up from the open cans and was carried down the block by the same wind that carried in the cold off the river.

If enough people complained maybe the city would send a few guys over to clean it up. Being a garbage man wasn't much different than being a cop, Lou thought. They both were responsible for cleaning the streets and their methods were often strangely similar.

He remembered how he used to listen for the sound of the garbage truck rumbling up Meridian Avenue. The garbage cans were made of metal back then, from the days when their houses were warmed by coal and the burnt ash had to be carried out every morning. He'd rush to the window in his pajamas, his father already up in his uniform and pouring his first cup of coffee. He'd watch these dark, strong men lifting the dented metal cans, tossing them from the moving truck, hearing the sound of the cans hitting the street and wondering how early these men had to wake up, if it was still dark when they crawled from their beds and drove around the city on that massive truck as if they were riding on the back of an elephant.

Lou squeezed into a spot about halfway down the block, backing up and using the mirrors on both sides and pulling forward until he touched bumpers with the car in front of him. Maggie screeched like a bird and Lou made a production of walking around and inspecting the damage. He put his hand to his chin, waiting thoughtfully for Maggie to come around with her skeptical frown.

'Not a scratch. Pretty soft touch, huh?'

'Is that what you call it? I call it poor judgment.'

'It's a tight spot.'

'I've seen tighter.'

They walked down the block with the wind at their backs and a full moon hiding behind steadily moving clouds. It would poke out its white grinning face just long enough to cast a few ominous shadows across the sidewalk and laugh silently at Lou and his daughter for their fear of the dark and their susceptibility to the cold.

They reached the front steps of the house, the stairs cracking again where Lou had patched it. They were careful about where they placed their feet and they were able to navigate the six or seven steps without much trouble. They were careful also not to lean too heavily on the loosened iron banister. A set of keys jingled in Lou's hand as he turned the deadbolt and grabbed the handle with his thumb on the latch as if he was opening a bottle of soda. The small front porch was just a slab of concrete running into the evening shadows.

It was Maggie who first saw the blood.

Her eyes had grown accustomed to the dark and she followed the trail of red spots to a man slumped in the chair at the edge of the porch. She'd only ever seen her father in that chair, sitting in the dark and smoking, leaning his head back against the brick wall of the house and blowing the smoke up towards the light. The glass ashtray on the floor was still there like a single polished stone in a rock garden. The man in the chair moved and his bloody arm fell, his fingers dangling just inches from the floor as if he was reaching in vain for the blood spilling from his body and gathering in a small puddle beneath him.

Maggie screamed and a black drop trickled from the man's hand and landed with what seemed like an explosion in Lou's head.

Jimmy Patterson was still alive but he wouldn't be for much longer. Lou tried to imagine what Jimmy must have looked like crawling up on that porch and into the chair with the two fresh bullet wounds he had in his stomach, the blood running freely now into his lap. Jimmy had lost the strength to keep pressure on his bleeding abdomen. He'd dragged himself the six long blocks from his house to Lou's front porch and was exhausted. There was nothing left for him to do but die.

Lou lifted Jimmy's head and looked into his dull black eyes. He smelled the blood and the alcohol that saturated it.

'What happened, Jimmy?' Lou yelled, begging the question though he knew Jimmy was drifting, the world of sight and sound falling away. 'Jimmy, can you hear me?'

Jimmy opened his mouth to speak and blood gurgled in his throat and spewed over his chin and onto his blood-soaked shirt. His left leg kicked out, going suddenly rigid and then circling under him, his ankle catching in the leg of the chair. Jimmy groaned from somewhere deep in his chest and coughed up another clot of thick red blood. In the next instant his body went limp as if he were a marionette and his strings had been cut all at once. Lou looked down at Jimmy's hands, one that lay motionless in his lap and the other hanging limp to the ground. His fingers relaxed and gravity seemed to pull them toward something floating in the pool of blood at his feet.

Jimmy's hand hadn't been pointing. It was reaching. Lou saw it now. He'd been reaching toward something partially submerged in the congealing puddle of blood. Lou bent to one knee and plucked out a gold ring. He held it up to the street light, turning it over and examining the oval-shaped diamond in its center, cloudy and red with blood.

Maggie had been on her cell phone, frantically telling the little she knew to the dispatcher on the other end of the line, something about a man covered in blood sitting on her front porch. A female operator with a very matter-of-fact voice asked Maggie if he was still breathing. A logical question followed by another one asking just how much blood there was. Both logical questions that Maggie was finding impossible to answer, her voice caught in her throat. The ambulance was on its way and so were the cops and they'd be there as soon as they could. But it was Philadelphia, the dispatcher told her, what the hell did she expect?

TEN

The ambulance arrived first and by the time Philly's finest rolled onto the scene Lou had Maggie inside, calming her down at the kitchen table. He'd turned on the stove, the gas jets heating the room. She was still trembling but the color was returning to her face. He'd quickly put together a cup of hot chocolate from a packet of powder. She seemed to be handling it pretty well, he thought, better than Jimmy Patterson was handling the two holes in his belly, his body chilling on the front porch, the last of the urine emptying from his bladder and mixing with the blood on the ground.

Lou had checked the body one final time before the uniforms arrived and sealed the place off in a maze of yellow crime scene tape. He'd pocketed the cigarette lighter from the window ledge behind Jimmy's head. He'd attempted to follow the trail of blood down the stairs and onto the sidewalk. It led him across the street and to the end of Meridian Avenue, droplets of blood heavier in some places and lighter in others. He'd followed it to the edge of Morris Park where it seemed to have disappeared. His eyes had swept across the open park and into the deepening darkness, taking in the swaying cluster of pine trees at the top of the knoll and the moon casting long moving shadows over the yellow grass. Morris Park was known to have kept its secrets over the years, much as Judy Garland Park and other parks in the city had, and it would have to keep one more. Whatever the cops found here, Lou thought, they could have. He'd keep the ring to himself, for now.

Lieutenant Kevin Mitchell was standing on the porch when Lou got back, a small congregation of uniformed officers standing in the yard below him. Mitch wore a black trench coat, black boots and gloves. A transparent plume of steam rose from his mouth every time he took a breath, like a musk ox on a snow-covered hill. He didn't look happy to get a call at home, the type of call that brought him out on a cold night after he'd already slipped into a pair of flannels and downed his third bottle of Yuengling lager. The fact that an ex-Philadelphia cop lay dead not ten feet from where he stood was incidental. Mitch wasn't shedding any tears over Jimmy Patterson. A body was a body and he was a police lieutenant and he'd want straight answers about what Lou was working on and why Jimmy would pick a place like Lou Klein's porch to die.

Lou weaved between the officers and ducked under the line of yellow tape. Someone should have stopped him but no one did.

'Looks like being friends with you is getting kind of dangerous, Lou.'

'Never used to be.'

'Not since you went all private on us.'

'It's a job, Mitch. I don't always like it. Like you don't always like yours.'

'Tell me about it.'

They stood side by side on the porch, not looking at each other and not looking at Jimmy Patterson. Their furtive policeman's glances tended to be drawn to the street light that burned like a low-hanging moon. The cops searching the ground for clues would turn their heads toward the two, watching them curiously as if they were two actors on a stage, their destinies inexorably linked.

'What do you know about the Haggerty family, Mitch?'

'Whoa, let's stop right there, Lou. I'm asking the questions and you're giving the answers.'

'Is that the way it works?'

'Suppose I humor you just this once. I don't know any more or less about the Haggertys than I ought to. And neither should you.'

'Well, if by chance you do know who Brian Haggerty is, then you should know that's his brother-in-law over there bleeding all over my porch.'

'That much I do know.'

'And what are you going to do about it?'

'Same as I'd do for anyone else.'

'The Haggertys seem to be a family that are pretty good at getting away with murder.'

'Wait a second, Lou.'

'Just hearsay, Mitch. Nothing but a lot of rumors that have been running around this town like ghosts in a graveyard.'

'Ghosts don't make the kind of noise you're making.'

Lou took Mitch by the arm and led him into the shadows. He wanted to avoid the rapt attention of a growing audience that seemed to have forsaken their task, preferring to await some sort of climax from the stage. The two men stood over Jimmy Patterson and continued the conversation in hushed tones. Jimmy didn't look the least bit interested.

'Listen, Mitch. This morning, at that accident, Jimmy asked me to look into a little trouble his sister was having with her husband. Next thing I know the sister shows up on my doorstep and she's scared. She's trying real hard not to show it but she's never been one to hide her feelings very well.'

'Takes after her big brother.'

'She's shaking like a fucking leaf and apparently she has good reason.' Lou's hands began fumbling in his pockets, finding the lighter and wishing he had a pack of cigarettes to go with it. 'It turns out she's Haggerty's alibi for that nasty little business with his first wife and his father. That alone would be enough to make me nervous but there's more. Haggerty's first wife, the former Miss Valerie Price, began her illustrious rise to fame as a dancer at the Arramingo Club, Haggerty's place on the waterfront. And she was fooling around with more men than just Haggerty's old man. Rumor has it the list was pretty long, names you and I might recognize, including our friend here.'

Lou pointed at Jimmy's ashen blue face with his thumb as if he was hitching a ride on a cold night on the Schuylkill Expressway. But nobody picked up anybody on the Schuylkill Expressway, not if they wanted to make it home alive.

Mitch looked as if he wasn't buying Lou's story. He was nodding his head but he wasn't buying it and Lou knew why. There wasn't a cop on the force willing to dig up any dirt on the Haggertys, especially one with thirty years on the job and a fat pension to protect. Mitch pulled his gloves on a little tighter.

'You expect me to believe that Brian Haggerty pumps a couple of bullets into Jimmy Patterson because he might know something about a ten-year-old murder or his sister might, or because he slept with his dead wife or because he's sending some kind of a message to his current wife? And he drops him off on your porch because Jimmy is just too drunk to drive himself. Maybe Haggerty thought you'd sober him up and take him home.'

'I'm not saying that's the way it happened. I'm saying Brian Haggerty is a suspect, a strong suspect and maybe in more than one murder.'

'Let us handle the murder investigations. OK, Lou? The Philadelphia police are still capable of solving a homicide, in case you've forgotten. Let's just wait and see what comes back from the lab and ballistics. Maybe we'll get lucky.'

'Someone's going to have to break the news to Franny.'

'I was hoping you'd do the honors. Better coming from you than me.'

'I'll handle it, but you might want to talk to her yourself. If she knows anything, she could be in danger. She could even be a witness.'

'I doubt that.'

'I'd just keep an eye on her if I were you.'

'Sounds to me like you're doing a damn good job of that yourself.'

Lou went back in the house to check on Maggie. Her trembling had subsided to an occasional shudder. Her eyes were closed and she was holding her head in her hands as if she was trying to reach inside and pull out the memory of what she'd seen and dump it out onto the table like so much spilled coffee, wipe it up with a wet rag and rinse it down the drain. Lou sat next to her and put his hand gently over hers.

'It's like a bad dream.'

'I know, honey.'

'That's the first thing I thought when I saw him, that I was dreaming and I'd wake up and be somewhere else, back in my bed. Have you ever felt like that?'

'Sometimes. It happens when reality becomes too painful to deal with.'

'Turn it into a dream and dreams aren't real.'

'Sort of.'

'No wonder you have nightmares.' She tried to force a smile. 'But this isn't a dream. Is it?'

'No.'

'He just looked so relaxed sitting there. It wasn't what I expected. I always thought if you got shot and you knew you were going to die you'd be screaming, writhing in pain. But he seemed so calm. The look on his face: he seemed content. It was like he was made of wax, like he wasn't a real person. It gave me the chills, watching someone die like that. I won't ever forget it.'

'I'm going to try to find out what happened to him. But first I'm going to call Joey, have him come up here and sit with you for a while.'

She stood up and walked to the kitchen sink, spilling out what was left of the now-cold hot chocolate and rinsing out the cup. She pulled a dish towel from a drawer and started drying the cup, continuing to wipe it even after it was dry.

'I don't need a babysitter. I'll be fine. You should take Joey with you. You'll need him more than I will.'

Lou put his hands on her shoulders, kissed her on the top of the head and turned to go. One of Mitch's investigators was still on the porch, photographing Jimmy from a variety of different angles, snapping pictures as if he was the paparazzi and Jimmy was on the red carpet, real celebrity. The medical examiner had a team there, ready to take him away once Mitch was done. They stood on the street, snapping on their rubber gloves and leaning against a tan-colored van. The back doors of the van hung open and they'd pulled out a thin metal stretcher with a black body bag flat across the top of it. It didn't look big enough to hold Jimmy Patterson. They'd have to squeeze him in and zip him up and it would take all three of them to carry him down the stairs.

Lou pulled out his cell phone, flipped it open and found Joey in his list of contacts. He hit the speed dial and held the phone to his ear as he watched a detective rummaging through Jimmy's pockets like an ordinary thief. Joey picked up on the fourth ring. His voice came back with the loose texture of bourbon in it.

'How soon can you get over here?'

'Why, what's up?'

'I just found Jimmy Patterson sound asleep on my porch. He won't be waking up any time soon. By the time you get here they'll have him down at the morgue and they'll be checking his belly to see what he had for dinner other than two thirty-eight-caliber pieces of lead.'

'Shit.'

'Maggie's a little shook up. Could you stay with her a little while?'

'Where you going?'

'First, I'm going to try to find Franny. Then I'll hit the Arramingo Club.'

'You sure you don't want company?'

'I'd feel better if you stayed here with Maggie.'

'You got it.'

Lou snapped the phone shut and clipped it on his belt. He took one last look at Jimmy Patterson and then at the floor of the concrete porch that Lou had recently painted battleship gray and was now a shiny crimson, still slick with blood. He craved a cigarette. It wasn't the first time he wanted one since he quit but this time it was more like need than want. He longed for the feel of it in his hand, the warm smoke in his mouth, the burning in his nose, the calming effect of the nicotine. Maybe it was because of Jimmy. He laughed to himself, recalling that Jimmy had just quit smoking. Everybody was quitting except Joey. He could have bummed a cigarette from one of the cops parading around his property. They'd already littered the yard with smoldering butts. They were searching the ground with their flashlights, looking for footprints or spent bullet casings, poking their noses under the thin bushes against the house and around the steps where the dirt had begun to subside. They wouldn't find a thing.

His eyes locked onto a pack of cigarettes on the window ledge directly behind Jimmy's left shoulder. Lou couldn't seem to remember now if they were one of his old packs and he'd just left them there or if maybe Jimmy had brought them.

He took a few steps across the porch, careful to miss the puddle of blood, and palmed the pack of cigarettes. If the crime scene guys suspected that he was removing evidence they didn't show it. They must have just assumed the pack was his and they all understood how possessive a man can be when it came to his cigarettes, especially cops, who always seemed to be dishing them out to suspects and confidential informants to loosen their tongues. Cigarettes were like money in prison and they seemed to understand the language. As he turned and started down the stairs, Mitch caught him by the wrist.

'I thought you gave those up.'

'I started again.'

'All that running and you top it off with a smoke?'

'It's a tough habit to break.'

'Yeah. If it wasn't for people's bad habits, we'd be out of a job.' He released Lou's wrist, opening his hand with an exaggerated motion as if he were releasing a trapped bird. 'Call me if you find something out.'

'You got it.'

Lou trotted down the steps and jumped into his car. He tapped a cigarette from the pack and put it to his lips. There were matches wedged behind the cellophane. He struck one between his cupped hands. It flared in front of him, illuminating his face in the rearview mirror. He took a hard drag on the cigarette. It was his first in over a month and it tasted good. He looked down at the matchpack. In the flickering light it read 'The Arramingo Club,' with the silhouette of a woman on the cover, just a black shadow, all legs and breasts and hair. The match went out and he was left in darkness.

He put the car in gear and eased slowly past the police cars, thinking that he couldn't remember the last time he'd seen Jimmy Patterson with a cigarette in his hand. He picked up a little speed toward the end of Meridian Avenue. Jimmy Patterson didn't smoke anymore. He'd given it up just as Lou had. But Franny still smoked, like a chimney.

ELEVEN

Remington Road was quiet and dark. Thick, bare branches threw shadows over the narrow street. The same pale-faced moon cast a trickle of light past the overhanging trees and made Remington Road look more like a muddied river run dry. Lou pulled up in front of the Patterson house. He shut off the car and sat in the quiet. The house was shrouded in darkness.

There weren't any cars in the driveway or parked in front. That very morning Lou had been standing there watching Jimmy rub the long scratch on his car door, listening to him wise off to the cop and wave with his big paw in the air like a grizzly bear with his nose in a beehive. Jimmy had been the first one to help Catherine Waites after the accident, rushing to her aid because that's who he was; it was the only way he knew.

Lou wondered what Franny's involvement was, if she'd been there when it happened or if she was up in bed and hadn't gotten the news yet. He wondered if she'd sprung awake at the very moment Jimmy had taken his last breath, letting her ring fall from his bloody hand. It happened that way sometimes. She would have run to the window, knowing something was wrong, death hovering in the night like a low-hanging cloud. The stillness of the night wouldn't have fooled her, though. Somehow, she would know.

Lou sat for a moment more in the stony silence. There were plastic trash containers and yellow recycling bins in front of every house on the block except Jimmy's. Lou had a sudden urge to take Jimmy's garbage down to the curb for him, stack it in a neat pile so when the garbage men came in the morning they wouldn't wonder why, for the first time in fifteen years, Jimmy Patterson didn't have his garbage ready and waiting to be collected. Surely the city owed him at least that. Haul the man's trash away. Send a cop down his street once in a while. It wasn't that much to ask.

Lou climbed the front steps and stood on the porch looking down at the street, seeing it as Jimmy had every morning, the same people and the same cars, the same trees with the bark peeling off like the mottled skin of the old men that came to the Regal on Sunday mornings for bagels and tea. Only today had been different. It was the last time he would see it and Lou wondered if Jimmy had ever thought about that, if he took the view of the world from his front porch for granted.

The view from Lou's porch was much the same, a view like so many others in this city where everything looked the same, like a movie set, a facade that got packed up in a truck at the end of the day and hauled away. But it was the only view they had. It's not like they paid anything extra for it. They could have left at any time if they didn't like it, sold everything and moved into an apartment nearer their children, where the deafening silence of the suburban nights would keep them awake at night, an imposing silence that could drive a sane man crazy. There was still cheap land out in Lancaster County; they could live like the Amish, without cars, without phones, without electricity or television. Wear a straw hat and a smile and try to forget that the heart of man was still vicious, the heart of an animal, and he'd always find the tools to kill.

Lou couldn't blame the neighborhood for what happened to Jimmy Patterson. Shit like this could happen anywhere. It just happened in Philadelphia a little more often.

There didn't seem to be anyone home but Lou couldn't just drive away, not after what had happened. And if he'd decided to sit there on Jimmy's front stoop dreaming about all the years Jimmy Patterson had spent in that house, one of the neighbors would eventually notice him and call the cops. They'd do that for Jimmy. It was still that kind of neighborhood. They watched out for each other. They might even get a license plate before he left, if they could see it in the thick darkness. And if there were any more corpses lying around for Lou to trip over, he'd prefer to find them before the law arrived and not hear about it from Mitch afterwards.

He tried the handle on the front door, giving it a little rattle first but it held fast. He cupped his hands over his eyes and put them against the window. The glass was cold and it was all darkness inside. He could make out the shapes of a sofa and chairs, a lamp with an oversized shade on a table between them, the faint outline of pictures on the wall, the flat black screen of a television across the room. His eye caught movement, a lean black cat bounding from the couch and over the dark carpet. It was light and fast and moved like a shadow, like a stone skipping over the placid surface of a frozen pond.

He walked around toward the back of the house, following a narrow stone walkway between the houses. A spotlight clicked on, the flash blinding him, forcing his eyes shut as he turned his head away. He must have activated a sensor, one of Jimmy's security set-ups, for all the good it did. The spotlight threw long dark shadows almost to the street, lighting the thin branches of the young maple tree in the yard, its sinewy gray trunk twisted and cracked, its shrinking leaves transforming from red to orange to a rusty brown. Under the tree a crusty layer of ice had formed on the grass and hardened like crystal. The windows on this side of the house weren't at ground level. They were higher up and looked securely fastened with the curtains drawn tightly closed.

There wasn't much room between the houses in that neighborhood: two-story, red-brick colonials, most of them separated into twins, the space between them so small as to be almost touching like hotels on a Monopoly board, close enough to see into your neighbors' windows, hear their arguments, smell what they were having for dinner, near enough to see what color underwear your neighbor's wife was wearing. At least it wasn't the projects – the chicken coops as the cops had called them: fourteen stories of filth, one crowded floor stacked upon another, its residents squeezed together like rats in the sewer and all that shit running downhill like a polluted river.

Once you were in there you'd never escape. There was no hope of it. You were trapped every second of the day and night, unable to get a breath of fresh air or see the sun in the sky or walk down a street that wasn't congested with people, no respite from the world of men. Not a moment's privacy, not a moment's peace. And for many the only way out was death, a quiet, peaceful death if you could manage it, fall asleep and never wake up. But more likely it was violent, a hail storm of bullets raining down from the heavens, the gods of the city playing some pathetic game with humanity.

The back door was locked as tightly as the front with what looked like a newly installed deadbolt. Lou could see into the small kitchen, a white coffee maker on the counter, an open box of cat food on the table and a cordless phone, quiet in its cradle. The backyard ran right up to an alley with a wooden shed angled in the corner and a worn patch of dirt where Jimmy might have parked his car if there were no spaces on the street.

Two garbage cans sat next to a side door that probably led to the basement. One looked brand new with a set of black handles that locked down the lid. The other was mildewed brown, half the size of the other one, with a longitudinal crack in it from top to bottom. The lid was held down with a brick, its rough edges and points worn smooth.

Lou's mother used bricks the same way. It was a good way to keep the squirrels and the raccoons and the stray cats out of the garbage. If they were hungry enough they'd find a way to gnaw through the plastic and in the morning she'd find debris strewn across the back porch. She'd spent more than one evening at the back door waiting for them, discovering that some animals only came out at night. They came out to feed and were impossible to stop. She'd shaken her broomstick at them, set traps, used sprays to keep them away like they were weeds in her garden. But all her attempts proved futile and she had begun to question the effectiveness of her bricks and her fence.

She'd stack them along the bottom of the chain link fence that bordered the back of her property. She'd stack them around the small garden in the backyard. She'd spent most of her days in that garden, weather permitting, cultivating and working like a bricklayer, building a small wall around her frail tomato plants. Lou had always wondered where she got the bricks from, picturing his mother standing in front of a mound of rubble, sifting through the wreckage of some demolished apartment building, loading them into her metal shopping cart and wheeling them down the uneven sidewalk. They could have weighed a ton but she would have gotten them home. She could have built a wall with those bricks, a great brick wall separating her from the rest of the city.

Lou picked up the brick and the garbage can toppled over. He tossed it into the wet grass where it landed with a dull thud. He pulled a pen flashlight from his jacket pocket and aimed the beam down at the contents that had spilled onto the walk. There were two plastic bags still inside, thin white plastic stretched to the breaking point like the skin of a bloated corpse. He poked one of them with the pen and it split open, white maggots tumbling from the broken bag in a choppy torrent of cracked eggshells, rotten vegetables and steak bones with slivers of flesh and fat still clinging to them. Lou picked up a broken branch lying in the grass, a thin brittle stick that had fallen from the neighbor's poplar. He prodded the bag gently with the dry, fragile stick. A few cans of Campbell's soup tumbled out and clattered on the walk as if they were tied to the bumper of an old Buick with a couple of newlyweds inside making for Interstate 95 and points south.

A light came on in a first-floor window in the house adjacent to Patterson's. Lou saw a figure peel back the blinds and peer out. It was a woman, thin and hunched, her fingers like bone against the glass. Lou could see through the sheer curtains to the lighted room behind her, a neat little parlor that appeared frozen in time, like a miniature English manor dropped into a row home in West Philadelphia. Lou raised his hand and gave an innocent wave, trying to put her mind at ease, this old lady, maybe drying herself after a hot bath, about to put her tired body to bed and hearing a sound outside and climbing down those stairs one last time, afraid of what she might see but afraid also of falling, remembering the time she'd fallen before, coming down those stairs for a cup of hot tea with milk and a touch of whiskey that she hoped would help her sleep. No matter what Lou did now, she'd be calling 911.

He flipped the lid off the other can. Six pizza boxes sat wedged inside with another white plastic bag on top. Lou reached in and tore it open. A vacuum cleaner bag rolled over, spilling its contents of thick gray dirt and dust. Jimmy had never run a sweeper in his life. It must have been Franny, cleaning the place up if she was going to be staying there for a while. It would have been good therapy since her romance with Brian Haggerty had gone sour. She would have fallen into a routine she was used to, one she'd followed before, taking care of her father and three brothers, two of them cops, one a firemen, living with the memory of their dead mother and the baby brother who'd never come back from Iraq. Lou poked at the garbage bag, thinking of Jimmy Patterson and his sister, the two having never said their last goodbyes.

Mitch's boys were surely on their way by now. But they wouldn't take the time to sift through Jimmy's garbage. They wouldn't want to hang around that long. They had better things to do. There were other murders and other crime scenes and honestly, they didn't have the patience. And what did they really expect to find? To get a conviction these days they'd need an eye-witness or a confession. And they weren't going to find either at the bottom of a garbage can.

But it wasn't the first time Lou had searched through people's garbage and found something valuable. It was an old police trick, a way to collect evidence without a warrant, without setting foot inside a suspect's house. Trash was considered abandoned property, fair game for anyone willing to sift through someone else's junk to get a glimpse of their discarded life beneath the surface. It had the smell of eavesdropping, sticking your nose in where it didn't belong.

His mother would always curse the men she'd see cruising the neighborhood at night in noisy, beat-up pick-up trucks, picking through stuff at the curb as if they were at a rummage sale or a flea market, referring to them as garbage scouts. The police did the same thing, commandeering a city truck for the day and grabbing what they wanted from a list of addresses, bringing it all back to the station and sorting through it, wearing rubber gloves and particle masks. It was a good way to find out about a person, see what they threw away, what they no longer had any use for. Turned out there wasn't much difference between a cop and a trash man after all.

Needles and empty baggies were what the cops had been looking for, packaging from over-the-counter cold medications, certain chemicals, cleaning products, receipts. They'd always find enough beer cans to get a few bucks for the aluminum at the recycling center. Now, Lou wasn't sure exactly what he was looking for.

He shone the light down to the bottom of the can, the fractured beam growing dimmer, losing power. He used the stick, pushing aside paper plates and plastic cups and soiled napkins. It looked as if someone had a birthday party with a sheet cake from the Superfresh and a few soggy gallons of WAWA ice cream. The beam of light landed on a wad of paper towels rolled into a ball, damp and dark with moisture. Lou used the stick like a divining rod, pushing on the clump of paper towels until they broke open. It looked sticky, like a used bandage saturated with matted blood.

He used the stick to ease the bloody towel out onto the driveway. He gave it a nudge with the stick and then another and it began to unravel. And then he saw it, a severed finger, gray and swollen, like a sausage link ready for the grill. It was a woman's finger. He wasn't sure just how he knew, with the nail torn off and the knuckle twisted as if it had been caught in a car door and crushed. First the ring and now a finger and still no sign of Franny.

Lou suddenly found himself fighting the urge to vomit. It started as a tingling deep in his throat and then his insides beginning to churn and whatever was left in his stomach began moving around. He swallowed hard and felt his mouth fill with saliva. He threw up in the frozen grass.

He caught his breath and turned his gaze back to the severed finger. He looked down at the dappled skin and the ugly black vein protruding from its base like a worm from the ground and the jagged shard of bone from which a grizzly ounce of flesh still clung and he wanted to kick it into the dirt, bury it like a dog buries a bone. He wanted to go home and gather up his daughter and keep driving until they were somewhere warm and sunny, somewhere safe near the ocean, where the body parts that drifted ashore belonged to people he'd never known, people he'd never cared about, people who'd lived on the other side of the goddamned world.

TWELVE

Lou flipped open his cell phone, got Mitch on his private line and told him to send one of his boys over if he hadn't already. Lou didn't have any more room in his pockets for another piece of evidence. He had the ring in one pocket and the pack of matches from the Arramingo Club in the other. He figured this long-lost finger belonged in a laboratory somewhere deep in the bowels of the Philadelphia Police Department where it could be properly dissected. He walked up the driveway toward the back of the house, out of the reach of that stubborn spotlight, where he lit up another cigarette.

The shed in the corner of the yard looked like a dilapidated doll's house, with small shuttered windows and a shingled roof. It was a replica of a Tudor mansion, just large enough for a child to climb inside and hide if he had the courage to brave the dark tangle of spider webs anchored in the ceiling like angry black clouds. The whole thing sat on a concrete foundation that had begun to crumble at the edges where the rainwater rolled off the roof and eroded the stone. As Lou got closer he noticed that the door of the shed was warped and hung open, a rusty metal hasp hanging unlocked.

Lou pulled on the hasp and stood back from the swinging door. A bare bulb dangled from a frayed black cord, a pull string hanging from that. He reached inside and gave it a tug and the light came on and a hundred spiders seemed to move in that instant, retreating into the concealment of the pitched ceiling. The bulb swung like a pendulum, the shadows on the wall moving in time with the swinging light. Lou steadied it and stepped in.

A lawn mower sat on the concrete floor, a couple of red plastic gas cans beside it. And beside that lay Franny Patterson. It looked as if she was floating on a river of blood, lying on her side, curled up and fetal as if she meant to die in the same position in which she was born. But she wasn't dead.

Her arms were pulled in against her sides as if she could stop her own blood from flowing, wrap her arms around herself like a clamp. More blood, Lou thought, so much blood. He was sick of it. He knelt at her side and rolled her onto her back and saw the puncture wounds on her chest and the defensive wounds on her arms. He couldn't see how deeply she'd been stabbed but he could see the blood in her mouth as it opened and closed like a fish mouth with a hook caught in its throat. She was trying to speak, forcing words through the blood with the last shred of air left in her collapsing lungs.

'I'm sorry, Lou.' Guttural and rasping, a trailing whisper and a trickle of blood. 'I'm sorry. I should . . . I should have . . .'

She couldn't finish the sentence. She fell unconscious in Lou's arms. But he knew what she was going to say. He heard it in her voice and finished the sentence for her.

'You should have told me the truth. I know.' He took off his jacket and slid it under her head. 'I know.'

He flipped open his cell phone again. This time he called for an ambulance.

He stayed at her side and held her head in his lap, pushing the hair from her face and counting the seconds until he could hear the sirens getting closer. His eyes scanned the cluttered shed. There were an assortment of tools in matching green buckets lining a low shelf and other tools hanging from hooks on the back wall: a weed trimmer with a strand of fluorescent green wire dangling from its base like a tongue from the head of a snake, a long silver tree saw, a hack saw next to that, a hedge trimmer and a pair of snips and a shovel with dried dirt caked on the blade.

On the top shelf cans of paint were stacked in three neat rows. The paint cans looked as if they'd been sitting empty for a very long time, their labels obscured with dried paint smeared over the face of each can. They reminded Lou of the painted faces of Native Americans he'd seen in grade school history books and on record albums, conquered tribes with nothing left worth fighting for, the painted faces of defeat, faces turned into masks, masks that mimicked death.

Lou's eyes continued to scan the small shed. There was a square window in the back with a screen and an open vent. Nails came through the ceiling where the shingles had been tacked down, their pointed ends protruding through the wood like sharks' teeth. On the right a pile of newspapers sat on the shelf and a case of beer next to that and a sleeping bag next to that. Why the sleeping bag? Lou wondered.

Franny's breathing was shallow but steady. A good sign. He let her head rest on the jacket and stood to examine the contents of the shelf. He pulled out an empty bottle of beer from the case and held it up to the light. Cigarette butts lay at the bottom of the bottle, soaking in warm beer. He slid the bottle back into the case. He thought he'd smelled body odor when he first entered the shed. It didn't smell like Franny. Someone else had been in there. And not just to hide Franny's body.

He grabbed a newspaper off the top of the pile and looked for a date. He picked up a few more and did the same. They were relatively recent, from the last month. Most of the headlines dealt with the sudden rash of violence in Philadelphia, the stabbing of a stripper off Delaware Avenue and the body of a man found in Judy Garland Park. Violence was like a rash, Lou thought. It got under your skin and just when you thought it was gone there it was again, back with a vengeance.

Lou peeled off a few more papers. They were smudged and worn like the ones at the Regal, as if they'd been handled by a thousand greasy fingers, used to swat flies and mop up spilled coffee. He read under the light from the bare bulb. It was more of the same: dead bodies turning up in public parks, most of them women, and none of them out for an afternoon stroll with the tikes in a baby carriage. Supply and demand, Lou thought. In Philadelphia there weren't many good reasons to be in a public park after dark. You either had a bad habit to feed or you were looking for the kind of fun you couldn't find at home. And that's what it was: good, clean fun. Until you brought a disease home to your wife or some politician got pinched in a sting and ended up in the morning paper. Then it got serious.

He lifted another paper from the top of the pile and that's when he saw it. The blue-steel barrel and the checkered wood grip and the iron sights resting harmlessly within that bed of old newspapers, and yet seemingly emblazoned with the glow of death as if it had just been pulled from the forge and left to cool. Sixteen ounces of cold steel. Unless it was in someone's hand, it was nothing but useless metal. But metal with a history and unless he was mistaken, he'd guess a long, violent history.

It was a thirty-eight, with a little rust around the hammer and the trigger worn to a smooth, silvery finish. Lou had seen plenty of guns in his day but this one was special. Not just because it was an old revolver and nobody carried revolvers anymore, but because of the way he'd found it. It was always special when you found them like that, when you weren't looking for them, when they're lying around in a drawer or in a woman's purse or on a shelf just waiting to be found. It was the kind of gun that made the ballistics boys' mouths water.

A car door slammed somewhere on the street behind him, followed by the sound of boots coming up the driveway, the uniformed officer inside of them yawning as he made his way toward the back of the house. Another rookie with a crew cut over a shiny white scalp and blue eyes that seemed to sparkle like two blue diamonds. He didn't seem surprised by Lou's presence. Mitch must have warned him.

'This is a crime scene, Officer. You'll need to seal off this shed and the entire backyard. Franny Patterson is in there. She's the daughter of one police officer and the sister to another. So see if you can't expedite that ambulance. There's a gun in there as well and it might have been used in a murder. If you have any of that pretty yellow tape in your trunk, you may as well get it out. You're going to need it.'

The officer looked at him with that confused expression rookies get when they're asked a question whether they know the answer or not.

'I'll radio Lieutenant Mitchell. Let him know the situation.'

'You do that.' Lou took a few steps down the driveway and picked up the trash can lid with the severed finger on top of it. He carried it over to the officer like a waiter with a tray of hors d'oeuvres. 'And when your boss gets here, give him this. It's evidence, lad. And if you can find the person who did this, they'll probably make you a captain. And if Mitch wants to take credit for it, let him. He'll owe you for the rest of his life.'

Lou left him standing there, looking down at the finger, at the purple skin and the ugly black vein and the jagged shard of bone protruding from its base like a root. The ambulance had arrived and Lou kissed Franny on the forehead as the techs loaded her in. He drove away knowing the neighbors' fears were allayed now that the police had arrived and they'd have a show to watch outside if they were still restless and they'd have enough gossip to last them a lifetime.

Lou drove the darkened city streets paying little attention to the road. Occasionally, one of his front wheels would smack into a pothole and the car would shake on its frame and Lou would grip the wheel a little harder. He fought against the dull throb of sleep behind his eyes. Even at one o'clock in the morning, with the temperature hovering around thirty degrees, people were still out on the street, men with their faces hidden under knit hats and fur-trimmed hoods and puffy-down coats. They seemed to shuffle in place, sliding from one foot to the other, their suede boots unlaced and doing a dance choreographed to keep their toes from going numb. The West Philly Shuffle, Joey used to call it.

They kept their hands in their pockets to keep that same numbness from gripping their fingers.

One was indistinguishable from the other in Lou's eyes, a

generic brand of city life prone to dwelling in dark corners, sleeping in the day and coming out at night, brandishing a multitude of improvised weapons primarily designed to kill cops but which they more often used against themselves.

Lou didn't know how to react to these guys anymore, driving past them in the night, walking past them in the WAWA parking lot, smelling the smoke from their cigarettes, the bottles of cheap wine and the forty-ounce quarts of beer. He didn't know if he should meet their stares the way he did as a cop or look away, avoiding eye contact as he'd been doing lately. He felt like he had no other choice since he often had his daughter with him and had given up carrying a gun. He'd hoped that the cold would've kept them off the street but he'd given up on that idea long ago. Nothing kept them off the streets. And just as he had to be out there, so did they. It wouldn't have been the same city without them and he wouldn't have been the same man.

The light snow had stopped but the temperature was still dropping and the road ahead of him sparkled as if it were made of glass. The small car was buffeted by a sharp gust of wind. It made him wish he was still driving the old Thunderbird. That car would go through anything, never missed a beat. It was time to get it out of storage, he thought, out from under the tarp in Joey's garage and back on the road. To hell with the gas it burned and the exhaust fumes and the tinted windows. The car had balls and Lou had been feeling lately like he needed to get that back, a set of balls.

He let his thoughts wander to Franny Patterson, how he wished he'd found her sitting pretty in Haggerty's house in Torresdale, sipping tea with the mother-in-law she hated, both of them waiting for Brian to get home from the bar, wondering if he'd get home at all. Not that either of them cared all that much. Judging from what Joey said Brian Haggerty seemed to skate through life unscathed, even while tragedy struck all around him. He didn't give a shit about anyone and no one gave a shit about him. It was a hell of a way to live.

Everyone sort of assumed he'd hook up with one of his new young dancers, one who hadn't learned the ropes yet, who hadn't learned that after a few rounds in bed with Brian Haggerty she might not look quite so pretty anymore. The bruises on her arms would turn from red to blue to purple and to black and eventually disappear entirely but there would be no question about how they got there. And they could be put there again. She might even lose a tooth and if she was smarter than the average stripper, she'd take pictures and show them to Haggerty and make plenty of copies and convince him to buy her a new set of teeth and a pair of breasts to go with them.

But if she had that hint of desperation about her that was common in the trade or the smell of fear, she'd let Haggerty continue to beat the shit out of her, thinking it was a good career move, thinking she could get ahead in a business where there was no getting ahead. And soon enough she'd be working for some low-rent pimp in Kensington and spending her leisure time sucking on a crack pipe.

Franny Patterson up in the big house, he thought, but not anymore. And during her last days there she'd probably stopped caring what the hell Haggerty did or who he was with as long as it wasn't her shaking her tits up on that stage at the Arramingo Club. And now with her brother dead and her fighting for her life, Lou wondered if Franny Patterson still thought it was all worth it.

Lou twisted in the seat and reached for the cell phone on his belt. He held it at arm's length, scrolling through contacts as he jumped onto the ramp for the Schuylkill Expressway. The luminous screen glowed in his hand, a picture of Maggie on its face with her tongue sticking out and her glasses sliding down her nose. Lou had taken the picture himself. She'd been hugging an enormous purple gorilla with a big white belly, a stuffed animal he'd won for her that summer at the Allentown fair. He'd won it throwing baseballs while Maggie cheered in the background. The stand had advertised a full-size cardboard cutout of Steve Carlton in a Phillies uniform standing next to a table with five milk bottles stacked like a pyramid. But the milk bottles were made of thick plastic and they were filled with concrete and they were heavier than bowling pins. The three balls they'd given him were filled with sawdust. He threw them as if his life depended on it.

He put the phone against his ear and listened to it ring. An eighteen-wheeler roared past him, a garbage scowl carrying ten tons of municipal waste to a landfill in Jersey. When the roaring stopped Maggie's voice was on the line, the tremble still audible as she repeated his name.

'Dad? Dad, is that you?'

'Yeah, kid. It's me.'

'Sounded like you were in an accident or something.'

'One of those big trucks just about blew my doors off.'

'I hate those trucks. I stay as far away from them as I can. I think those guys are half-asleep most of the time.'

'They're just in a hurry to get where they're going.'

'Aren't we all.'

'How are you making out?'

'Pretty good. I'm playing poker with Joey. He's letting me take his money.'

'OK. Try to get some sleep. I'm going to be late.'

'Joey wants to know if you found anything over at Jimmy's.' Lou could hear Joey reciting his list of questions in the background. 'And did you get down to the Arramingo Club yet?'

'Tell Joey I'll talk to him later.'

'He heard ya.'

'And I'll talk to you later, too.'

'OK. Good night.'

'Good night, kid.'

He snapped the phone shut and let it rest against his thigh. Another few trucks rumbled past, the trailer of the last one fishtailing over the broken white line as the road merged from four lanes into three. He passed the exit for the zoo and he could see the Art Museum lit up like a monument across the river. He passed the 30th Street Station and veered south, coming up on the right side of all those trucks hugging the guard rail in the left lane. The Philadelphia skyline looked ominous through his side window, everything dark except for the statue of William Penn standing guard in the spotlight atop City Hall, asleep at his post. Lou still had the phone against his leg when it began to vibrate.

'What's up, Mitch?'

'I got the little present you left me.'

'Merry Christmas.'

'Thanks. What the hell are you getting me into, Lou? A straight-up shooting, I can deal with. I don't like it but I can deal with it. But when body parts start showing up that's getting bizarre, even for me.'

'It looks like the Pattersons pissed off the wrong person.'

'Yeah, maybe. And maybe Jimmy was doing a favor for his little sister. And maybe you're doing a favor for her, too. You just better be careful.'

'Careful is my middle name.'

'The surgeons are going to have a field day with your girlfriend. That finger didn't just fall off.'

'I figured as much.'

'And I got a man going over that shed with a fine-tooth comb. We should know a lot more once he's done.'

'This is a nasty business, Mitch. Something's not right. Jimmy was shot. Franny was stabbed. That finger looked like it was snipped off. It doesn't add up.'

'Even killers need a little variety in their life.' Lou was quiet and Mitch went on. 'Hey, listen, Lou. I'm already feeling the pressure from upstairs. I can't let this go on much longer. You know what I'm saying.'

'Tell me about it.'

'Every time some broad nicks herself shaving or takes off a piece of skin making a salad, the boys upstairs want to make it into a sex crime. What you got, though, is a crime of passion and considering the history of the Haggerty family in this town, the chief inspector will be salivating at the prospect of wrapping it up with one high-profile arrest. Am I making myself clear?'

'Sounds like I don't have much time.'

'Time for what?'

'To find out the truth.'

'Bullshit. You know how it works.'

'Yeah. Another long night.'

'They're all long nights, Lou.'

THIRTEEN

Oregon Avenue was a street that burned with activity and the later it got, the hotter it burned. Young people wandered from club to club, mingling on the street. Their voices mixed with traffic sounds, creating a hum like a swarm of bees. Jets circled overhead, waiting to land at the airport nearby. The night air always seemed charged from the friction of all those warm bodies bouncing off each other. Cars circled the block slowly, their polished skin gleaming under the street lights, reflecting the neon in streaks of bold color. And at the heart of all that warm circulating blood was the Arramingo Club.

It was small compared to some of the other clubs springing up on the waterfront. But there were still nights when they'd line up outside, waiting for hours sometimes. It wasn't just about size or location. It was about what was happening inside. It was about the girls. And Brian Haggerty knew how to pick 'em.

The Arramingo Club was a perfectly square building with white marble columns and white-washed concrete. Between the pillars were a series of shallow porticos cut into the concrete just above eye level. Inside the porticos, carved stone statues stood like sentries, life-size stone replicas of men and women, their perfect bodies angled to hide those parts that are best kept hidden. Their faces were chiseled and strong, their lips and chins and noses like Roman gods. But their eyes were blank, empty orbits of polished stone, staring blindly down from their pedestals at the mass of human traffic parading on the street before them.

The Arramingo Club hadn't always been on Oregon Avenue and it hadn't always been the jewel it was now. It hadn't always sat on the waterfront with a deck overlooking the harbor, where dinner was served by women in short black cocktail dresses and high-heeled shoes and sheer black stockings with a line crawling up the back of their legs. And the fare hadn't always included a view of ships floating slowly down the river, passenger ships and freighters sailing under the Burlington-Bristol Bridge, a drawbridge with its mouth agape like some medieval fortress. And it wasn't just food the clientele had an appetite for, then or now.

The original Arramingo Club sat at the end of 27th Street somewhere between Grays Ferry and the muddy waters of the Schuylkill. A Laotian restaurant occupies the building now and Haggerty still owns it, still owns a few apartment houses in the neighborhood too and a couple of bars, his hands still reaching into the pockets of people he'd forgotten about almost as soon as he'd moved out.

His father, William Haggerty, had first opened the doors to the Arramingo Club in 1972. Draft beer was a quarter a glass and a shot of good Irish whiskey was never more than a buck. It had caught fire and burned twice in the next twenty years and he'd rebuilt it both times. It hadn't been turned into a strip joint yet but even back then cheap women were as abundant as cheap booze. And if you worked for William Haggerty you could run a tab at the club, no questions asked. Haggerty understood that hard-working men needed a good stiff drink at the end of the day and he wasn't about to begrudge his men a few beers whether they could afford it or not. And if the tab ran too high, Haggerty would see the balance was taken out of their paychecks in increments that kept the pain tolerable. And as long as you made it to work the next day, the agreement held. That was the rule.

And for all his labors he'd never had any trouble with the cops or with the church. Haggerty took care of business all week and the church got them on Sunday. Haggerty put a crisp fifty-dollar bill in the basket and the priests nodded and shook his hand and looked the other way, same as the cops.

Lou didn't need anyone to tell him about the Arramingo Club. He didn't need Joey to tell him and he didn't need Mitch to tell him and he didn't need to read it in the papers or hear it from Franny Patterson. He'd heard it and seen it all before. Though, what he remembered most wasn't just about the Arramingo Club. It was just as Joey had said. It was about William Haggerty. It had always been about William Haggerty.

*   *   *

The Philadelphia Police Department had never been in much of
a hurry when it came to responding to bar fights. It wasn't official
policy. It's just the way it was. They'd take their time and hope
the brawl would punch itself out before they arrived. They'd pull
up in their cruisers and the crowd would scatter and whoever
was still standing would spend the night in the drunk tank and
whoever wasn't would go away in an ambulance. They weren't
called to many fights at the old Arramingo Club. Not that it didn't
have its share. It's just that they were over soon after they began
and no one dared call the cops.

Lou had responded to one such fight. He'd taken his time but
was still the first officer on the scene. He'd expected a crowd
but when he'd pulled up there were just two guys, grown men
standing toe to toe punching the shit out of each other. They'd
seemed to be enjoying it, the fight choreographed as if they'd
been taking turns, a certain politeness to the style though the
blood was running freely from their noses and mouths. At the
same moment Lou had stepped from his police car, William
Haggerty had stepped from the club.

He'd been wearing a white button-down shirt with a stiff, white
collar and an apron around his waist and a touch of sweat on
his chest as if he'd been working behind the bar and had just
come out for a breath of air. His hair had been a steely gray, flat
and colorless with a hint of white at the edges like rain-soaked
clouds. It had been the same color as the slate sidewalk and the
roof, the same color as the freighters floating down the Delaware,
the same color Lou had painted his mother's back porch. He'd
looked sternly at the fighters, set his chin and spoken with the
brogue still heavy in his voice.

'I'll take care of this, Officer.'

It was all he'd said and everyone, including Lou, knew he
meant it. William Haggerty's reputation preceded him and Lou
had seen it first-hand: a man who recognized men's needs and
gave them what they wanted but not without conditions. They
needed money and they needed drink and they needed a woman
now and then that wouldn't be there in the morning to knee them
in the balls. And men needed to fight. Haggerty would give them
that too, let them get it out of their system and leave it on the
street. But then he'd sober them up and dry them out and carry

them home and tuck them in if need be and even have them
picked up the next day for work. No one doubted his methods.
Not the politicians that got paid to look the other way, not the
bosses at the Philadelphia waterfront that needed to keep the
barges loaded, and not the Philadelphia Police Department who
needed to keep the peace.

He'd grabbed each of the men by the scruff of the neck and
loaded them one at a time into the back seat of a black Chrysler
Imperial with suicide doors and clean whitewalls – managed it
without getting a drop of blood on the hood, on the seat or on
himself. He'd driven away leaving Lou alone on the street with
only his report left to write.

Lou glanced at the naked statue now, giving it one last, hard look
before walking through the wide front doors of the Arramingo
Club, wondering if William Haggerty's son could handle men
the same way his father had. There didn't seem to be much of
a question how he handled women.

The low vibration from the music inside reached him even
before he tugged on the heavy glass doors. A deep electronic
beat throbbed with the steady, resounding tempo of war drums,
distant but coming closer and with a purpose behind them. Lou
heard it as a kind of warning, primitive and malevolent. Its
meaning was clear. Something was coming and if you stood in
its way, you'd be trampled. It shook the walls and the sidewalk.
It rumbled like thunder, like an earthquake rippling beneath the
foundation of the building, threatening to bring it down like a
house of cards.

A sea of people moved in broken waves. They were men
mostly, the smell of alcohol thick in the air, mixing with the
scent of cologne and perspiration. It clung to them like the soupy
aroma of sex, of fluids mixing together and bubbling up like
chemicals heated in a test tube. He could feel the pounding base
in his chest. Narrow beams of blue and green light cut through
the darkened space and strobe lights flickered from all four corners
and Lou's first impression was that it was utter chaos. It took
him a second to get his bearings, the mirrored walls distorting
his depth perception.

There were two circular bars in the center of the room with

a long, elevated ramp that ran like a trolley track between them. Around the ramp was a narrow ledge where customers could set their drinks and lean their elbows and flash some green and get a better view of the girls who strutted down the lighted runway as if they were modeling the latest summer fashion. There was an open second floor, a balcony of sorts with a yellow iron rail and those oversized binoculars on yellow posts, the kind that cost a quarter at the zoo in case you were interested in a closer look at a grazing zebra or a sleeping tiger.

Spotlights shone up from the stage, rotating wildly, capturing the girls in their nakedness, following them as they danced and mimicked the ecstatic convulsions of sex.

They all seemed to be cut from the same mold: lean and muscular, smooth and tan with long legs on high heels that accentuated their height. Their features seemed exaggerated, just a little too perfect, like the statues outside. Lou hardly considered himself an expert on the female form. He hadn't seen more than a handful of women in his life and the girls on stage at the Arramingo Club constituted a whole hell of a lot more than a handful. But still, they seemed unreal, more than most men could handle.

And the patrons of this Arramingo Club looked more like boys than men, standing around the stage raising dark green bottles to their lips and clanking them together and surveying the women as if they were bidders at a slave auction. One of them yelled out, the others laughed and they all took a drink as Lou weaved his way past them.

On stage a skinny, very white-skinned girl moved slowly and seductively to the music. She had bright red streaks in her dyed blonde hair. She wore it short and her face was painted in shades of powdery blue around her eyes. Her lips were slick and red and her teeth sharp and white through her open mouth. She cupped her breasts in both hands, running her palms lightly over her nipples until they stood sharp and erect.

The bartender came over and bent his ear toward Lou, trying to hear over the music and the laughter and the catcalls and the electric hum that would ring in his ears well into the next day. Lou ordered a beer and asked to see Brian Haggerty.

The bottle was cold and wet in Lou's hand. His eyes remained

on the girl as she centered herself over her spiked heels and
lowered her swiveling hips until she was an inch off the floor.
Her head swayed hypnotically and her hair splashed across her
face. She was remarkably thin, her ribs showing beneath the
bulging artificial breasts. She would allow her tongue to dart
from her open mouth and Lou noticed a thin scar on her upper
lip, a horizontal slash that seemed to give it a permanent curl.
She'd tried to hide it under a coating of heavy red lipstick but
it only made her appear more inanimate, like a doll in a Race
Street sex shop. Her eyes looked provocatively around the room,
lurid and unashamed, two rolling black irises. She was high as
a kite.

Lou turned his back to the stage and, leaning against the bar,
took a long swallow from the bottle.

A sliding door opened at the end of the bar and a well-dressed
young man stepped through. He wore a navy blue sport jacket
over a black T-shirt and jeans. His brown hair was streaked with
blond. Lou assumed it was Brian Haggerty. He carried himself
with the same self-confident demeanor as his father. The physical
resemblance wasn't immediately evident but Brian Haggerty
seemed to have learned a few things from his father, things he
didn't necessarily inherit but, like the best lessons, learned by
example. Haggerty came up opposite Lou and put his hand over
the twenty-dollar bill Lou had dropped on the bar, pushing it
back so Lou would have to take it or it would fall to the floor.

'You're my guest, Mr Klein.'

'If I had known I was welcome I would have called first and
made an appointment.'

Haggerty put his hands up in a gesture of surrender and his
eyes moved to the dancer making her way down the runway.

'Please, Mr Klein. I knew my wife spoke to you. I was just
sitting here thinking of what I would say, trying to talk myself
out of believing that maybe this whole thing was my fault. I can
see by the look on your face that you might not think I sound
very convincing.'

'Guilty conscience or something else?'

Lou raised the bottle to his lips. He emptied it in one long
swallow and replaced it on the bar.

'The doctors called me from the hospital. They told me what

happened. Whether you believe me or not, I'm worried about her.'

'Then how come you're here and not there, with her?'

'First of all, she doesn't want me there. Second, she's heavily sedated. She'll most likely sleep through the night. I'll be there when she wakes up.'

'The sincerity sounds genuine. But right now I have no way of knowing for sure that you weren't responsible for what happened to Jimmy Patterson or Franny. I'd be lying to you if I said I was the only person wondering about that.'

'You mean the police. I don't care what they think.'

'You should.'

Haggerty invited Lou back into his office, ushering him around the end of the bar toward the hidden door. The bartender was fixing a pitcher of some exotic drink, pouring in four different types of alcohol and mixing it with a variety of tropical fruit juices. It was intended to get someone plastered without them knowing it, the kind of drink that could sneak up on anyone regardless of their size or their age or how fat their wallet was or their sexual orientation. It was sweet and smooth and icy and easy to take and, after the first sip, all your problems were on hold. It was like liquid Valium in a fancy glass.

The bartender gave Haggerty a knowing smile as he shook the mixture in a stainless steel cylinder, shaking it in time to the music like a maraca. Lou turned and took another look at the girl on stage. She was down on her hands and knees now, her hair falling around her face and her painted fingernails extended like claws as she crawled plaintively toward the group of leering men. Haggerty was watching as well.

'She's good, isn't she?'

'Sure.'

'You'll never guess where I found her.'

'Where?'

'Waiting tables at a diner in Port Richmond. Had to drag her out of there. Do you believe it?'

'If you say so.'

'That girl could raise the fucking dead with a whisper.'

'Is that what you think?'

FOURTEEN

Haggerty's dimly lit office was well appointed with a dark green leather sofa and chairs around an oak desk. A brass lamp rested on the edge of the desk, a glimmer of soft yellow light illuminating its polished surface and glinting off a brass pen set, a large walnut humidor and a sailor's barometer. A deck of cards were arranged in a game of solitaire that Brian Haggerty still had hopes of winning.

Autographed football jerseys hung on the wall in glass frames. Some looked old and some new. Haggerty had other memorabilia in the office, all from Philly teams past and present. There were Eagles football helmets and baseballs signed by the Phillies, a hockey puck that allegedly penetrated the net in the '74 Stanley Cup. Lou couldn't read the names scribbled on any of them.

The smell of musty perfume seemed to emanate from the walls and the floor and the furniture as if every woman who'd set foot in that office had left their scent. And there had been a lot of them, no shortage of women willing to take their clothes off for a price. Haggerty pointed to a thickly padded chair but Lou ignored the offer and strode to the darkly stained bookshelf adjacent to Haggerty's desk. He began perusing titles, his head canted to one side as if he'd spent hours a day in a moldy old library and had developed a permanent stiff neck.

'You have no idea how sorry I am about Franny and Jimmy, Mr Klein.'

'I'm sorry too, Brian.'

'I had nothing to do with it. You've got to believe me.'

'Convince me why I have to believe you.'

''Cause it's the truth. I'm not a killer, Mr Klein.'

'That's not what the police think.'

'And what do you think?'

'I don't know. I haven't made up my mind. Not yet. But Jimmy was my friend and so is Franny. I don't know anything more about you than what I was told.'

'I never killed anybody in my life.'

'Even if I accept that I still have to believe you know a lot more than you're telling. You can't throw words like "truth" around and then expect me to just believe your denials. There's obviously a lot going on here and I'll need to know the whole story. Until you're willing to give that to me you're just another liar. You're not accustomed to anybody questioning your word. That's because of who you are. But that doesn't mean they believe you. It means they're afraid of you. Maybe they don't really want to know the truth. But that doesn't change anything. You can't manufacture the truth, Brian. I've been around a long time and the one thing I've learned is the truth always comes out. It has a will of its own.'

Haggerty was leaning forward on the desk, his hands covering his face. The light caught the blond streaks in his hair.

'Are you working for Franny?'

'Indirectly. I was working for her brother.'

'And now that he's dead?'

'When I spoke to Franny she wasn't happy. She didn't want Jimmy to talk to me but she did end up asking me to help her. She wanted me to get some of her things back. As a favor. Personal items that belonged to her. Said you wouldn't return them. I guess she assumed the marriage was over.'

'It's not, Mr Klein. I hope *you* realize that. We were angry. We might have said things we didn't mean. But it's not over. Not by a long shot.'

Haggerty was up now, leaning back in his chair.

'How much does Franny know about your first wife? I know it's a sore spot but it keeps coming up. And now there's been another murder, so naturally the cops might decide to reopen the case.'

'What happened with my ex-wife was a tragedy for our entire family. And Franny knows everything. The whole goddamn world knows what happened. And for your information, the coroner ruled that a murder-suicide. I was never charged with a crime.'

'That doesn't mean a thing to me. I don't care what the cops can prove or what they can't.'

'Are you able to put yourself in someone else's shoes? You think it's easy to air out my family's dirty laundry for everyone to see. What we did, Mr Klein, we did to ourselves. It's nobody else's business.'

Lou pulled a book down from the shelf and ran his hand over the dusty spine. The corners were frayed and the lettering was worn and he couldn't read the title. He opened it and turned a few soft mildewed pages to the table of contents. It was a book of romantic poetry. All those Irish balladeers who'd composed those meandering love songs in their twenties and then drank themselves to death by the time they were forty.

'It seems to me the Haggertys have been pretty fortunate.'

'You mean the ones that survive? You're joking, Mr Klein. The dead don't suffer – the living do. Surely you don't need me to tell you that. My family's fucking cursed.' Haggerty reached into a cabinet behind his desk and pulled out a bottle of Jameson and two shot glasses. He poured one for himself and offered one to Lou. The aroma reached him from across the room. He looked at the liquid that spilled onto the dark wood and the open bottle on top of it. 'Would it surprise you to learn that William Haggerty is not my real father?'

'Nothing surprises me anymore, Brian.'

Lou raised the glass off the desk and held it in front of him, turning the glass in his hand, the dull yellow light from the table lamp filtering through the amber liquid. Brian Haggerty quickly emptied the entire contents of the glass into his mouth, the burn visible in his face as the whiskey hit the back of his throat. He grimaced and closed his eyes and let his head roll back against the soft leather of the chair.

'Not only wasn't he my father, he never really liked me very much. I would say he hated me. I was a burden to him. He let me hang around out of a sense of obligation to my mother. But that's it. And he took a sick pleasure in letting me know it. Liked to see me squirm. Every time he looked at me I could see what he was thinking. I'd never be him, never live up to his idea of what a son should be. If it hadn't been for my mother, William Haggerty would have tied me up in a burlap bag like the runt of the litter and tossed me into the river.'

'I'd say I'm sorry but it wouldn't mean anything, would it?'

Haggerty poured himself another drink. He turned the bottle to face him on the desk so that he was able to read the label. He looked like a kid reading the back of a cereal box at the breakfast table. There was a gold ring around the neck of the bottle and a gold cap above it like a crown. Lou watched Haggerty stare at the bottle of whiskey, watched his eyes go out of focus as if he was falling asleep, seeing his own distorted reflection in the cross-cut glass before slipping into unconsciousness. He raised the drink over his head.

'To the great William Haggerty! And his subtle tortures.' The liquid was gone with a quick flick of his wrist. He flung the shot glass across the room. It skittered on the rug and banged into the corner. 'I wasn't fit to walk in his shadow. Just ask my mother. She'll be happy to tell you all about it.'

Lou walked over and picked up the glass and replaced it gently on the desk. He replaced his own glass as well, still untouched.

'I'll be sure to ask her when I see her.'

'And while you're at it, ask her about my real father. She'll have a few choice words to say about him, too.'

'Why don't you tell me?'

Brian Haggerty was playing with the shot glass now, sliding it across the wooden desk from one hand to the other. Lou wondered when he'd learned to take his medicine like a man and if he'd learned it from his father or his mother.

'They were never married. At least that's what she said. The way she tells it he took off soon after he found out she was pregnant. It was a sore spot with her. She didn't like to talk about it, not even to me.'

'So you never met him?'

'I didn't say that. He came around one time, looking for my mother. He wanted money. Money to go away and leave them alone. Money to not see his son and not make a stink about it. If he didn't get it there'd be lawyers and custody battles and he'd make himself a thorn in their side for as long as he could.'

'So William Haggerty paid him off?'

'Yeah.'

'That was the last time you saw him?'

'I saw him one other time. He'd been locked up in a prison upstate. It was actually William who told me, couldn't wait to tell me. He enjoyed it, I'm sure. He liked to remind me that if I didn't watch myself I'd end up in jail like my old man. Liked to remind me where I came from, how easily I could find myself out on the street. He was fond of the phrase "the apple doesn't fall far from the tree." Like he would know. Well, anyway, I went upstate to visit him. He wasn't expecting me. Had no idea who I was and you know what he did when I told him?' Haggerty had poured himself another drink. The bite didn't seem as sharp this time. 'He laughed. That's it. Just laughed.'

'How long ago was that?'

'Ten years or so. And you know what? When I walked out of that prison, I wasn't mad at him. It was William Haggerty who I hated. I had him to thank for everything I had and I hated him for it. He'd drilled it into my head that just because he was married to my mother and I had his name didn't mean I would ever get my hands on his money. Isn't that a laugh, Mr Klein? Because I never cared one bit about his fucking money.'

Haggerty pulled out a fresh pack of cigarettes from the desk drawer. He peeled it open and offered one to Lou and lit one for himself. He took long drags and seemed content to let the smoke just drift in the still air around him. Haggerty tossed Lou the lighter and Lou came around the desk and sank into one of the soft leather chairs. He lit a cigarette and let it smolder in a crystal ashtray on the coffee table.

'You haven't touched your drink, Mr Klein.'

'I'll pass. Thanks. How did your mother ever get hooked up with William Haggerty?'

'How does anyone get hooked up with William Haggerty?'

'You tell me. You talk about him like he's still alive.'

'In a way he is.'

'I think you're overestimating even him.'

'Don't be so sure. Some people have a way of hanging around even after they're dead. And believe me, he finds a way to make his presence felt. Just look at the way people talk about him, like they were waiting for him to come charging through the door and kick them in the balls.'

'Everyone leaves some kind of legacy. It's rarely all good or all bad.'

'People were afraid of William Haggerty. That's his legacy. A legacy of fear.'

'Were you scared of him?'

'That's part of the problem, Mr Klein. I'll always be afraid of him.'

There was a knock at the door, three quick raps and they both turned their heads from the rising smoke. The music came through the door first, followed by the bartender's shaven head, his scalp slick with sweat. He was breathing heavily and his face was flushed. The large diamond stud in his ear sparkled like cut glass. He turned his attention to Haggerty.

'We got trouble, boss.'

FIFTEEN

The place was emptying quickly, the crowd pressed against the walls on both sides and rushing toward the exits. The strobes still beat in time to the pounding music. The same dancer who had been on stage earlier was now nestled into the arms of one of the bouncers, holding a bloody towel to her mouth. Another bouncer was wrestling with someone near the main entrance. He had the curled end of one massive bicep wound around the guy's neck. He didn't seem to be having much trouble controlling him. It looked like if he squeezed any harder, the guy's head would pop off.

Haggerty grabbed the bartender by the arm and pulled him within earshot.

'Check on Angel. Make sure she's OK.'

The dancer removed the towel from her mouth and looked down at the blood and then looked over at the man that had obviously just punched her in the face, seemingly satisfied that he was getting a good working over. She returned the towel to her mouth and nestled herself deeper into her doorman's bulging chest. He didn't seem to mind and his partner didn't seem to mind dancing with this idiot who thought he'd taken one look at Angel Divine and found the girl of his dreams.

The bartender took Angel by the hand and led her away, past Haggerty, who reached out and stroked her naked arm as she slid through the paneled door and into his office. But

Haggerty's eyes remained locked on the man caught in the grip of his two goons, getting a better look at him now that he'd stopped struggling. He looked more like a boy than a man, no more than nineteen or twenty. Haggerty stared at him for a few seconds but the seconds seemed like hours and in that instant Lou got the feeling they knew each other, even hated each other. He sensed something almost tangible pass between them.

Lou had seen it before. He recognized the look. Whatever this kid had seen in Angel Divine, it set him off. But it wasn't Angel he wanted, not really. His steel-gray eyes focused on Haggerty with the intensity of an animal caught in the teeth of a steel trap. Lou glanced back at Haggerty and saw the anger in his face melt away into uncertainty and then into fear. He'd seen that look before, too.

Haggerty seemed to stare across the room as if he was caught in a daydream. His eyes seemed to have lost their glow, the emotion draining out of him. He looked at the slight figure and feminine features and the close-cropped hair and the suppressed rage of this young man as if he was looking at a ghost. At that moment Haggerty looked like the last man on earth, standing at the edge of the world and deciding whether to turn around and go home or leap to his certain death.

Lou remembered seeing the same look on the old women in Our Lady of Peace Church, sitting before the God they both loved and feared. He remembered now what his father had said about people who were confronted with circumstances beyond their control, things they didn't understand, things they had no way to measure. The word he'd used was *awe*. Their belief in a higher power seemed always being tested. Lou saw it now on Haggerty's awestruck face. His continued silence was proof enough.

Then the music stopped and the strobe lights stopped and in that sudden quiet Haggerty seemed to remember where he was.

'Is this the kind of drama you expected, Mr Klein?'

'Do you know him? Who is he?'

'He's no one.' Haggerty yelled at the bouncers and pointed toward the door. 'Get him out of here.'

'No, wait!'

The bouncers were dragging the man toward the exit. One of

them leaned on the crash bar with his hip and shouldered the door open. With a good push in the back, they sent the man tumbling into the dark alley behind the bar. The two double-steel doors slammed shut behind them.

Lou squeezed between the two bouncers who were standing there, satisfied and smiling with their tongues hanging out like two dogs waiting for a biscuit from their master. He got outside and the guy was gone.

He ran to the corner and down Oregon Avenue and into an adjacent alley, his eyes searching for movement. He looked past the row of loading docks, gray metal doors with no handles and green metal dumpsters and potholes that littered the ground, half-filled with muddy water and the stench of rotting garbage that seemed perpetually trapped between those buildings. He came back out and looked down the crowded street but it was impossible to distinguish one person from another. There was no telling which direction the guy ran or if he'd come down that alley at all. But Brian Haggerty knew who the guy was. He was sure of it.

Lou walked back around to the Arramingo Club and was met by the same two overgrown bouncers. They informed him that the bar was closed and that Mr Haggerty had decided to escort Angelica Divine home after her frightening ordeal. Haggerty hadn't mentioned when or if he'd be back. There was no sense in arguing. He'd already seen the alley. He didn't need to see it again.

The entrance to Interstate 95 was only a few blocks away and he was sailing along the highway within minutes. He thought about taking the scenic route, maybe jump on Torresdale Avenue and wind his way up through some of Philly's oldest neighborhoods. It would be like a trip through time, through some ancient ruin, the remnants of a lost city built ten thousand years ago by one of those primitive civilizations now doomed to extinction. But he knew what he'd find; more ghosts. And there was no sense in waking them now.

He decided on the interstate, preferring cold, flat pavement for as far as the eye could see, nothing in his way to slow him down, no stop lights, no speed limits, the world going by so fast it was reduced to a blur.

He waved a faint goodbye to Society Hill as he followed 95 north along the river, gliding past Fishtown and Port Richmond like they weren't even there. And soon Kensington was looming dark over his left shoulder, a lament of late-night sirens and screams rising like the agonizing cries that must have reached God's ears as the cities of men burned under his vengeful eye.

Lou crossed himself as he passed, one hand on the wheel and the other inches from his furrowed brow, saluting all those nights he'd spent there as a cop, standing over some crime scene on Lehigh and Allegheny, on Girard Avenue at 34th Street, streets with proud, historic names, streets with more murders to their name than he could count. And if these streets were somehow responsible for what happened on them, just as responsible as the men who had committed murder upon them, they'd draw the same death sentence. But nobody got put to death in Philadelphia these days. No electric chair, no lethal injection, no gas chamber, just a life sentence which meant they'd live to kill again.

Lou turned his head away and focused on the road, hoping this day's journey would soon be over. He was tired but he kept driving. He passed the Betsy Ross Bridge and thought how great it would be to take the exit into Jersey and roll into Pennsauken, see if Katz's Deli was still in business. He could drive past the old Capitol Theatre where he'd seen Neil Young in concert on a cold Halloween night over twenty years ago. It seemed like yesterday. He'd taken Franny Patterson. She'd only been out of high school a few years and Lou was a rookie patrolman and this would be their first date. They'd taken the train out of 30th Street Station with Franny dressed as the catwoman. She'd succeeded in convincing Lou to dress up as well.

He'd been a cop, of course, worn one of his father's old uniforms with a thick leather belt cinched tight around his waist and a French-blue polyester shirt that scratched his skin and a tarnished badge on his chest and a crumpled hat and a pair of heavy black boots with the trousers tucked inside and a plastic squirt gun wedged into the holster. Franny was in a black catsuit with a tail and gloves to her elbows and heels and a black mask. Coming home she'd sat on Lou's lap and he'd slid his hand along her leg, the thin material like a silken web over her warm skin.

They had both gotten drunk and they had sex that night for the first time in Lou's car. He always suspected that Franny had told her brother all about it.

Interstate 95 continued north parallel to the Delaware River past Frankford and Holmesburg, Penny Pack Park directly underneath, the hardcore skateboarders still out dodging the cops as they would be well into the morning. The airport wasn't far away and the jets were circling like vultures, waiting for their turn to land.

Lou exited onto Academy, letting the car glide down the long ramp and through the green light at the bottom, past Reedy's Tavern, still going strong, a few patrons saying their drunken goodbyes on the corner. He drove past the vacant lot where Eden Hill Chapel had once stood before it was leveled by a city bulldozer just last year. Demolished in the name of progress and safety, city inspectors had said. Depended on your definition of progress, Lou thought. Progress in Torresdale was measured by how close it came to returning things to the way they were in the old days, better days. It was the same with so-called improvements in most of the city. But in Torresdale those better days hadn't been so long ago. They were still alive in the collective memory of its residents, most of them hanging around wondering where the hell they were when it got so bad.

Lou often wondered if Sister Paulette Mercedes would have considered it progress if she'd lived to see the demolition of her beloved chapel, if she hadn't been struck and killed by a hit-and-run driver on Cottman Avenue and dragged thirty feet and left to die in the middle of the street on her way to morning mass at St Matthews.

The whole city of Philadelphia mourned that day. And it had seemed like it wasn't just Sister Paulette they were mourning.

It was Captain Mike Mercy who'd picked up the case, Lou remembered. Mercy was a good cop but even he couldn't bring back the dead. The reward was 10G's for information on the maroon pick-up truck last seen rolling to a stop on Hawthorne, stopping just long enough to look in the rear-view mirror and see what was left of Sister Mercedes before it sped off. But the money wasn't enough. An off-duty fireman thought he'd seen the truck jumping onto Roosevelt Boulevard and that was the

last anyone had ever heard. It was never seen again and no one
was ever caught.

By the time Mercy had his press conference on the front steps
of the Frankford-Torresdale Hospital, the vigil had already begun
and the spot where she was killed was already laden with wooden
crosses and candles and flowers and plastic dolls and Bibles and
cards. And someone had claimed to see a vision of the Virgin
Mary visiting that spot and that brought more people out, the
pious and the orthodox, the grieved and the curious. The cops
put up barricades at both ends of the street and posted an officer
to stand there all night and the vigil continued through the day
and the next night and wouldn't end until Sister Paulette Mercedes
was laid to rest a week later at St Catherine's Cemetery.

East Torresdale amounted to a couple square miles of big brick
homes clustered at the inner edge of Northeast Philadelphia and
it seemed constantly under siege from the expanding wilderness
to the south. These were houses occupied by the descendants of
the same families that had built them a few generations before
and had never left. They'd stayed out of stubbornness and they'd
stayed out of pride. The signs of change were springing up all
around them and they weren't easy to miss but they chose to
ignore them. They were being told to get out while the getting
was good, before their property became completely worthless.
You didn't want to be the last one left standing in Torresdale.

But they had stayed and they'd compelled their children to
take up the fight after them. What they couldn't admit to themselves was that their children didn't have the stomach for it; the
children that sold to the highest bidder, the children that divided
their parents' homes into apartment houses and showed up once
a month to collect the rents.

Eleanor Haggerty was one of those that stayed. And though
it was late, if Lou didn't find Brian Haggerty at home, he had
every intention of speaking with his mother, even if he had to
wake her up to do it.

He parked on the street and found the address. It was the kind
of street where the porch lights stayed on all night as if the
residents were afraid of the dark. There was a narrow driveway
and a four-door, gold Mercury sitting in front of a detached

garage. The garage door was closed and looked like it hadn't been opened in quite some time, used only for storage now, junk from the big house finding its way out the back door and into the garage where it was piled to the rafters.

Lou moved slowly up the front walkway. A couple of the slate tiles were loose and shifted under his feet. He rang the doorbell and listened for the echo of chimes behind the dark double door. He heard dogs barking inside. They sounded like small dogs, more than one, ankle-biters from the sound of them. He waited for what seemed like a very long time before he pushed the lighted button again. The wind had picked up, blowing the brown dead leaves down the driveway and into the street in a swirling torrent. A cold drizzle had started as well, a light misting rain that didn't seem to be falling but was suspended in the air. A first-floor light came on and there was movement through the sheer curtains and the bolt turned and he was standing face-to-face with a very old woman in a blue housecoat and thinning white hair.

Lou's first impression was that Mrs Eleanor Haggerty was not the kind of woman that carried her age like an infirmity. She was in possession of years in the same way she owned her house and she was just as solid and rooted and unyielding. Other than stern annoyance, it was a countenance that gave away nothing. Square and stiff and pale like marble and, though it was closing in on midnight, she did not appear to have lost any of her energy. Her housecoat was royal blue and dripping with sequins that caught the light and seemed to flow over her like a waterfall. She seemed the kind of woman who valued precious stones, who preferred to keep her jewels always within reach as some women preferred to keep their children. She stopped the dogs barking with one quick look.

'Mrs Haggerty . . . I'm very sorry to disturb you this late. I was hoping to talk to you . . . about your daughter-in-law. It is important. And it affects your son as well. I don't know if you heard what happened tonight.'

'And you are?'

'Louis Klein. I'm a friend of the family.'

'A friend of the family? If you were a friend of the family, I think I would know it.'

'I'm sorry. I meant the Patterson family.'

'Well, then I'm sure you know that Frances hasn't lived in this house for some time now. A friend of the family would know that as well, Mr – what did you say your name was? I'm getting so bad with names.'

Lou looked at Eleanor Haggerty and wondered if he hadn't made a mistake, wondering where she got off speaking to him as if she were scolding a small child and if she spoke to everyone like that. It was the privilege of age, he suspected, her belief that she knew that much more about life than he did. What could she have possibly learned about life behind these brick walls, Lou asked himself? He'd learned his lessons the hard way, not having locked himself away as Eleanor Haggerty seemed to have done, guarding herself jealously as if she was a national treasure.

'My name is Klein, Mrs Haggerty. I'm also a private detective. I knew Franny's brother, Jimmy. We worked together a long time ago at the Philadelphia Police Department. Jimmy Patterson is dead, Mrs Haggerty. He was shot and killed just a few hours ago. He died on my front porch and I'd like to find out why.'

'I can't imagine how I can help you, Mr Klein. I barely knew the man.'

'A few minutes of your time, that's all I ask.'

'Well, if you'd like to come in, I suppose I could spare a few moments. My husband was always a great supporter of the police in this city. But of course, maybe that was somewhat before your time.' She stepped aside and ushered him in with a wave of her hand. 'On second thought, I think maybe you're somewhat older than you look. Am I right?'

She smiled a very full, very perfect smile, her false teeth like pearls in her mouth. The two Scottish terriers hovered behind her and then jumped up onto a love seat, curling up and watching her like a captive audience.

'About my age, Mrs Haggerty? Or about what I know about your husband?'

She laughed heartily. It was a man's laugh, with her mouth open wide like a man who'd already had too much to drink and planned on having a few more before the night was over, a few more drinks and a few more laughs.

Lou had followed her into a dimly lit parlor where he sat at her direction in a wide-set, round-backed chair. The furniture appeared to be antique, the upholstery a pattern of pink roses clinging to a faded green vine and swirling in an off-white sky of marshmallow clouds. It still smelled brand new. She took her time parading around the room, switching on a few oversized table lamps of frosted glass and gold stitched shades. She sat adjacent to him on a long, low couch with her arm slung across the back and her legs crossed, making a show of it, posing in the manner of a much younger woman.

SIXTEEN

'What do you know about my husband, Mr Klein?'

'Mostly what I've heard.'

'What you've heard. The things people say, I assure you, are based largely on rumor. You make assumptions about a man from the things you've heard, what you've read in the papers. Believe me, it's false. Exaggerations, fairy tales to whet the public's appetite. Nothing more.'

'I didn't come here to pass judgment on your husband. As you say, I'd prefer to hear the truth from you. I don't believe everything I hear, Mrs Haggerty, any more than you do.'

'I seem to find myself defending my husband's reputation out of habit, even when it's not called for. Perhaps I'm just a self-indulgent old woman.' She paused for a second, her eyes fixed on a portrait of William Haggerty hanging over the fireplace in a heavy gold frame. He seemed to be staring back at her with a pair of cold gray eyes. 'Maybe a bit defensive, too. But I have the right to be.'

'It sounds like you loved your husband very much, regardless of the rumors. Sounds to me like you still love him.'

'Controversy comes with the territory.' She rose and took a long time walking across the room to a service table where bottles of liquor in a collection of crystal decanters lined up in a neat row. She set out a couple of glasses and a couple of linen napkins and started to pour. 'Brandy?'

'No, thanks.'

'I don't think you understand me, Mr Klein, any better than you could have understood my husband.' She made another slow elaborate production of sipping from the glass of brandy, her pinky finger outstretched, her Adam's apple bobbing in her throat as she swallowed. 'My husband was the toughest son of a bitch you'd ever want to know, tougher than me if you can believe that.'

'Toughness runs in your family, then. Is your son anything like his father?'

She slammed the glass down hard on the table, some of the liquid staining the white tablecloth.

'I don't appreciate innuendo either. The difference between my son and William Haggerty is a matter of their experience. My son has had all the advantages I could afford to give him. William wasn't raised with those same advantages. He was never given anything. He fought for everything he had. That's the difference between my generation and yours, Mr Klein. We don't walk around with our hands out like beggars. Now, if you have something to ask, please ask it.'

She refilled her glass, wiping the table with a fresh napkin. She turned like a skater pirouetting on the ice, her head spinning around, followed by her shoulders and then her hips and all before she took a step, returning to the sofa and facing Lou with a set of venomous, red-rimmed eyes.

'Everybody seems to talk about William Haggerty as if he was still alive.'

'Some men don't die so easy. They stick around a while.' The mantle clock chimed once and she paused. 'People have long memories, especially when it comes to the Haggerty family. Don't underestimate the power of memory, Mr Klein.'

'I wouldn't dream of it.'

'I'm afraid we've gotten sidetracked. I'm terribly sorry about Mr Patterson. Please believe me. But how does his death have anything to do with me? And how is poor Frances taking it? It's no secret that she and I didn't always get along. But I'm not unsympathetic. She must be devastated.'

'I haven't spoken to her yet. She's in Lankenau hospital. I won't be able to see her until tomorrow.'

'The hospital?'

'She was attacked earlier tonight at her home, probably by the same person that killed her brother.'

'My Lord!'

'I'll be completely honest with you, Mrs Haggerty: the police think Brian had something to do with it.'

'They would think that. They've been dying to hang a charge on him.'

'Since the murder of your husband . . . and Valerie Price?'

She drained the second glass of brandy, stood quickly and wobbled a bit as if her first step would send her falling to the floor. She fumbled with the empty glass and it slipped from her hand and cracked on the hardwood at her feet. Lou jumped up and grabbed hold of her arm, sidestepping the broken glass and leading her back to the couch where she sat with her eyes closed and her fingers pressed to her temples. Lou knelt and picked up the larger shards of broken glass and set them onto the white napkin.

'Do you think Brian had something to do with it, Mr Klein?'

'No, but the police believe there might be a link between what happened to Franny and the women that are being attacked in the city.'

'You mean prostitutes. Don't say women, Mr Klein, if you mean prostitutes.'

'They've been dancers, Mrs Haggerty. And a few worked at the Arramingo Club. That's no coincidence. The police have been crawling all over that place. They're going to catch the guy. It's only a matter of time. The question is how many more people will get hurt before they do. There was a disturbance there tonight. The guy that caused it got away. Brian seemed to know him.'

Eleanor Haggerty seemed to recover from her momentary weakness, the color coming back to her face, her voice regaining its resonance.

'Slipped through your fingers too, then.'

'I guess so.'

'The club . . . it's been nothing but a curse on this family.'

'Brian said the same thing – called it a curse. I'll tell you what I told him. I don't believe in curses any more than I believe in ghosts.'

'I really don't care what you believe. If you're telling me the Arramingo Club is a wretched place filled with wretched people, then we found something we can agree upon. If you told me the devil himself stopped in there for a drink every once in a while, I wouldn't be surprised. I wish it would burn to the ground and everybody inside can burn right along with it for all I care.'

'It burned once before if I'm not mistaken.'

'And William never should have rebuilt it. I begged him not to. It's a dirty business and it was the perfect opportunity to get out of it.'

'I take it he didn't listen.'

'Contrary to popular belief, William Haggerty never listened to a word I said. He was the kind of man who preferred to keep his business and personal life separate. He wouldn't have allowed me to set foot in his precious gentleman's club even if I'd wanted to. In other words, Mr Klein, I didn't have a say in the matter.'

'Can you think of anyone who might have hated your husband – or you or your son for that matter, hated enough to kill?'

'That list is a long one. My husband wasn't in the business of making friends. But he treated people fairly.'

'So this probably isn't business related, at least not directly.'

'How should I know? Would you pour me another brandy? I think I'm just about ready for one.'

Lou stood and went to the table and poured a glass of brandy. He filled the glass with ice first and then poured in the liquid. The two terriers, responding to Lou's movement, were suddenly up off their cushions, exercising their stubby legs and sliding over the floor and growling, more at each other it seemed than at Lou, as if they were quarreling over who would get the first bite. Lou capped the bottle and set it in line next to the others while the dogs sniffed at his heels. He thought about giving one of them a good kick but it wasn't their fault they acted like a couple of spoiled kids. They'd probably taken a few shots to the jaw already. It might have been the only attention they ever got.

Lou passed the drink and a fresh white napkin to Mrs Haggerty, pressing it into the bony fingers of her two hands, hoping she wouldn't have another accident.

'Tell me about Valerie Price.'

The way Lou said it, making it sound more like a command than a question, caused Eleanor Haggerty's head to spin around as if she'd been slapped in the face. Her eyes were blazing behind the thick oval lenses and translucent gold frames of her glasses. She jerked them off her face and let them dangle from her neck by a strand of frayed elastic, her jaw clenched as if she was going to hiss at him and then spit like a cobra.

'Mr Klein, I've never so much as uttered that woman's name in all my life. I'm not about to start now.'

'She was killed right here in this house. Certainly you must have spoken to the police about her.'

'It was more like she was exterminated. And my husband paid the price for his sins. I'm sure if he had to do it all over again, he would have thought twice before he allowed that girl to set foot in this house. The police were nothing but a nuisance, traipsing around my house with their muddy shoes, snickering and asking all sorts of ridiculous questions. The police prefer to fabricate the truth, Mr Klein, not discover it. Of all people, you should know that.'

'And I suppose I'm just another meddlesome cop sticking his nose in where he's not wanted.'

'You are what you are, Mr Klein.'

'I am at that.'

Lou started for the door and Eleanor Haggerty followed, remarkably steady on her feet now even after her third full glass of brandy. The dogs began their yapping again and Lou looked down at his wristwatch and turned it until it caught the light. It was after two in the morning. He breathed out a long, groaning sigh.

'Before you go, tell me, what kind of a name is Klein?'

'I'm not sure I understand.'

'Your nationality, just out of curiosity.'

'What does that matter?'

'I didn't say it mattered. My God, you act as if you had something to be ashamed of.'

They were standing at the front door, Lou's body half-turned and Mrs Haggerty facing him, her complexion still pallid and waxen, the blood draining again from her face but gathering in her throat which was throbbing now with a venal redness.

'My father was Jewish.'

'And I take it your mother was not.'

'She was Italian.'

'An interesting combination. I would have thought you'd be a little darker skinned.'

'You don't seem to have a very high opinion of me, Mrs Haggerty.'

'I have no opinion. You remind me of someone, though. Your nose isn't small but it's straight. Your parents must have been an attractive couple.'

'My parents are dead.'

'Both of them?'

'My mother was murdered in her house in Overbrook Park. She'd been there a week before they found her.'

'For heaven's sake. How often did you check on her?'

'Not often enough apparently. Not as often as your son checks on you, I'm sure. He probably checks your pulse at night while you're sleeping.'

'I suppose you think I deserve that. Maybe I do. And your father was a cop, like you.'

'No, nothing like me. But yes, he was a cop, and he was killed in the line of duty a long time ago.'

'I'm so sorry.'

'Don't be. The badge meant everything to him. He died doing what he loved.'

'And how about you?'

'If I cared that much, I might still be wearing it.'

'Oh, that's right. You're a private investigator. Why aren't you still on the force? Or is that the one thing you don't want to talk about?'

'Let's just say there's no love lost between me and the Philadelphia Police Department.'

Lou opened the door and stepped out onto the front porch. The breeze whistled through the trees and he waited for it to pass and then went to the pack of cigarettes in his pocket. Eleanor Haggerty leaned into the doorway.

'You don't like me very much either, I'm afraid. Don't bother to answer. I know what you'll say. You'll be polite and smile and tell me it's not like that at all. You'll say that it's not that

you don't like me, it's that we don't understand each other. You'd
patronize me, wouldn't you, Mr Klein?'

'I might say that.'

'It's OK. Because I stopped caring what people thought of me
a long time ago. They all have their own reasons for hating me
and they all believe they're justified. They think I have money
and connections and I can get away with murder. So, it's OK to
hate me. But the truth is, they need someone to hate.'

'Maybe you hate them as much as they hate you. Have you
ever thought about that?'

'Maybe you're right. Then I'm no different than they are. I'm
just held to a higher standard. As a former cop, you must know
how that feels.'

'Good night, Mrs Haggerty.'

Lou started down the front porch steps.

'Now I know who you remind me of. That statue, in Rome I
think it is. The statue of David. That's it. King David. All strong
and serious but with a certain weakness, too.'

'I guess I should be flattered.'

'Don't be. For all his greatness, he had his flaws. An eye for
the women. One he couldn't control. It was his Achilles heel,
Mr Klein.'

SEVENTEEN

Roosevelt Boulevard was the fastest way out of there and all
Lou could think about now was getting home. He'd had
enough drama for one night and enough of the Haggertys.
He circled onto the southbound ramp and had it up to sixty as he
merged onto the deserted highway. He continued to pick up speed
and was quickly through Rhawnhurst, coming up on the Roosevelt
Mall, all dark and empty below him. He continued south, flinging
the last of the cigarette out the window, North Philadelphia
spreading out all around him. He passed over Harbison Avenue
and then Devereaux, through Lawncrest to the west and Friends
Hospital to the east, its lights like beacons in the night.

He rolled through Hunting Park, feeling the bottom of his foot cramp against the gas pedal and letting his mind go blank, just driving, on automatic pilot. He drove through Germantown, slowing as he crossed the river, deciding whether it would be West River Drive and through the park or if it would be City Avenue or the Schuylkill Expressway. Philadelphia was a city of neighborhoods connected by ribbons of highway and yet no one could really know it as a whole. It would always be divided. There would be times when the Phillies or the Eagles or the Flyers would bring people together but that unity was an illusion. He jumped on City Avenue, stopped at a 7/11 in Wynnefield for a pack of cigarettes and then he was home. Not much was moving in Overbrook and he was thankful for it.

Joey was asleep in a chair, a full cup of cold coffee still in his hand, balanced on the armrest. He hadn't spilled a drop. If Joey woke up now, the first thing he'd do was take a sip, cold or not. His head was back and he was breathing through his open mouth and snoring loudly, his chest rising and falling like a billows. The cup still didn't move.

Lou slid it out of Joey's hand. Joey's eyes opened and Lou poured the coffee into the sink while Joey got his bearings.

'What time is it?'

'Pushing three o'clock.'

'Shit. I must have dozed off. Whad'ya find out?'

'Not much. Nothing you hadn't already told me. Eleanor Haggerty is a bitch but you knew that. And you did warn me. Her son, while I wouldn't put anything past him if he was pushed hard enough, seems like just another troubled kid trying to fit into a pair of shoes way too big for him.'

'The long shadow of William Haggerty. What did I tell ya?'

'You'd think these people would want to bury this guy so deep they'd never hear from him again, wouldn't you? If you were his wife and he'd been cheating on you since day one or if you were his son and he'd been banging your wife. I don't care how much money they stood to inherit.'

'That's you, Lou. They're not you.'

Lou felt the coffee pot; it was still warm so he poured two fresh cups and passed one to Joey. They both drank it black.

'It's the old lady that's obsessed with it. I think the kid would like nothing better than to let it die.' They both sipped their coffee. 'There was a bit of a ruckus at the Arramingo Club tonight.'

'What kind of a ruckus?'

'A guy got fresh with one of the girls. Bloodied her lip. Not a guy, though, Joey. He was more like a kid, early twenties at best, maybe less. Whatever he was doing in there, I didn't get the impression he was a customer.'

'Then what?'

'The way he was dressed, maybe a waiter or a busboy.'

'An employee?'

'Yeah, maybe.'

'Then Haggerty would have to know him.'

'That's another thing. Haggerty did seem to know him. And even after all the shit that's been going on, Haggerty let him go. A couple of bouncers had him by the neck and tossed him into the alley.'

Joey nodded and they drank more of the coffee.

'How bad was the girl hurt?'

'Not bad. Looks like she got punched in the face. That's it.'

'That's considered foreplay to the girls at the Arramingo Club.'

'How would you know?'

'Did you forget about Candy?'

'Oh, yeah.'

'That little fling cost me my marriage and my job. I'd be collecting a captain's pension right now if I'd never hooked up with Candy Bell. Just one of the advantages of staying in the good graces of Petey Santi.'

'Marrying his daughter was about the best deal you ever made. Man, did you fuck that up.'

'Coincidentally I heard Petey resigned from City Council about the same time your boy, Vincent Trafficante, bowed out of the mayor's race. Next thing you know they're in business together.'

'So what else is new?'

'Nothing. Not only are these guys hauling garbage upstate by the truckload but they got involved in some kind of land deal, thinking they'd open up a few more landfills, give them some-place to dump all that Philly garbage. Lots of cheap land up there, ya know. Now I heard they found pockets of natural gas and they're making a fucking fortune on it.'

'Jesus Christ! What is it with those people up there? First it's coal mines, then garbage dumps and now they're digging around again, this time for gas. The ground's already like an open sore.'

'They're coal crackers, Lou. What do you expect?'

'That they'll wake up.'

'Keep dreaming.'

They took their coffees outside and stood on the porch. Joey had a cigarette going before Lou shut the door behind them.

'You ever hear from Candy?'

'Nope. She went from a high-priced call girl to a suburban housewife. Ends up with a township commissioner in Trevose. Guy divorces his wife and kids. Six months later he's married to Candy. Of course, she's Candace now.'

'How do you divorce your kids?'

'You haven't met Candy.'

'Why don't you see if you can contact her? Ask her about the Arramingo Club and the Haggertys. Maybe she knew this Valerie Price.'

'You mean before she started spreading her legs for father and son?'

'Yeah. Well, before she was killed anyway.'

'I'll see what I can do.'

'Thanks, Joey, and thanks for hanging out tonight. You were a big help. I know it meant a lot to Maggie.'

'No problem.' Joey took a last sip of coffee and placed the cup on the window sill. He took a last drag off the cigarette and put it out in the ashtray right next to it. 'That's too bad about Jimmy and Franny. We don't really know who did it. Do we?'

'No, but we will.'

'How can you be so sure?'

'It's a pretty tight circle here. We're talking about the Arramingo Club, the Haggertys and the women that fall inside that sphere of influence. Trust me, the truth will come out eventually, no matter how much they try to keep it hidden. We'd have a harder time trying to prevent it.'

'I know your philosophy on truth, Lou. But what if the truth comes out and no one's listening, no one cares?'

'Not our problem. Our job is just to unlock the door and let it out.'

'Tell me this. How do you think it will all end?'

'Not well, Joey. Not well.'

They stood on the porch for a few more moments in silence, staring at the place on the porch where their friend had taken his last breath. They stared at the empty chair and the blood stain which seemed to have permanently discolored the concrete. Joey hobbled gingerly down the steps, protecting the knees that had grown stiff from too much sitting. Lou listened to the car start and watched it move away, leaving the street bathed in that late-night stillness that he'd come to cherish. The sky was dark and cloudy, with no stars to count and the night suddenly more quiet than he'd ever remembered. It wasn't the peace in his life that he'd always hoped for, though. It was more like the peace of the grave. He shuddered against that thought as the breeze picked up and seemed to go right through him.

He went back inside and prepared a bed for himself on the couch. He positioned one of the throw pillows under his head and unrolled a thin blanket. He lay on his side facing the television with his eyes open, trying to relax and will himself to sleep. It took a good half hour before he began to feel the muscles in his neck loosen and his eyelids slowly close.

This was the simple ritual of sleep to which he'd become accustomed: a lumpy couch, an oversized pillow and a threadbare blanket, accompanied by a fear of relinquishing his hold on consciousness, never really knowing what to expect from the dream world to follow. He'd spent many nights fighting against it. But every living thing must eventually sleep. And now that the face in his dream had come to life once again, unconscious and alone in a hospital bed only a few miles away, maybe he could finally put it to rest.

What must her dreams be, Lou wondered, her mind buried in a coma? And in those last fitful minutes before he drifted off, he'd prayed that the faces of Jimmy and Franny Patterson wouldn't be joining Catherine Waites on the list of apparitions haunting his sleep.

He woke to the smell of coffee and the sound of Maggie dropping a couple slices of bread into the toaster and hammering it down. He sat up and rubbed his red, swollen eyes. Maggie brought over a mug of steaming hot coffee and set it on the table. With his hands still over his face, he looked at it through the cracks in his fingers. The mug had the emblem of the Philadelphia Police Department on it, a gold shield with a blue crest depicting an old Yankee Clipper with its sails unfurled and a golden eagle over that and two rearing horses framing the skyline of the city. He raised the mug to his lips and sipped the hot coffee. The toast popped, startling him and some of the coffee spilled into his lap.

'We still going to the hospital today?'

'Yep.'

'Thought you'd forget.'

'Thought or hoped?'

'Drink your coffee. And try not to spill it on yourself.'

If he'd had any dreams during the night he didn't remember them. Another reason to be thankful. Maggie returned again from the kitchen, this time with the toast on a plate and a jar of strawberry jelly with a big tablespoon stuck in it.

'Breakfast of champions.'

'I thought that was cold cereal.' She sat next to him and started digging into the jar of jelly. 'You know I was up last night when you got home.'

'You should have come down.'

'Well, actually I heard you come in. I woke up and then I heard you talking to Joey.'

'Sorry.'

'No, I didn't mean it like that. I hadn't been sleeping very well anyway.'

'I could see why.'

He spread a thin layer of jelly on a slice of toast and took a bite. He washed it down with a swig of coffee.

'You've known Joey for a long time, huh?'

'I've known Joey longer than I know you.'

'How about Jimmy Patterson?'

'Him, too.'

Lou took another sip of coffee, his eyes drawn to the television which was still on from the night before. The morning news had replaced the endless array of infomercials playing through the night, most of them trying to sell a pill that promised to make his penis grow three times larger and stay erect twice as long. They'd interviewed all kinds of woman who'd attest to the fact that size matters, each successive claimant having a bigger smile on her face and more exposed cleavage. Lou had managed to sleep through most of them without giving much thought to the size of his penis.

The morning news didn't have much more to offer than the infomercials, correspondents trying to convince viewers that politicians really had their best interests at heart. Journalists doing public relations for politicians, Lou thought. When did that start happening?

'You guys are like a family, aren't you? I mean, the cops.'

'Yeah, we are.'

'You stick together, help each other out, right?'

'Yeah.'

'All of you?'

'Most of us.'

'But not all?'

'No, not all.'

'How about me? Am I in or out?'

'You're in, kid.'

'Then it's not just the cops. It's their families, too.'

'Yep.'

'That's nice to know. I mean, for some people who might not have much of a real family, you know what I mean, their cop family must be very important to them, like it's all they got.'

'I guess so.'

Maggie went back into the kitchen and put her cup of coffee into the microwave to heat up. She looked out the kitchen window while she waited, the first rays of sunshine splashing the grass with yellow light. A sprinkling of melting ice had formed overnight and she had the urge to walk in it, to feel it cold and sweet on her bare feet.

'You learn anything last night, like at the Arramingo Club?'

'You were listening.'

'Isn't that what detectives do?'

'You're too smart for your own good.'

'The Arramingo Club is a strip joint, right?'

'Yeah.'

'So what happened?'

'I spoke to the owner, Brian Haggerty. That's the reason I went there.'

'Do you think he killed Jimmy?'

'I didn't at first but now I'm not so sure.'

'Why's that?'

'You know, you're spending way too much time with Joey. You're starting to sound like him.'

'That's because both of us waste half our time trying to get a straight answer out of you.'

'Brian Haggerty's got a lot of hate in him. He seems to have a lot to hide as well.'

'That doesn't mean he killed Jimmy Patterson.'

'Jimmy knew the father, William Haggerty. Worked for him for a time or so rumor has it.'

'You mean, according to Joey.'

'Yeah. Knew Haggerty's first wife, too. I mean, *knew* her.'

'There's always a bimbo, isn't there?'

'I don't see jealousy as a motive.'

'Why not?'

'I just don't. Call it a hunch. But it is interesting that Jimmy's sister became Haggerty's second wife and his alibi for the night Valerie Price was killed. I have no doubt that Jimmy knew more than he was telling and if Haggerty thought he was going to blow the whistle on him . . .'

'Maybe Jimmy should have been more honest with you from the start. I'm not saying you could have prevented anything, but you never know.'

'Jimmy wanted to protect his sister.'

'By lying to you?'

'Well, there's lying and there's not telling the whole truth.'

'I didn't know there was a difference.'

'You'll make a good lawyer some day, you know that?'

'Not a cop?'

'No. Not a cop.'

Lou carried his empty cup and plate into the kitchen and set them in the sink. The sun was climbing higher now and just starting to come through the window. He leaned against the counter and looked at the table and chairs, the same ones that had been there since he was a kid. He looked at the cabinets and the counter top, also unchanged. The whole house was like that. He'd never even thought about remodeling. He thought about it now,

'Either way, you're a liar.'

'You might be right, Maggie. I don't know.'

'What time do visiting hours start?'

'At the hospital or the cemetery?'

'Very funny.'

'I think ten.'

'Well then, we better get ready.'

'I am ready.'

'I mean, shower and shave and put on a clean pair of pants.'

'Oh, that kind of ready.'

He let the hot water run against the back of his neck. Hot showers seemed to be one of the few luxuries he had left. He could lose track of time in there, standing with his eyes closed and the water washing over him like it washed over the statue of St Francis outside the Girard Avenue soup kitchen.

He stepped from the shower into the steamy bathroom, wrapping a towel around his waist and getting a cigarette going in the ashtray on the sink. He hit the switch for the overhead fan and got a look at himself in the clouded mirror with the cigarette dangling from his lips and his hair wet and slick against his head. And then it came to him. He was smoking again. He almost had himself convinced that he'd quit for good this time. But he was going again full force now and he had little doubt that the drinking would follow. He took another drag, the smoke mixing with the steam. Denial was a wonderful thing, he thought.

EIGHTEEN

Lankenau Hospital looked more like a college campus than a hospital with its long rectangular parking lots connected by narrow winding drives and surrounded by scenic waves of green lawn that would make the members of the Merion Golf Club envious. It seemed all dressed up to fool the trauma patients coming out of West Philly into believing it was worth the ambulance ride. They could get a bullet removed from their belly and enjoy the view for twenty-four hours before getting wheeled out with a six-inch scar under their shirt and a free token for the 100 Line. They could ride the trolley back into the heart of the city, trying to pull off their wristband and thinking that the food in the hospital was better than the food in prison. They just didn't keep you as long.

Maggie walked through the sliding glass doors ahead of her father, who nodded at the uniformed security guard. He got a cold stare in return.

'Nice place to visit.'

'Check in at the front desk.'

'Just like at the Marriott.'

'You can't afford this hotel.'

'I'm still covered under your insurance, compliments of the City of Philadelphia.'

'Don't pay your bill here and they check you out in a body bag.'

'You're morbid.'

'Hey, don't say anything about Franny Patterson. They may not let me see her. We're here to see Catherine Waites. That's it.'

'You got it, Chief.'

Maggie spoke to the guard so Lou wouldn't have to, so they wouldn't get into that whole cop thing, Lou wasting half an hour getting on this guy's good side, one ex-cop to another.

'We're looking for Catherine Waites.'

He typed the name into a computer and directed them to the third floor and pointed toward a bank of elevators against a far wall. Maggie thanked him and Lou smiled and the guard went back to his coffee and morning paper.

They waited by the elevator doors with a man and a woman and their three small children. There were two girls and a boy, scrapping with each other like a litter of puppies, each one taking a turn pressing the elevator button as they ran past. They had light brown skin and jet black hair and they spoke Spanish in short melodic phrases that Lou couldn't understand. Lou had the feeling that the two girls were teasing their brother, making him chase them around the lobby while their parents stood conspicuously quiet. The elevator door abruptly opened and they all piled in. Lou got on last, pushed three and asked the man what floor he wanted.

The two parents exchanged a desultory glance, neither of them speaking, as if they'd forgotten what floor they were going to. Maybe they didn't understand English any better than Lou understood Spanish. But the glance that passed between them was grave, as if it didn't matter how many children they had at their feet. There was one missing.

The woman said something to her husband in Spanish and he turned to Lou.

'*Quatro.*'

It sounded like some lonesome bullfrog croaking in the night.

The elevator grew warm and stifling and when the doors slid open to the sound of pinging in the ceiling, Lou practically fell out into the hallway. He was hyperventilating, sucking air in through his mouth and wiping a layer of sweat from his forehead. He looked down at his wet fingers and wiped them repeatedly on his pant leg and then began to tuck his shirt in his pants and adjust his belt and his jacket.

'What's wrong with you?'

'Claustrophobic.'

'You never were before.'

'I just really don't want to be here.'

'Then let's leave.'

'Let's just get this over with.'

*   *   *

The nurses' station bustled with activity. Everybody seemed to be talking at once, on the phone, to patients, to each other. They were talking and writing at the same time, opening and closing drawers, putting away files, bumping into each other in the cramped space behind the counter. It was a perfect square centered between three long corridors with patients' rooms on both sides. A fax machine whined against the back wall and Lou followed the sound, thinking that he must be the only one that could hear it.

About halfway down one of the hallways an old woman was screaming. She was down on one knee and Lou could see blotches of red beneath her thinning white hair. She appeared to have fallen and was having some difficulty pulling herself to her feet. She was clawing at the hand rail that ran the length of the wall, screeching like a bird as she screamed for help. She'd managed to get up onto one knee and could go no further, either from exhaustion or weakness. She was so thin, Lou thought, her legs looked like popsicle sticks poking out from under the hospital gown.

Lou turned his head toward the woman and back toward the nurses, who all seemed to be focused on the computer screens in front of them. It was Maggie who got their attention.

'Isn't anyone going to help her?'

There was no answer at first, the nurses in their blue smocks and white sneakers busy ignoring her question and still ignoring the screaming from down the hall. One of the nurses did look up and spied Lou over the top of her glasses.

'Lock up the med room, girls. We got the law here.'

'Hey, Betty.'

'Hey yourself, Lou.'

'Hey the both of you. There's a lady that needs help down there.'

Betty looked from Lou to Maggie and back to Lou.

'This one belong to you?'

'My daughter.'

'Congratulations. She full grown?'

'Almost.'

'Hey, honey. She does the same thing every day. She lays on the floor and cries until one of us walks down there, picks her up, puts her back to bed and tucks her in.'

'But isn't that your job?'

'No, honey, it's not. That old girl can walk just fine. There's not much more we can do with her here. We could strap her to the bed but she'd scream even louder. Once she's cleared medically, they'll ship her to a rehab facility.'

'You mean an old-age home.'

'Not necessarily. Assisted living, maybe.' Betty turned her attention back to the computer screen. 'Wonderful girl you have there, Lou.'

'Thanks. She reminds me a little of you.'

'I don't even know why I'm talking to you. You show up once a year, make nice, promise to call and then disappear.'

'I never thought you really wanted me to call. I thought you were just being polite.'

'Stop it. When you're ready, you know where to find me.'

'Behind those thick black glasses?'

'Yeah. Ya like 'em? A buck at the dollar store.'

'With them or without them, you're still beautiful, Betty.'

'Sure, Lou. And if I had a buck for every time I heard you say that . . .'

'I mean it.'

'You know what, I think you do mean it. You just don't know what to do about it.' She pulled the glasses off her face and rubbed her nose with the back of her hand. 'Now tell me what you're here for. 'Cause I know it's not to see me.'

Maggie had already gone down the hallway and was helping the old lady to her feet. They seemed to be hitting it off pretty well.

'We're here to visit a girl. Catherine Waites.'

'She's here. Hasn't regained consciousness yet.'

'That's what I heard.'

'It's a sad state of affairs, Lou. A young girl like that. She may end up brain-dead.'

Lou didn't appear to be listening. He was looking down the hall at the old lady, who was now smiling a toothless smile at Maggie and hanging tightly onto her arm. And watching them together, Lou thought what a good nurse Maggie would be.

Her youthful enthusiasm was evident. Rookie cops brought the same thing to the job, Lou remembered. He had it once upon a time, too long ago to remember now. Both jobs also came with a promise, an oath that in the long run was often impossible to fulfill. Nurses and cops seemed to have always walked hand in hand. Half the cops Lou worked with had married nurses. Most of them were divorced now but that wasn't the point. They'd helped the weak and they'd helped the sick and dying, cops working the street and nurses in every hospital in the city and for all their efforts, death only laughed in their face.

'I'm sorry, Betty. What was that?'

'I said you're goddamn brain-dead and you should wake the hell up.'

'Yeah, you're right. What room did you say Catherine Waites was in?'

'I didn't say.'

Lou spun and faced Betty and looked into her eyes, at the dark circles below her eyes still puffy with sleep and the thin nose and full lips of a once beautiful woman, older now but still in possession of those qualities that make a woman attractive at any age. And something passed between them, an acknowledgement of sorts, a recognition of who each of them had become since they'd last seen each other. They had changed and yet they were still the same in many ways. They had taken different paths but seemed to have moved through the stages of life, arriving at the same place. And what had attracted them to each other all those years ago was still there.

Neither one of them was smiling, both of them wondering what to say to the other. The few seconds that their eyes had locked seemed to pass like an eternity and in the next second they looked away and the moment was gone.

'She's in room 310. The end of the hall.'

'Thanks.'

He took the long walk down the hall, letting his hand rest lightly on the railing. He stayed close to the wall as he passed where the old lady had fallen. Though she was gone now, back in her room under an extra blanket, he could still smell her. It was a sour smell, a strange combination of too much medicine and body odor, the kind of smell found only in the very old. It lingered in the hall like some chemical by-product of the life and death struggle being waged in that old woman's body. Then again, he thought, maybe all hospitals smelled like that.

He thought he saw a couple spots of blood on the floor where the old woman had lain. It could have been old blood but, whether it was old or new, there was no mistaking it. It was definitely blood, just a few scarlet drops left to congeal on the cold floor. The janitor could go over it with his mop a dozen times, knowing that if he really wanted to get the floor clean he would have to get down on his hands and knees with a bucket of hot water and a strong dose of ammonia and a good stiff brush and scrub it away.

Maggie came out of the old lady's room at the precise moment Lou was walking by. They almost ran into each other.

'Good timing.'

'For another errand of mercy?'

'Is that what this is?'

'Why, what would you call it?'

'I don't know. A deathwatch?'

They continued down the hall, a red exit sign over a fire door marking the end of the line.

'I got a question for you.'

'Shoot.'

'Do you believe in fate, like something is meant to be?'

'Yeah, I believe in fate. I also believe in chance. Sometimes they're one and the same. Why do you ask?'

'Well, like, I think I was meant to be here, to help that lady and to see for myself what I'm capable of. I think stuff like that happens and it's a way we discover ourselves.'

'If you believe it then it's true. You asked if I believe in fate. Maybe it's the belief that makes it real. Fate couldn't exist if there wasn't someone to believe in it.'

'Well, now we know I believe in it. The question is, do you? You never really answered the question.'

'I guess I wouldn't be here if I didn't.'

NINETEEN

C atherine Waites lay motionless on her back. A white bandage covered half her face and most of her head, which looked oddly misshapen under the bandage. Her mouth hung open and a thick gray tube ran out of it and snaked along the side of the bed to a machine that hummed and hissed like a copy machine with a paper jam. The arm with the IV had already begun to bruise and her complexion had grown perceptibly jaundiced.

Lou closed his eyes and tried to picture the girl he'd met more than ten years earlier, the girl from his dreams, thinking that she bore little resemblance to the girl lying here on this bed and that perhaps he was mistaken in thinking that it was really her.

There was a chair in the corner and Lou sat in it while his daughter walked around the bed and leaned over the girl and looked at her face, studying Catherine Waites as if she might recognize her too from her father's descriptions. And though they'd never met Maggie didn't see her as a stranger. She gently stroked the back of the girl's hand as a mother might do to wake a sleeping child.

'She could be just resting, you know. Isn't that what a coma is, the mind trying to heal itself?'

Lou's eyes were closed again and he was rubbing the thick skin on his forehead as if he was shielding his eyes from the sun.

'I don't think anybody really knows.'

'Then it's possible she can hear every word we say.'

'I suppose so.'

'Then say something to her, Dad. Let her hear your voice.'

He took his hands away from his face and shook his head.

'I wouldn't know what to say.'

'Say anything.'

'There's nothing for me to say.'

They stayed there for a while, Lou looking at the floor and

Maggie taking the chart out of a plastic bin at the bottom of the bed, trying to pronounce the names of the medications on what seemed like a very long list. The textured drop-ceiling diffused the fluorescent light in the room and the flat, white walls were the color of eggshells. All that artificial light beat down onto the face of Catherine Waites as if she was in a tanning bed, her pallor turning a sickly yellow instead of golden brown. It reminded Lou of the bare bulbs on the cell block at Eastern State Penitentiary that never went off, day or night.

Lou rose slowly from his seat in the corner and, giving Catherine Waites one last glance, he pushed hurriedly through the door. He made his way back to the nurses' station where he dropped his elbow onto the counter and spoke without looking down, his vision still lingering in the direction he'd come as if he expected Maggie to be following right behind. But she wasn't and Betty hadn't yet noticed him standing there.

'You know, I meant to ask you. How are your kids doing?'

'Back so soon? That was a quick visit.'

'I wanted to see her. That's all. Nothing I can do.' A young doctor in green scrubs stood across the counter, holding a clipboard and scribbling notes onto a lined pad. 'You have two, don't you?'

'My daughter is still in high school. My son's in Afghanistan. The Marines.'

'I'm sorry.'

'Why would you be sorry? It was something he always wanted. He wanted to be a Marine before he was old enough to shave. My ex-husband was in the military. He used to say it was a noble profession. He'd say there was no higher calling than being a soldier.' Betty removed her glasses and closed her tired eyes and dropped the glasses on the counter and leaned back in her chair. 'Nobility is something you read about in books. Not a way to characterize your son.'

'I don't know.'

'You don't know?'

'I've seen noble men, Betty. I've known them. And I didn't read about them in books or see them in the movies. I saw them in action. It's our actions that define us as noble. It's one of the few things I've ever been sure of.'

'Then, I suppose, you classify yourself as noble.'

'I didn't say that.'

'I think you just did.'

Maggie was coming down the hall now, side-stepping the blood stains as Lou had done. She stared alternately at her father and then at Betty as if she'd just entered her parents' bedroom and interrupted a domestic dispute.

'Betty, I do have one more favor to ask you.'

'You haven't asked any yet.'

'Franny Patterson was brought in here last night. I know she's in pretty bad shape. I'm just wondering if you can tell me what room she's in?'

'Jimmy's little sister, right?'

'Yeah.'

Betty rolled her eyes and turned to the computer screen in front of her. She started pounding the keys and then turned the computer screen toward Lou so he could see it over the counter.

'She's still in intensive care.'

'Thanks, Betty.'

Lou and Maggie rode the same elevator back down to the main floor and proceeded through a long hallway connecting separate wings of the hospital. The hallway was essentially a glass tube, two thick glass walls on each side with a view of the parking lot, cars going silently by on Lancaster Avenue and clusters of sparse, bare trees littering the grounds. The trees didn't appear to be arranged in any particular order, each one looking like a crippled hand emerging from the earth. Air whistled down the hallway like it was a wind tunnel. Lou picked up his pace, Maggie walking a few paces behind. She was running now to keep up.

Franny wouldn't be allowed visitors, not if she was in intensive care, not from anyone other than the immediate family or a parish priest if things looked that bad, someone to administer the last rites so her soul could enter Paradise as opposed to wandering the streets of Philadelphia looking for revenge. All things considered, she'd probably have a cop outside her door; maybe it'd be a friendly face, one of her brother's old friends.

The detail would have come down the seniority list with very short notice and whoever was looking to pick up a little overtime would have to do it after eight hours on the midnight shift with no sleep. Lou had done it plenty of times, babysitting a witness or a victim in the hospital, grabbing a chair from the waiting room and parking it in the hall and slugging coffee from the machine.

'I think I should handle this myself, Maggie. Sorry.' He pulled a crumpled five out of his pocket. 'Why don't you meet me in the cafeteria?'

'If I knew you were going to blow me off I wouldn't have come this far.'

'It kind of just dawned on me. It's going to be hard enough getting myself in.'

She folded the five-dollar bill and slid it into her back pocket. 'Big spender.'

It was Donny Weeks sitting outside Franny's room. Lou recognized him instantly. Donny was a career patrolman. In twenty-five years he'd never managed to climb even one wrung on the promotional ladder. After a while it had become a badge of honor to him. There were days on end when he and Lou met outside Tony Luc's, sitting car to car, inhaling cheese steaks and talking with their mouths full and washing it all down with Diet Pepsi. Thinking about it now, Lou couldn't remember what those conversations had been about. Yet he felt he knew Donny pretty well. Donny felt the same. Who knew why?

Approaching from down the hall Donny looked like a caricature of his earlier self, the same long, thin face, always a little pasty. He was in his early fifties now with a dark pompadour and only a touch of gray. He'd never had a chin. What he did have was this slim, rubber-like neck that protruded over his collar and twisted spasmodically every so often, his whole head twitching. Lou remembered watching Donny over the door of his police cruiser, waiting for his head to spin all the way around, thinking he looked like a nervous rooster.

Donny held a white Styrofoam cup and his head was back against the wall. Lou was a little surprised to see him still on the job. He was another one of those guys with enough time to retire and just waiting for the right time to do it, wondering if there was ever going to be a right time, always finding something else to spend his money on: a boat, a motorcycle, a cottage in the mountains, a twenty-something girlfriend.

Lou remembered hearing that Donny had bought a place in South Carolina. A lot of the guys in the department seemed to be going that way lately. Their pension money went a lot further down there, a little place a few blocks from the beach, the same ocean but touching the shores of a more civilized society, southern manners and hospitality, where the man was still the man and graffiti was something they threw at the Thanksgiving Day parade. You could drive along the same stretch of road for mile upon mile and not see an office building or a strip mall or an industrial park or an oil refinery, just one shanty town after another, poor upon poor living side by side, unchanged for a century. It was everything an ex-Philly cop could ask for at half the price.

Donny had known Jimmy Patterson as well as Lou had, all of them assigned to the Seventeenth District early in their careers, keeping the blacks in Point Breeze and the whites in Grays Ferry from killing each other.

'Hey, Donny.'

Donny's eyes fluttered open and he casually put the cup to his lips before turning to the sound of Lou's voice.

'Hey, Lou. Long time no see. How's things?' He used his shirt sleeve to wipe the dribble of coffee from his chin. 'I heard you were back in town. Someone said they ran into Joey G down at the Ivy, said you guys were starting a PI business.'

'It's not much of a business.'

'It's the kind of business that takes connections, that's for sure. And come to think of it, Lou, I don't remember you havin' a lot of connections. And I know there ain't no money in cheatin' housewives.'

'I've met a few housewives that have made a pretty good living at it.'

They laughed out loud and any tension between them melted away.

'You ain't shittin'.' Donny got slowly to his feet and placed himself in front of the door. 'That's a shame what happened to Jimmy. It's got a lot people pissed off. The fuckin' Haggertys. For Jimmy's sake, I don't mind keeping an eye on his baby sister but she should have known better, gettin' mixed up with them.'

'It's not always easy knowing what the right thing to do is.'

'You don't believe that, Lou. Her old man's a cop, she got

two brothers who are cops and she throws in with a gangster. There's a problem there.'

'The father and the son, Donny, they're two different people.'

'The apple don't fall far from the tree. You know that.'

'Maybe she thought she could change him.'

'Hey, you don't have to defend Franny Patterson to me.'

'I know, Donny.'

'She was like family. You know what I'm sayin'?'

'You never know. Maybe it wasn't Brian Haggerty who killed Jimmy.'

'C'mon, Lou. After all that shit that went down with the old man. Hey, like I said, I don't blame Franny. Women get a little crazy when it comes to money. And I don't put it past Jimmy to have a few friendly words with Brian Haggerty, just to keep the record straight. If it was my kid sister, I'd do the same. And I don't put it past this Haggerty clown to think he can put the hammer down on anybody he damn well pleases, cop or not.'

'Can I have a few minutes?'

'I don't even think she's awake, Lou.'

'A few minutes, that's all I ask. If someone comes, one knock at the door and I'm out of there.'

Donny nodded and stepped aside and Lou went in. His first impression was that Franny looked worse than Catherine Waites. But head trauma and blood loss were two entirely separate types of injury and Franny had obviously lost a great deal of blood; she might have bled to death if Lou hadn't found her. It had only been the night before but it seemed now like it had been a lifetime ago, as if it had been one of his dreams. But he would always wake from his dreams and know they weren't real. Reality, however, was becoming problematic: a burden, always there regardless of how he chose to define it. It never went away.

Franny's face was pale, ghostlike. Her eyes were closed and her hair spread out on the pillow under her head. The wave of light that pulsed across the monitor seemed like a silent bolt of lightning on the horizon. Lou went to her bedside and lightly touched her arm. The skin felt cool. A large needle protruded through layers of clear plastic tape. There was the beginning of a black, burgeoning bruise. The hand had been heavily bandaged, a yellowish stain forming over the missing knuckle of her ring finger.

Her eyes twitched under her thin, almost transparent lids, rippled with red, web-like capillaries. They looked like the wings of a butterfly.

'Franny? It's Lou.' His hand moved to her shoulder. A sliver of white slowly emerged as her eyes came open. She was still far from consciousness. 'It's Lou, Franny.'

The groan that emanated from her seemed to come from deep in her throat, the pain in her body pushing to the surface.

'Who did this to you, Franny?'

'Oh, Lou.'

'Who was it, Franny? I want to help but I can't if you don't tell me the truth.'

'Where's Jimmy?'

'Tell me what happened, Franny. Please.'

'Lou. Where's Jimmy?'

'He's gone.'

'Where, Lou? Where is he?'

'He didn't make it, Franny. I'm sorry. I . . .'

Franny began crying but the crying sounded more like gasps, like hiccoughs cut short through lack of air, like maybe she might stop breathing altogether. And her eyes were so dry and her mouth was so thick that she couldn't even produce a tear and her cracked lips just trembled.

'Oh, God help me. It should be me, Lou. I should be dead.'

'It's time I heard the whole story, Franny. There's no other way.'

'I can't.' She seemed to take a gulp of air but nothing went in. She was struggling for a breath. Her lungs seemed to be shutting down. She couldn't remain conscious much longer. The effort it took to speak was draining her.

'Franny, stay with me.' Her lids fluttered again, only a thin rim of white showing now and her two eyes moving beneath the surface of the lid. 'You have to talk to me, Franny. Please. It's now or never.'

Lou heard the knock and before he could move the door opened and the same resident in green scrubs was standing there, his glasses making his eyes look three times their normal size. He hadn't moved from Franny's bedside and her last words came to him in a whisper.

'Sapphire. It was Sapphire.'

'What the hell is going on in here?' He turned his head quickly toward Donny, addressing him in the same tone. 'Did you have knowledge of this, Officer?' Donny was standing behind the doctor, holding the door open. 'I want an answer. Did you have knowledge of this?'

'No, Doctor, he didn't.' The doctor moved past Lou, putting the stethoscope into his ears and placing the business end of it against Franny's chest. 'I needed to speak to her. It was important.'

'Important enough to jeopardize her life?' He pressed a button on a bedside panel and two nurses came rushing into the room. 'Who the hell are you, anyway? You're not the police. And how the hell did you get in here?'

'I'm a family friend. A private detective hired by this woman.'

'This woman is a victim. Does she look like she's in any condition to be hiring private detectives? You could have killed her.'

'That wasn't my intention.'

'Famous last words. I want your name, Mr Private Detective, and believe me, this won't end here.'

'Lou Klein, Doctor. My name is Lou Klein.'

TWENTY

Out in the parking lot, Lou handed Maggie the keys. 'You mind driving?'

'You OK?'

'I've had better days.'

Maggie guided the car down the ramp toward the street and they sat waiting in a long line of idling cars while the light cycled through. There was a little bit of sun and people looked happy to be out driving around though it was still cold. It was already past lunchtime but there were still cars going in and out of the fast-food joints along Lancaster Avenue.

'You hungry?'

'We can get something at Heshy's.'

'OK.'

'You working today?'

'Supposed to be. But I'm already late. I think Heshy was expecting me there for lunch. That's when he really needs me.'

'He'll survive.'

The lunch crowd was filtering out of the Regal Diner as Lou and Maggie showed up, a lot of construction workers in Carhartts and work boots and dusty caps coming from the project down the street, a new bank going up in record time, supposed to help with new money for new business, new blood for an old neighborhood. They looked disappointed, walking past Maggie as if they'd come expecting to see her with her apron and her ponytail and her smile, a communion of working stiffs. Most of them said hello and Maggie said hello in return.

'Nice of you to show up. Not a call? Nothing? I'm here by myself.'

'My fault, Hesh. She was with me.'

'A lot of good that does.'

'You had Joey here.'

'Joey?'

'He's a good helper.'

'He's a good eater.'

'And that's why you love him.'

'Loveable. Yes, he's a very loveable man.'

Lou smiled and Joey looked around the side of the newspaper he'd been holding in front of his face. He closed the paper and folded it in half and reached for a cup of coffee.

'Well, she's all yours now.'

'Good. She can clean up. Bus the tables, get the dishwasher going and then start on the counter.'

'See what you got me into,' Maggie chimed in.

'More like what I got you out of.'

Maggie took off her jacket, hung it up and tied an apron around her waist. She began clearing tables, pocketing a couple single dollars. Lou sat next to Joey at the counter. There were only a couple of other people left in the place, two women Lou recognized as employees from the liquor store in the strip mall around the corner. They were both middle-aged. One was black with a red hue to her skin and one was white with red hair. They were both wearing striped polyester pants suits and had blue nametags pinned to their chests. They were looking down the counter at Joey and Joey was staring back at them as if he was trying to read the names on their nametags.

'I heard back from Candy Bell.'

'Glad to see you weren't wasting any time.'

'No comment.'

'What'd she have to say?'

'She wants to meet. Seems like she might have a lot to say but wasn't going to say it over the phone.'

'Why do you suppose that is?'

'Well, let's put it this way. When I mentioned the Haggertys, her voice got that little quiver in it and I'm not talking about a scared quiver. I've never known Candy to be scared of anything. It was an angry quiver, angry like if there was something in her hand, she'd throw it at your head. And if you knew Candy like I knew her, you'd better duck.'

'Where does she want to meet?'

'The Taurus Club. In Delaware.'

'Delaware?'

'Says she can't afford to be seen talking to me. Said she'd meet us at the Taurus Club in Wilmington around five. It's right across the street from the Wilmington Trust Bank. Can't miss it, she says.'

'Ex-call girl, ex-stripper doesn't want to be seen in public with ex-cop. That's good.'

'We all have a history, Lou, especially me and Candy. It's common knowledge in certain circles. She's just protecting her interests.'

'And isn't the Taurus Club private?'

'She says to tell the doorman we're there to see her. It won't be a problem. We buy her dinner; she tells us what she knows. And we're out of there.'

'Great.'

The Taurus Club sat in the middle of Fayette Street across

from the bank, right where it was supposed to be, with a big black bull hand-painted onto the tile façade. The bull looked ready to jump down and gore someone through the chest. Its broad black head was bowed; its horns were long and curled and smooth with a glistening point at the tip. The silver handles of two jewel-encrusted swords protruded from its arched back and its brows were deeply furrowed as if it were in excruciating pain. The ring in its nose pierced two red flaring nostrils and all four hooves of the animal were off the ground as if it had been drawn leaping into the air, its eyes glowing in the night like two sparkling emeralds.

Lou couldn't help but sympathize with the portrait of this animal on the wall, the wretchedness of the beast plain on its face, animated and alive like a tattoo on the skin that moved and flexed and twitched with the striations of the muscle underneath. Whoever drew it meant for it to be seen that way, that it should be examined and understood, the agony evident in this most sensuous of creatures. And everyone passing through that door would look at it and feel its power, perhaps even fear it. And by the end of the night they would need more than a few drinks to erase it from their memory.

Lou and Joey had both worn sport jackets for the occasion and they tugged at their ties nervously, obviously uncomfortable with the formality. Lou unbuttoned his jacket and gave their names to a hostess in a long black dress that clung to every curve of her narrow frame. She was all business.

'Ms Bell was just a little delayed. But she wants you to know she's on her way. Would you gentlemen care to wait at the bar?'

'Not a bad idea.'

They preferred the bar to the dining room and by Taurus Club standards it was probably where they belonged. The drinks were overpriced but they didn't have to wait long. Candy Bell arrived without much pomp or circumstance. The door came open with a rush of air and she appeared in a brushed wool pants suit, black over white, with zebra stripes and a matching waistcoat and black gloves and boots and a small purse that she held by the handle at her side as if it was a mace. She noticed Joey at the bar and with the slightest nod of her head made him understand they were to meet at the booth she'd reserved in the back.

'Thanks for coming, Candy. Sorry about all this. You know how it is.'

'It's Candace, Joe. Please. And I do know how it is. Believe me, I'm not here to do you any favors. But if I can say something that'll put Brian Haggerty away . . .'

'Ah, you remember Lou Klein, don't you, Candy? We were on the job together back in the day.'

'Doesn't ring a bell.'

'That's good. Yeah, I like that.'

Lou took a sip of the beer he'd brought with him from the bar and set it down. Joey did the same and they both leaned across the table. Candy pulled a pack of cigarettes from her purse and lit one. She took a long drag, blowing the smoke into the air. She let the cigarette rest in a gold ashtray.

'What we were hoping is that you could tell us something about Valerie Price. You know what I mean. The kind of stuff you can't read in the papers. Joey says you got started at the Arramingo Club so you might have seen things you weren't supposed to, or heard things. There are still a lot of rumors going around and we figured you might be able to help us separate fact from fiction.'

'Joey, tell your friend here that if he doesn't shut up real soon this is going to be a dinner for two. And the only thing I'll be talking about is how you used to chase me down Woodmere Avenue in your skivvies.'

'Shut up, Lou, and let the lady talk.'

'The first thing you guys ought to know is that Valerie Price wasn't the only girl to get something going with William Haggerty. He was the owner and he liked to sample the merchandise. None of us are naïve, so you guys know what I'm talking about. We did what we had to do. I'm a much different person now than I was then.' She took a quick drag on the cigarette and waved over a waitress, a young woman in black tights and a white button-down, tied in the front. 'Well, maybe not all that different, but I am in a different place in my life. I'll be honest: I didn't like Haggerty, the old man or his son. Brian wasn't as bad as the old man. I'll give him that. But it doesn't change the way I feel.'

The waitress stood by waiting for Candy to finish her sentence.

The menus still sat in a pile at the edge of the table. The dim lighting in the booth obscured their faces and the waitress seemed well versed in avoiding eye contact, making the patrons of the Taurus Club feel anonymous, which was the way everybody wanted it. Candy ordered the shrimp salad and Lou and Joey ordered blue-cheese burgers and sweet-potato fries. The waitress grimaced and wrote it all down without looking up from her pad.

'I take it Valerie Price played it a little different.'

'That's one way to put it.' She took one last drag and snuffed the cigarette out. The waitress brought over a bottle of white wine and poured a few ounces into a glass with a long, thin stem. 'Valerie was beautiful and smart but she was reckless. She had a plan and it was a good plan. Most of the girls had the same plan. Hook a rich guy.' She took a sip of the wine, trying to look dainty with her pinky finger curling over the table. It was a good act. 'Some girls become cheerleaders and go for a big-ass pro football player. And some girls prefer to take their clothes off. They just like politics better than sports. Some girls are faster workers than others but the end result is usually the same.' Candy took another sip of her wine. She seemed thirstier this time. 'Valerie had a wild streak. She would drink and she was out of control. Her eyes would go black and fuzzy like she was gone somewhere; another fucking planet. But William was definitely taken with her. Everyone was. That was part of the problem. She spread herself too thin and pretty soon all the boys are fighting over her.'

'I didn't think Haggerty was the type to let a woman get to him.'

'I didn't think so either. Until he showed me otherwise.'

'Showed you how?'

'You see this scar on my lip?' She pointed to a slight discoloration on her upper lip. If she hadn't pointed it out Lou never would have noticed it. Seeing it now, he noticed how the orange light from the ceiling seemed to catch it just right, a blemish on an otherwise perfect set of pink lips. He noticed too that Candy Bell never once smiled. 'I called Valerie Price a whore. I told him she'd fuck anybody with a hundred-dollar bill in his pocket or an ounce of coke to put up her nose. I told him she was after his money and doing a pretty good job of getting it. Other than being naked in bed when I said it I didn't think my comment would have much of an effect on him. He wasn't much of a listener and he was used to girls looking for a piece of the action. But he flipped out. Didn't say anything. Just slapped me across the face with the back of his hand.'

They all sipped their wine. Candy's salad came and she laid a napkin across her lap, stabbed a baby shrimp with her fork and pulled it off with her teeth. She chewed silently while Joey and Lou fumbled with their burgers. For a few minutes all that was heard was the sound of silverware scraping against the porcelain plates. Joey filled their glasses with wine.

'A lot more to the story, though. Huh?'

'Yeah.' Candy took another sip of the wine. She held the glass aloft, looking through it, the two men following the movement of the glass in her hand. She caught a glimmer of herself in the thin glass and the bittersweet aroma of the alcohol seemed to catch in the back of her throat. She replaced the glass on the table. 'Nobody was surprised that Valerie ended up dead. But William – that was a shock.'

'People assumed he was untouchable.'

'As you said, there were a lot of rumors floating around.'

'And then there was the truth.'

'Yes, Mr Klein. The truth is that Valerie got herself pregnant. Whether it was on purpose or not, I can't say. Who was the father? The assumption was Brian Haggerty since officially the two of them had been an item for a while. But who really knew? Could have been the father just as easily as the son. And there were a lot of big shots in and out of the Arramingo Club back then – lawyers, judges, politicians, cops – and Valerie had her turn with most of them.'

Lou turned a wary eye toward Joey and then back to Candy.

'What about Jimmy Patterson?'

'What about him?'

'Did he go in there?'

'He worked there. And when he wasn't there on business, it was pleasure.'

'Was there anything between Jimmy and Valerie?'

'You know damn well there was. Jimmy couldn't keep it in his pants any more than Joey could. You're all the same. Believe me, I understand. It's human nature. But Jimmy was the jealous type, to say the least. He'd get drunk and the wheels would start turning. He'd start thinking, Valerie Price in his head. Then he'd get angry and all hell would break loose. He was in a tough spot, a cop working for William Haggerty on the side. His sister trying to climb the same ladder he was on. It was only a matter of time before someone fell off.'

'Looks like they both went for a fall.'

'Franny was good. I'll give her that. Anyone who gets what she wants and doesn't have to take her clothes off to get it.'

'But Jimmy wasn't crazy about the idea.'

'He didn't approve of her relationship with Brian Haggerty but he had no one but himself to blame. He practically handed her over to him. Got her a job. A kind of nanny for Valerie's kid. But she didn't stay a nanny for very long; she had her sights set a little higher. Maybe Jimmy figured if Brian went for his sister he'd have Valerie to himself. Maybe he just wanted to be part of the family. Who knows? No one can say what's going on inside a person's head, especially when there's a woman involved.'

'Or in their heart?'

'Please don't get sentimental on me, Mr Klein. Lou. These people, every last one of them, were heartless fucks. Their idea of love was a stiff prick and the almighty dollar.' She pushed a lock of bleached blonde hair off her face and threw her head back and looked Lou in the eye. 'Anyway, Valerie decided to put the squeeze on the Haggertys. And I don't blame her one bit. She had them by the balls. She was pregnant and she had a big mouth. Either Brian stepped up to the plate on his own or an arrangement was made.'

'What kind of arrangement?'

'Brian and Valerie were quietly married. Valerie seemed to have just disappeared and a lot of the girls were saying she lost the baby. Then I heard the baby was born and arrangements were made to have him taken care of. Valerie wasn't exactly the mothering type.'

'Is that where Franny came in?'

'Haggerty paid her to watch the kid. Jimmy set it up. But like I said, it didn't last too long. Pretty soon Franny and Brian and Valerie's baby were playing house and walking around like they were a happy family.'

'Sounds cozy.'

'William didn't seem to mind. He could have Valerie whenever he wanted.'

'One big happy family.'

'And you know the rest. They found William and Valerie dead. Called it a murder-suicide. And we all moved on.'

'What happened to the kid?'

'They got a new nanny to watch him while Brian and Franny were off honeymooning. A girl from the club. Her name was Mary Grace Flannery. We called her Gracie. The second she agreed to watch that kid she wanted for nothing. The crazy thing was that it was the old lady, Eleanor Haggerty, who arranged everything. Everything went through her – what school the kid went to, what kind of clothes he wore, music lessons, karate lessons. I never understood it. Her husband knocks up an exotic dancer and she shows more interest in the little bastard than she showed in her own son, like she was going to turn him into some kind of gentleman.'

'Who else knew about all this?'

'Some of the other girls probably knew: Gracie's friends. I heard her tell people the kid was her nephew. Before the murder we all assumed that Brian would end up divorcing Valerie anyway and he and Franny would raise the kid as their own. She seemed like she was all for it. Seemed like that type: a nice, clean girl from a cop family. I don't think Valerie cared one way or the other as long as she was getting paid.'

Candy reached for the glass of wine and accidentally knocked it off the table. The thin stem cracked cleanly in two and what little was left of the white wine formed a small clear puddle on the floor. The shattered glass seemed to draw its share of sideways glances from other tables in the room. Candy was obviously uncomfortable with the attention. The hostess caught the sound of it and sent a boy over to clean it up and it was gone almost before the echo of breaking glass stopped ringing in Lou's ears. The waitress took the opportunity to clear the table and ask if she could bring a carafe of fresh coffee.

'So Franny was in?'

'She was in. Even Brian Haggerty knew a good thing when he saw it.' She dusted a few crumbs off the white tablecloth with the back of her hand. 'And neither of them told you a thing, not Jimmy or Franny?'

'Why do you think that is?'

'We all have our little secrets to keep, don't we?'

The waitress came back with a pot of coffee, three cups, a container of cream and packets of sugar. She began reciting from a list of desserts until they were all shaking their heads in unison like three stiff-necked bobble-head dolls on a bar-room shelf.

'It was all just a big game, with Valerie Price on one end and Franny Patterson on the other.'

'That's what the Haggertys do, Lou. They play with people's lives. They make their own rules. They make life fit their mold. A life to them is just something to be used.' Candy poured in the sugar and a little cream and stirred it noisily with a small silver spoon. 'I used to drink my coffee black. Now I like it sweet. Maybe I'm getting spoiled.' She stirred the coffee absently while she seemed to contemplate the swirling liquid. 'But you're right, Mr Klein. It was bound to blow up in their face.'

'I take it you didn't buy the official story?'

'William Haggerty wasn't the suicidal type and neither was Valerie. Homicidal? I can see that. It wasn't hard to believe they'd end up killing each other. But the stories in the papers and the police reports – all bullshit.'

'So, you think Brian pulled the trigger and got away with it?'

'I didn't say that. I don't like any of the Haggertys, Brian included, but I just don't picture him as a killer. He's got a lot of hate in him but there's something else. There's times he looks . . . defeated . . . broken, not like a guy who'd pick up a gun . . . more like someone who'd run away.'

'Then who do you think killed them?'

'My opinion?'

'Unless you were there that's all you can give, right?'

'That's right. If I had to guess, I'd say it was Eleanor Haggerty. That woman's got no conscience. I'm a good judge of men; maybe not as good a judge of women. But I think she's a ruthless bitch. If someone got in her way she'd find a way to get rid of them. She likes pulling strings from the background. And the only people she couldn't control were her husband and Valerie Price. I think she was pushed too far.'

'By William's infidelities, you mean, and then the baby?'

'This was a long time in the making, Mr Klein. We're not talking about six months here. We're talking about years. I was out of it by then but I stayed in touch with Gracie and she'd tell me about Valerie, about her behavior and her drinking. It was Valerie doing the pushing. She was living in the Haggerty house like a goddamn concubine, and if that wasn't bad enough she'd grab her son if the mood took her and parade him around the house, telling him stories about who he really was and how someday it would all be his. She'd even named the kid William. She was spitting in the face of all the Haggertys. She was playing with fire and she didn't care.'

Candy paused for a moment with the coffee cup still in her hand, looking over at the bar, at the line of men sitting there with their backs turned and their broad shoulders and expensive wool suits, gray and dark in the dim light, their conversation nothing but a low din like the engine of the taxis idling outside waiting for them to finish up their last drink and fall into the back seat for the slow ride home.

'Gracie seemed to think she was working some kind of blackmail scheme. Always had a lot of cash on her; spending money like crazy. Spoiling the kid, sure. But spoiling herself worse.'

They were all silent for a minute. Lou looked up at the ceiling, at the dark wood of the exposed beams, at the bronze chandeliers hanging from six feet of twisted chain and at the black glass of the Palladian windows and the checkerboard shadow they cast across the floor as the occasional headlights passed in front of the Taurus Club, veering off at what seemed like the last minute.

'Whatever happened to him? Where is he? He'd be almost twenty now.'

'If he's still alive. I married Paul Vannero and got the hell out of Philly. Moved to the suburbs, changed my name and lived happily ever after. I wanted to forget that part of my life. I wouldn't be talking about it now if Joey hadn't called. I don't know what happened to Billy. Probably ran away if he knew what was good for him.'

Joey smiled and Lou winked at him and they all polished off a final sip of coffee.

'Do you have children, Candace?'

Even in the darkness of that dining room her face seemed to droop a little at the question and then quickly stiffen. If she'd been taken off guard, it was only there to see for a fleeting second.

'I'm nothing like those other women, Mr Klein. Not like Valerie Price or Eleanor Haggerty or the girls at the Arramingo Club. Half of them ended up dead because of an overdose. The other half spent the rest of their lives taking punches from some drunken cop, present company excluded. I saw the world for what it was and I wasn't going to bring a child into it if I couldn't raise it right. And I learned enough about myself to know I wouldn't have made a very good mother back then.'

'How about now?'

'Not a day goes by that I don't think about it. But it's too late now, isn't it? Much too late.'

'I'm sorry.'

'Don't be. I don't like pity, Lou. I've never been pitied by anyone in my life. I had my years in the spotlight. I was young and beautiful and had my pick of men from all over the city. My stage name was Arabesque. And believe me, I was a jaw-dropper.'

'You're still gorgeous, Candy.'

'Thanks, Joey.'

Candy got up and excused herself to the ladies' room. Lou called the waitress over and paid the bill. Candy came back but she didn't sit down and it was obvious that the dinner and the conversation were over. Both Lou and Joey began to stand but she waved them back into their seats, letting them know she'd prefer to leave alone and for them to wait a few minutes until she was gone.

'Just one more question, Candy.'

'What's that?'

'Any idea where we can find Mary Grace Flannery?'

'I haven't seen or heard from her in a long time. Last thing I knew she was living on Catherine Street in Grays Ferry. She's old-school Irish. That's where Haggerty found her and if I had to bet, I'd say she's still there.'

'Thanks.'

Candy tucked her purse under her arm and walked away, her heels clicking lightly over the floor. Her calves were sleek and smooth with the black line of her stockings running down her leg from the back of her thigh to the top strap of her shoes.

'Oh, Candy. You mentioned that you went by the name of Arabesque. What name did Valerie Price go under?'

Candy turned and smiled for the first time that night.

'Sapphire. It was her birthstone.'

TWENTY-ONE

The front of the Taurus Club was quiet except for the occasional passing car. Lou stared at the mural of the tormented bull whose burning eyes seemed to follow his. Wilmington had become the kind of city that rolled up their streets soon after business hours, all those corporate types making a mass exodus to their suburban retreats. It seemed like the few left inside the Taurus Club needed some additional self-medication before going home to their wives and their children and the paradise that awaited them there.

The lights were out in all the office buildings on the block. Storefronts had gone dark. Across the street, the bank had locked its doors but on the concrete steps in front there was a strange assortment of homeless men setting up camp, wheeling their grocery carts from the darkness of the alley, using the long handicap ramp to the sidewalk. One of them stopped and unzipped his pants and began urinating in the fountain, red spotlights shining up on him from under the water, steam rising along with it. Lou watched him from across the street. There wasn't a cop in sight.

'Where to?'

'Grays Ferry.'

'Back to the Seventeenth District?'

'We cover a lot of territory, Joey. A lot of miles.'

'Yeah, but it seems like we keep going over the same ground.'

'It does work that way sometimes, doesn't it?'

Joey drove and Lou sat quietly in the passenger seat, the Wilmington skyline receding behind them and a lot of open road ahead. Philadelphia loomed in the distance, waiting for them just the way they left it with a light fog rolling in off the river, mixing with the industrial smoke and making it seem as if the sky itself was dropping down on top of them.

Lou looked at his watch. It was eight thirty. Neither of them said another word until they were crossing the South Street Bridge, looking out over the swollen river running black beneath them and then to Naval Square, where a condominium complex had replaced the old Navy Hospital. From the bridge, the attached units looked like cardboard cut-outs, like little green houses sitting side by side on a Monopoly board. They came off the ramp, Lou leaning into the long, sweeping turn, and stopped at the light in front of Callahan's.

'Brings back memories.'

'Yeah.'

Lou knew what memories Joey was talking about – memories of two rookie cops riding like young cowboys into hostile territory for the first time, memories of the chases and the fights and the murders and the dead bodies and the abandoned children and the house fires and the hold-ups. Memories of friends too, the friends they'd made in the most unlikely of places, friends that might even help them now if they were still around.

Larry Staples had been one of those friends.

He had an upholstery shop on 27th Street near Willow in Point Breeze. It had been Lou's first stop when he started walking the beat. Larry's door had always been open to him. Not that Larry ever locked his door, but his was an open door for two white cops when all the other doors in that neighborhood had been closed to them. They'd have their coffee in there when they were working the day watch and maybe a couple of shots of Hennessey when they were working nights. They could use Larry's phone to call their wives. They could eat lunch in there. They could read the paper and do crossword puzzles and get out of the rain.

Larry was also a wealth of information. He'd been around a long time and he knew things and he would hear things and he wasn't afraid to speak his mind. Not everybody in that neighborhood appreciated his candor. And then he was killed and suddenly everyone was his friend again. Lou wondered now, the way things were, whether Larry Staples was better off dead than alive.

The upholstery shop had been far enough down on 27th to put it in that border area where Grays Ferry and Point Breeze met. Dodging bullets had become an occupational hazard back then. It was like a war zone. And soon after Larry's death the shop had been boarded up like many of the storefronts in that neighborhood.

Lou remembered the last night he'd spent there with Larry. They'd been celebrating his eightieth birthday. Larry's son had called and wished him a belated happy birthday. He was still trying to convince Larry to move into a condominium complex out in Montgomery County, a little efficiency overlooking one of those mega-malls, with the Turnpike running behind it and round-the-clock security and an elevator in the building to take him up and down and a laundry room in the basement where he could slip and fall and not be found for days. For the first time in his life, Larry had been considering it.

Larry had a speckled, caramel-colored head and every time Lou had come through the door of the shop, the first thing he would see was Larry's bare dome, gleaming under a dotted coat of sweat. He'd be sitting behind the counter next to an old chair, turned over on its side with the stuffing all torn out. His eyes had a greenish tint to them that seemed to brighten with his quick smile. He'd inspect the marred wood and use a staple gun to secure the new material. Lou would watch him work from the other side of the counter. Then Larry would take out a bottle of Hennessey and set out a couple of glasses.

They'd drink and Larry would get dreamy and begin to talk about the old days, preaching to Lou like he did to the kids in the neighborhood. He'd tell them about a time when Philadelphia had real greatness, when the jazz clubs on South Street rang all night, the biggest names in the business making the rounds. And when the clubs closed they'd take it out on the street, their voices carrying through the neighborhood. And soon there would be a crowd gathered around, listening to the music, letting it get inside them. People weren't afraid to be out on the street back then. It didn't matter what time it was. Even the cops that came to break it up were touched by the sound and could only just stand there and listen.

Larry would have a few more drinks and his head would start to droop and then he'd start in on the prostitutes and the transvestites up in Judy Garland Park and how many dead kids there were that year and that if they didn't get out of Point Breeze pretty soon they'd end up dying there and how nothing would ever be the same unless someone did something about it.

But no one ever did, except maybe Larry in his small way. Lou knew that Larry Staples would never have left Philadelphia, even if he'd known what the future would bring. He just ran out of time.

'What do you think Larry would say if he could see the two of us driving around Grays Ferry like a couple of lost souls?'

'He'd say we were crazy.'

'You think?'

'He'd tell us to go home and forget the whole thing. No matter what we do, we can't bring Jimmy back, can't change what happened. And Larry Staples isn't comin' back either. He'd say we're just spinning our wheels.'

'Then why are we here?'

'We're crazy. Remember?'

Joey took 27th Street down to Grays Ferry Avenue and then onto 30th where he pulled into the lot at St Andrew's. He circled slowly through the lot and stopped. He rolled down his window. The last time they sat in that lot they were wearing the uniform of the Philadelphia Police Department.

Lou looked up at the old church, the red brick and jagged gray stone and the school next to it and the dark, deserted playground next to that. Shadows from a couple of shaky wooden backboards spread across the lot. Rusted rims with no nets on gray, metal poles, loose in the ground, wobbling as if a stiff wind would bring them down. A sagging fence surrounded the lot and the playground, making it look like an old reformatory, a forsaken scrap yard of condemned men, where prisoners were allowed out of their cells once a day and would spill into the yard and glare at the ravaged baskets and the razor wire wound atop the ten-foot fence. And they were left alone for that hour to fight amongst themselves until some semblance of order was achieved. And the wind that spun the gilded weather vane balanced on the vaulted spire of St Andrew sounded like laughter from the sky.

The Holy Fathers had planted a row of cherry blossoms along a cramped portion of barren dirt on the fringe of the lot. Thin, twisted trees that had once bloomed in spring, the tender pink petals unfolding timidly, had soon gone dormant. The withered bark had sloughed off, revealing the stunted trunk underneath. They hung on like that for a decade, Lou remembered, gray and forlorn, their meager branches frozen and stunted.

Lou noticed a light on in the rectory. A woman had set her face against a second-floor window. A vigilant nun finishing her evening prayers and spying on the white Cadillac in the lot. St Andrew's seemed to have the city of Philadelphia under surveillance, judging it and its many crimes.

Lou snapped open his cell phone.

'Who you calling?'

'Information. See if they have a listing for a Mary Grace Flannery.' He listened and then snapped it shut. 'No dice.'

'How about we hit the Golden Rose? If she's from the neighborhood, someone over there'll know her.'

'And if not, I can always go for a good, old-fashioned Irish car bomb.'

'You are crazy.'

He snapped open the phone again and waited until he heard Maggie's voice on the other end.

'How you making out, honey?'

'Fine. I'm over at the hospital.'

'Why are you at the hospital?'

'I felt like paying Catherine Waites a visit.'

'At this hour?'

'They never were able to get hold of her mother. She's got no family here.'

'OK. I understand. But I'm going to be late.'

'Your friend Betty said she'd give me a ride home.'

'She did, did she?'

'She's a very nice lady, you know. You should give her a call sometime. You two have a lot in common. And she likes you.'

'Maybe I will.'

'Can you call me when you're on your way home? It doesn't matter what time.'

'You're something else.' Joey stopped at a four-way stop sign. A primer-gray, two-door Oldsmobile sped past with the music blasting. The driver was wearing one of those beaver-fur hats and gloves and a T-shirt with no coat. 'Yeah, I'll call.'

The Golden Rose didn't look like much from the outside. There was a lighted sign with a few burned out letters and a worn wooden door with an opaque square of green glass about nose high with an iron grate over it. A lot of red and green neon in the window made it look like some drunk's idea of a cheap Christmas.

'Did you ever think that the guy who killed Larry Staples could be sitting at the bar in there and we'd never know it?'

'And if you found out, what would you do about it now?'

'Lock him up.'

'You need proof for that.'

'Maybe I'd take him for a ride, leave him under the bridge.'

'You don't mean that. I agree with you, but you don't mean it.'

'Hypothetical question. Right, Joey?'

'You think that's what Larry would have wanted?' Joey found a spot on the street and parked the car. 'I was just as angry as you were when Larry died.'

'Larry was murdered, Joey. That never sat well with me.'

'Someone gets murdered in this city every day, Lou.'

'And whose fault is that?'

'Not yours or mine.'

'Larry never would have been out there on the street if it wasn't for me.'

'That's where you're wrong. Larry would have been there no matter what. His neighborhood was on fire. When the riots started Larry chose what side he was on.'

'He should have stayed in his shop, locked the door like I told him.'

'Larry picked his battles, Lou. He wasn't about to give up. He'd stand up to his own people if he had to. We know what Larry Staples was all about. He was willing to die for something greater than himself. It could just as easily have been me trying to break up that mob. I could have been the guy on the ground getting his ass kicked. There was good and bad on all sides back then, Lou. Larry was on the side of good.'

'The man was a fucking saint.'

'He was.'

'And what can we do about it? Canonize him at the Golden Rose?'

TWENTY-TWO

They went inside and grabbed two stools at the end of the bar. The place was going pretty good, plenty of locals primed and ready to go the distance. There was a pool table in a back room and the hard tapping of the balls reached them through the music. Last call was coming up quickly. Joey and Lou hadn't caused much of a stir when they walked in; they must have looked like a couple of regulars.

Two guys got up from a table and walked out. Another guy got up off his barstool and headed to the men's room. Joey and Lou settled into their spots at the bar. A middle-aged guy in a blue flannel shirt with dark gray hair under a Phillies cap and three-days' growth on his face came up behind them and tapped Lou on the shoulder. Lou checked the guy out in the mirror behind the bar before turning his head.

'You got a lot of fucking nerve comin' in here.'

'I didn't think anyone would mind. It's been a long time.'

'You don't remember me, do you?'

'Afraid not.'

'Denis McNulty. You put my little brother away for five years. Been a long time but not that long. Not long enough. I don't think my brother would've forgot about you while he rotted in a cell up at Camp Hill.'

'The McNulty brothers. Yeah, I remember. Armed robbery, right? We caught him buying a bag of crack with the stolen money, the stupid shit. You were too smart for that, though. You got away and laid low. He could have rolled over and it would have been you in Camp Hill. But he was afraid of his big brother,

wasn't he, afraid of what would happen to him if he came back
to Grays Ferry after squealing on Denis McNulty.'

'A lot you'd know about it.'

'I know you could have come forward and taken responsibility,
saved your little brother. Done the time yourself.'

'It don't matter anyway. My brother's dead. Never made it out
of prison.'

'Well, I hope you see his face every time you look in the
mirror,' Lou dropped a twenty-dollar bill on the bar, slid the pack
of cigarettes in behind it, 'if you're looking for someone to
blame.'

Denis McNulty's face burned red. He exchanged a glance with
Joey and walked back to his table in the back. Lou waited for
the bartender to notice them. She was a redhead, middle-aged
and built like a linebacker in eighties spandex, black and tight
from her neck to her ankles. She was putting out a cigarette in
a dented tin ashtray, ignoring them and waiting for them to leave
after their encounter with Denis McNulty. When she figured they
weren't going anywhere, she pushed the ashtray away and strolled
to the end of the bar.

They ordered beer and she put the glasses down on two
lime-green napkins. Lou slid the twenty in her direction and told
her to keep the change. The smirk on her face didn't move a
muscle but her eyes opened a little wider as if she hadn't seen
a twenty-dollar tip since she'd been doing lap dances at the
Arramingo, which would have been a very long time ago.

'What's this supposed to buy?'

'Answers.'

'I thought as much. What are you guys, cops?'

'Ask Denis McNulty. He'll tell you.'

'I don't need to ask Denis nothing. What the hell you want?'

'Mary Grace Flannery.'

Lou took a long drink. He eyed the woman over the glass.
She was still in pretty good shape, probably mid-forties, bleached
blonde hair. A little too much make-up but she needed it to cover
the nicks and scars and the wrinkles from all the long nights
she'd spent on both sides of the bar. She was just as tough as
she looked.

'What would she want with you?'

'Then you know her.'

'Sure I know her.'

'I was just wondering what happened to her. I haven't seen her in a long time.'

'Nothing happened to her. If I see her, I'll tell her you were asking. What'd you say your name was?'

'I didn't say. When's the last time you saw her?'

'Don't remember.'

'But she comes in here?'

'She used to come in all the time. Not so much anymore.'

'You said you knew where she lived.'

'I never said that.' She lit another cigarette. One of the other patrons called to her and she filled a few glasses of beer from the tap and came back. 'Gracie used to cover for me once in a while. That's it.'

'Listen, honey. Your friend could be in danger. Why don't you quit the act and help us out. You'll be doing her a favor.'

She was wiping her hands on a wet towel and then used the towel to wipe the red lipstick that had run to the corners of her mouth and formed little concentric circles, making her look a little like a clown: a sad, old clown.

'I think we have her on file in the back. Give me a minute and I'll check.'

'Thanks.'

Joey polished off his beer in two quick swallows. Lou took his time, the alcohol slowly catching up to him. The place was starting to clear out. A few couples, talking secretly in the dark booths, packed up and crept away with their heads averted. A guy fell off his bar stool but managed to stay on his feet, grabbing for the stool next to him and making it to the door. Lou could hear the guy throwing up on the sidewalk outside.

The door opened again and a black guy in a worn consignment shop overcoat came in. His blue jeans were brand new but three sizes too big. They hung dangerously low on his hips and the wide cuffs were rolled up at the bottom. He wore a pair of black hi-top sneakers unlaced on his feet. His gait was uneven as if one leg was longer than the other and he seemed to drag the shorter one along, his sneakers sticking to the floor. He pulled his bare hands out of his pockets and blew on them. His chin

was covered with gray stubble and he was wearing a purple
Minnesota Vikings cap perched high on his head.

He made his way to the bar and the first thing he did was bum
a drink from the guy next to him. Lou could hear the garbled
din of his voice and turned to see the guy's broken-toothed leer.
He finished his drink and moved on, bumming another drink
from the next guy and making the same drunken speech. It
wouldn't be much longer before he reached Lou.

'You ready to get out of here?'

'And miss the opportunity to buy this gentleman a drink?'

'What the hell's wrong with you?'

'Maybe it's this place, Joey. I never liked it. I thought I could
come back here and just do a job and just talk to people and
gather the information I needed and walk away. But I can't. I'm
looking into the faces of these people and I see myself in their
eyes and I don't like what I see. I hear their conversations, how
petty they all are and how empty, and it pisses me off. In all
these years not a damn thing has changed.'

'As soon as the waitress comes back with this Flannery girl's
address we're out of here. That's all we came here for. I don't
like hanging around this dump any more than you do.'

'I don't know. Maybe it's not just this place. Maybe it's me.
I don't have the right to judge anyone. You wonder what happens
to places like this in between visits, you wonder if anything
changes other than the rotting wood and the crumbling sidewalk
outside. Do the stories ever change? Do the voices ever change?
Do the people change?' He looked toward the man bumming
drinks. 'I guess I got used to avoiding places like the Golden
Rose. And I guess now that I'm here, I have my answer.'

'Well, here's your chance to do a good deed. Buy this guy a
drink and then we can get out of here.'

Though the man's face was a rich, dark black beneath the
stubble, there were washed-out splotches of faded pigment. And
on the back of his chapped hands, where he held the glass of
beer, the same patches of cracked, light skin came through as if
it was some kind of a rash which, if it kept growing unchecked,
might turn his whole body white. The man leaned against the
bar for balance. He seemed to be losing his coordination one
ounce at a time.

Lou was still on the stool, a few dollars left on the bar in front of him and the half-empty glass of beer going flat. He didn't want to look the man in the face, knowing now what he wanted. He wanted to skip the formalities. He wanted to spare them both the unnecessary small-talk. He wanted to spare this man the humiliation of telling his sad story one more time, of begging another glass of beer and admitting that he had no money and that when he got paid he'd come back to the Golden Rose and repay the favor, buy a round for everyone in the place.

Lou finally turned and looked at the man and was surprised to see that he was younger than Lou first thought. He'd looked like an older man from a distance, the grizzled face and staggered gait. But up close his age wasn't so well hidden and Lou thought now that maybe humiliation wasn't what the man was feeling, that humiliation was felt by the very old and the very young because they couldn't take care of themselves, because they'd lost their independence or had yet to find it. But this guy felt nothing, not while he had a drink in his hand, not anytime.

The bartender returned with a glass in her hand and she set it down a little harder this time, taking two dollars from Joey's pile without asking. She'd come out wearing a white tuxedo jacket over her black spandex like she was ready to close for the night. Joey watched in dismay as she plucked the bills off the bar. Before she walked away, she tossed a matchpack on the bar. It had an address written on it and a telephone number.

'The address is Gracie's. The phone number is mine. If you find Gracie, tell her to give Shar a call.'

'If?'

'I mean, when you find her. And you can use that number yourself, if you feel like it.'

'Thanks, Shar.'

Joey smirked and reached over Lou's shoulder and snatched the rest of his money. He folded the crumpled dollars in half and slid them into his pants pocket.

'Can we go now? Or do we both have to buy him one?'

'I guess that depends on how thirsty he is.'

Lou raised his glass; they all tapped glasses and some of the foamy beer spilled from the man's glass and dripped onto the floor.

They drank in silence and Lou and Joey got up to go. The man was obviously in no hurry and proceeded back to the other end of the bar, where he started the process all over again.

'Looks like he's pretty thirsty.'

'Do you blame him?'

'For being thirsty?'

'For accepting free drinks from these kind-hearted souls.'

These were mostly working men at the Golden Rose and while they didn't mind spotting someone a drink now and then, they wouldn't be willing to carry him all night. And there was no better person to give a voice to their collective will than Denis McNulty.

'That's enough!'

A hush fell suddenly over the bar. Everyone knew who Denis McNulty was addressing except for this poor black guy who only knew that his glass was empty and no one seemed in a hurry to fill it.

'Did you hear me? I said you've had enough.'

McNulty was standing by the table where he'd been sitting all the while, his thumbs hooked into his pants and his flannel shirt pulled back, exposing the black crew underneath. He was a hard man and there was enough of him showing to know he could make a lot of noise if he wanted to. The bartender turned up the lights and pulled the plug on the juke box. Lou could see what Shar was thinking. She didn't like the idea of telling her boss how his bar was wrecked when Denis McNulty beat the shit out of some drunken rooster and threw him out into the street and chased his ass all the way back to Point Breeze.

McNulty wasn't moving but the other guy seemed to have gotten the message and started for the door. He was taking his good old time, though, his feet threatening to get crossed with each step. With the lights on the place looked empty. Not much of an audience, Lou thought, for the show McNulty was putting on for his home-town fans. Even the Leprechauns in green-framed pictures on the wall looked bored by the charade, sitting on their glowing rainbows and their shining pots of gold. They'd turned up their pug noses and rolled up their sleeves and raised their fists but Lou could tell they didn't really mean it. Their heart wasn't in it. He could see it in their eyes, those emerald green eyes that might buy you a drink and then take a swing at you. And by the end of the evening, it would all be forgotten.

The man paused in the doorway and spun around as if he was determined to have the last word before he left. He'd pulled a gun from under the tattered winter coat and started waving it around. Shar froze behind the bar. But McNulty wasn't having it, not in his bar, not where he and his court had always convened, ruling with the sort of street-corner benevolence known only in Grays Ferry.

McNulty reached behind the bar and came up with a sawed-off shotgun. It was a relatively small piece of machinery, about twenty inches long, with a double barrel and duct tape on the handle and a serial number that had been filed off ages ago. McNulty racked one into the chamber and pointed it at the man, who took one look at it and ran, his limp suddenly gone.

McNulty chased him out the door and into the street. Nobody got up to follow them out. After about a minute, a few short blasts from the shotgun rang out. They were like explosions in the street as if someone had pulled the pins on a couple of hand grenades and dropped them out of the window of a moving car. A few of the old-timers still at the bar let out a laugh as if the sound jogged their memories of old days in Dublin. McNulty could be heard outside, punctuating each pull of the trigger with a tirade of epithets in which he summarized the nature of race relations in Grays Ferry for now and all time. Nobody dared to dispute it.

By the time the cops got there, everything was back to normal. The shotgun was back behind the bar. McNulty was back at his table with a full pint of dark beer in front of him. The lights were dimmed again and the juke box was back on, playing Black Thorn's latest rendition of 'Irish Eyes,' which even seemed to elicit a tear from one of the cops. Lou and Joey had made a hasty exit between the time McNulty had replaced the shotgun and the first few chords of that sad score issued from the jukebox.

They sat in their car and smoked, watching the patrol car double park and the cops listening to the heavy silence on the street. They watched them go inside the Golden Rose as if the cops needed one more drink before quitting time, just like everyone else. They watched a group of punks, not more than sixteen, behind the chain link of Battery Park. They were like ghosts in the night and they took turns hurling broken chunks of gravel at the last intact street light hanging over the western end of the playground. Lou and Joey heard the crash of the rock against the light and a second later the sound of broken glass hitting the ground. But they were moving already, on their way to Catherine Street to see Mary Grace Flannery.

TWENTY-THREE

Joey parked in an empty 7/11 lot on 25th. He locked it up and set the alarm and they started walking toward Catherine, the cold night air seeping into their bones and compounding the fatigue that was beginning to tie a knot at the base of their spines. Lou snapped the top button of his jacket and thrust his hands into his pockets. A couple of black girls stood on the corner chattering into their cell phones. They were both skinny and young and wore short fur coats. The fur was dyed white and Lou pictured the hundred dead rabbits it might have taken to make them. But they were most likely fake, Lou thought, only the girls didn't know that.

They were out of their turf and Lou knew the score there. They'd met a couple of white boys, did some business, which usually amounted to a couple hits of coke followed by a quick blow-job. Then they got dumped and were probably calling one of their brothers for a ride, still tasting the coke in their nose and the cum in their mouth.

Their hair was braided with iridescent beads that sparkled as their heads flitted around. They noticed Joey and Lou coming toward them and started walking quickly away. They made them for cops immediately.

The front door to Mary Grace Flannery's building was open. The lock seemed as if it hadn't worked for a long time. She lived in a two-story walk-up made of worn brown brick. The street-level windows had thick black bars over them. The vestibule was dark and cold. The overhead light didn't work any better than the lock. They stepped into the dark hallway and started up the steep flight of stairs. Gracie lived on the second floor. They didn't have an apartment number. There were three doors on the second floor, one on each side of the hallway and one at the far end that had a capital *B* and a *4* drawn in ornate calligraphy onto a piece of gray cardboard and held up with a thumbtack.

Lou had smelled it as soon as he'd entered the building. Joey had smelled it, too. It was sharp and bitter in their nostrils. They knew that smell and they looked at each other, wondering aloud how anyone could live there and not notice it, not knock on Mary Grace Flannery's door and ask her what the hell she was cooking in there. They both were on edge. Call it instinct or intuition, it was an early-warning system and most cops had it. Hopefully they had it before they ever became cops. If not they learned it soon after they hit the street. It could be triggered because something doesn't look right or, as in this case, something doesn't smell right. Some guys were just born with it. Some guys had it and some guys didn't and the ones that didn't usually weren't around very long.

Lou knocked on the door at the end of the hall and waited. He knocked again, the smell that much stronger with his nose against the door. He tried the knob, knowing it wouldn't turn but going through the motions while he contemplated just how much force he was willing to use to get in. Joey leaned against the wall watching him, the slight gleam in his eyes revealing the humor he saw in the situation, two ex-cops breaking and entering, knowing what they'd find and knowing that it didn't matter, that an enthusiastic DA would think nothing of charging them with criminal trespass regardless of what they found. The right thing would have been to call it in and let the cops do their job.

Lou had gone back down the steps and through the front door and around to the back of the house and up a set of wooden steps leading to a second-floor landing. There was no light at all in the back. Joey was right behind him, their combined weight causing the bare, unpainted wood to creak under them. At the top of the stairs there were two doors with windows side by side. Lou put his face against the glass of the one on the left. He cupped his hands around his eyes. The darkness was thick inside. He lit a match. On the other side of the glass was a buzzing swarm of black flies.

There must have been thousands of them, a living black mass that seemed to move as if it had a single consciousness. He'd felt the vibration of their wings through the glass as they were drawn to the light and he'd seen their round, bulging, metallic eyes, the blindly staring eyes of an insect that fed on death.

Lou dropped the match and turned his back to the door. He could still hear their buzzing behind him and he shuddered as if one of them had crawled under his shirt and up his spine and was biting the skin on his back. He stood there for another minute with his eyes closed, visualizing what it might look like in there, what might attract that amount of flies, just how much human flesh they could consume in a day, a week, a month. He'd seen how maggots can live and grow in a carcass that was once a human being, laying eggs, eggs hatching into flies and those flies laying more eggs until they'd grown into a dark, moving shadow.

'You see anything?'

'Flies. A lot of them.'

'Oh, shit.'

'You ready to go in?'

'Not really.'

'Light a cigarette.'

'Aw, c'mon Lou. This isn't our job. We know what we're gonna find in there. What else do you need to know? Let's just call it in. Call it a night.'

'I want to get a look around.'

'Of course you do.'

'OK, stand back.'

Lou pulled his balled fist into the cuff of his leather jacket and punched it through the glass. He felt it shatter and heard the falling glass hit the floor. He jumped back and watched the swarm of flies streaming from the window like thick black smoke. They hit the cold night air and sped away while Lou kept his hand over his mouth and nose and Joey waved the cigarette at them and blew out a heavy cloud of blue-gray smoke. The vibration of all those diaphanous wings pulsating at once seemed to crackle with electricity. The swarm flew from the house, the humming dissipated into the night and it grew suddenly silent as if someone had pulled the plug.

He reached through the broken window, turned the latch and pushed open the door. They stepped into a dark kitchen and Lou reached along the wall for a light switch. Something moved beside him and he pulled his hand back reflexively. A cat hissed at him and jumped from the counter and raced across the floor, a dull yellow glow emanating from its crusted eyes. Lou found the switch again and the animal seemed to cringe from the light. He could see it licking its dark greenish-gray fur, cleaning itself with a rough, pink tongue that looked as coarse as sandpaper. There was another cat moving behind it. Lou noticed a line of dishes on the floor, all of them empty.

The moment they'd come through the door, the caustic stench that seemed tolerable in the hallway was now a tangible, fetid odor, thick in the moldering air. Lou pulled the neck of his sweater up over his nose and mouth. Joey, who had thrown his cigarette off the back porch, was now lighting another one. The kitchen was small with a row of small cabinets against one wall. Against the other wall were two stools and a cut-out counter top that opened into an equally small dining room. The living room was beyond that. A dim light from a small table lamp glowed at the other end of the apartment. Lou moved toward it and Joey followed, careful not to step in the scattered mounds of cat feces littering the floor.

She was wearing a green and white Eagles T-shirt and green sweat pants. She was on the floor curled up in the corner. It looked as if she'd crawled there trying to escape until she had nowhere left to go. From what Lou could tell there were multiple stab wounds covering her entire torso. But there wasn't much left of her. She wasn't quite as beautiful as Candy had described.

She'd obviously been there a long time, a month or more, too long to leave a dead body lying around and expect the same person to be there waiting when you got back. He assumed he was looking at Mary Grace Flannery but there was no way to tell for sure. It wouldn't have mattered if he had seen her before or if Shar had given him a description or if he'd kept her picture in his wallet or if he'd dated her in high school. There was nothing left of her face to identify.

The cats had gotten to her, pushed to it by starvation, going first for the soft, mollified flesh of her cheeks and then her tender, succulent lips, ripping the meat away in thin, pulpy shreds from around her mouth and under her eyes and the side of her neck. All of it was gone, eaten away and exposed. The flies did the rest.

The cats had been her pets, her loyal companions. She'd cared for them, given them food and water, petted them and brushed them and held them and loved them. And yet they'd fed on her as any carnivore might. They'd succumbed to the hunger, reverted to their primitive selves and devoured her one small scrap at a time.

'If only these cats could talk. They must have witnessed the whole thing.'

'And didn't bat an eye.'

'I always preferred dogs. Never liked cats. You hear all those stories about dogs waking someone up in the middle of the night. The house is on fire. Or they find some lost kid. Ya never hear that shit about cats.'

'True. But an animal is an animal, Joey. Keep them warm and well fed and they're under control. Keep them starved, keep them cold, abuse them, and you have a wild animal on your hands.'

'We talkin' about cats and dogs now. Right, Lou?'

'What else?'

Lou wiped beads of perspiration from his forehead. Gracie must have liked it warm. Even now, Lou could hear the popping of steam rising through the pipes in the walls. He could hear it hissing through the iron radiator in the corner, the furnace working in the basement, keeping the water boiling hot. The tan curtains, the color of New Jersey sand, swayed gently as the heat radiated across the floor and a cat darted suddenly from behind its folds, bounding silently over the mint-green carpet. He looked into the cat's eyes. They were indignant, impugning eyes and he blew out the breath of air he was holding for what seemed like minutes before turning his attention back to the body on the floor.

One of those flies had decided to hang around, making itself at home in the ameliorated remnants of cartilage that were once this woman's presumably perfect nose. The insect crawled out of one hollow nostril and fanned the air with its wings as if it was warming up for a take-off. It had swollen red eyes; alien eyes with flashes of gold and metallic green on its head resembling a gladiator's helmet and a black and white checkered thorax and sharp prongs like fish hooks on all six of its primeval legs. Its arced mandible hung open and its antennae twitched with an instinctual awareness.

Joey winced and recoiled in disgust.

'Is this absolutely necessary?'

'We won't be here long.'

'I know I won't be.'

'Why don't you give Mitch a call, let him know what we've got.' Joey started walking away. 'Just tell him it's a body. Give him the address. Nothing about Haggerty.'

'And what are you going to be doing?'

'Looking around.'

'Looking for what?'

Lou looked down at Mary Grace Flannery, at the numerous stab wounds over her flayed torso, at the many defensive wounds, deep cuts on her fingers and hands, the gouged muscle of her arms, her hollowed eye sockets and yellowed teeth.

'Signs of a lost childhood.'

Joey stepped out onto the back porch and fished for the cell phone in his jacket pocket. He was coughing spasmodically and with his other hand he was reaching for the pack of cigarettes. He leaned over the loose wooden railing and retched.

Lou left Gracie where he'd found her, apologizing to her as he walked away, the words *I'm sorry* sounding strange to him, saying them out loud and no one in the room except him and a decomposing corpse. He wouldn't have much time. Joey and Mitch would trade jabs before getting down to business and then Mitch would send the cavalry and they'd secure the crime scene and Lou would be back on the outside looking in.

Two bedrooms sat in an adjacent hallway separated by a paper-thin plaster wall that ran the length of the apartment. He entered the first bedroom, found the light switch and stood studying the décor for a moment. It was a woman's bedroom, the bed neatly made with a lavender cover tucked under a pair of fluffy white pillows. A pair of pink fuzzy slippers sat at the foot of a bedstand with a lamp and a phone and an empty glass ashtray on top of that. The ashtray looked like it belonged to the Golden Rose.

He wandered across the room to where a mirrored chest stood against the wall. He lifted the lid of a silver jewelry box and found it still full with a tangle of necklaces at the bottom like snakes in a pit. There was an assortment of rings in a tray on top. Lou had never familiarized himself with jewelry beyond the lists of stolen property he'd documented over the years. He was no expert. He couldn't look at a diamond and know if it was glass, if it was real or fake or what it was worth. Other than the engagement ring he'd bought his ex-wife twenty years ago, he wouldn't know white gold from aluminum. He gently closed the lid. There seemed to be nothing missing.

He opened a closet door and briefly examined the rows of clothes hanging from two parallel rods. Looked like expensive stuff on one side: cocktail dresses, a lot of wool and leather. On the other side there were mostly T-shirts and faded jeans. A well-organized collection of shoes sat in pairs on the floor, everything from high heels to sneakers to hiking boots to sandals. Nothing seemed out of place. Other than the putrefied body in the living room, the cat feces on the floor, the broken glass in the kitchen and the flies, the place was in order.

The second door had a 'keep out' sign hanging from the door knob on a wire hanger. Lou remembered his daughter had made something similar and hung it from her door, *Keep Out* sewn onto a small pillow shaped like a blue heart. She would have been about eleven. Lou turned the knob and gave the door a little push with his foot, the dangling hanger rocking idly as he brushed past.

Lou repeated the motion of reaching for the light switch on the wall, hoping to find it in the same place as he had previously. He snapped it up with his forefinger and nothing happened. He flicked it up and down a few times and still only blackness, not even any light from the windows or from a street light or the half-moon that had been hanging over them since the trip back from Delaware.

He found the cigarette lighter that had fallen through the hole in his pocket and was floating around in the lining of his jacket. The flame from the lighter dimly lit a bedroom half the size of the other one, a room with a single unmade bed, a wooden desk and a wicker basket brimming with dirty laundry. The shades were drawn down tightly over the windows. The desk and the carpet and the mattress were scarred with burn marks from what looked like cigarettes. A coffee cup on the desk was overflowing with butts in a syrupy brown liquid and the surface of the desk was marred with carvings, deep indentations made with a knife or a screwdriver. In the darkness of the room they looked like stick figures.

The lighter began to burn his finger and it abruptly went out. He switched it to his other hand, the flame a little shorter this time. The walls were covered with hand-drawn pictures like a sort of mural. He held the light closer. It was done in black ink, a story that seemed to take shape, covering the entire wall like a tattoo that covers the skin of a human body.

Lou noticed a halogen lamp in the opposite corner. The brightness hurt his eyes briefly as he took a closer look at the world he'd walked in on. There was a portrait on the wall over the bed. It was of a woman, a very beautiful woman, her ivory face glowing as if the sun shone upon it morning and night. Her skin seemed made of white satin, a luminous complexion that radiated the warmth it had absorbed from the sun. But her eyes seemed glazed over, unable to reflect that light. They were dark, black orbs, soulless eyes like those on the statues outside the Arramingo Club.

Her hair was as dark as her eyes, flowing behind her as if blown by the wind, moving as if the wind and the light had brought the portrait to life. And her beauty had a savagery to it, the emptiness in her eyes reflecting the hand that drew it as much as the woman herself. It was Valerie Price. He was sure of it – as sure as he was that the woman on the floor in the living room was Mary Grace Flannery.

There was more to see. Beside the portrait was a cemetery scene, two open graves dug into the earth so there was only blackness within their depths and mounds of black dirt piled alongside them and two nameless gray tombstones.

Lou pulled out his cell phone, held it up until the image was in focus and took a few pictures. The police photographers would have a field day. These would be just in case Mitch decided to deny him access. He was like that sometimes.

Every inch of space was covered, some of it in pencil and some of it in ink, depictions of death by various forms of torture like something out of the Black Museum. Decapitation was a favorite theme, human heads rolling in the street, lying under guillotines and blocks of wood, hanging from decrepit old trees, impaled on the end of spears and sinking into a murky swamp. And all the faces on all these severed heads looked alive, heads separated from their bodies but still alive, their eyes open and staring. And finally there was the executioner, hooded and faceless, a grim reaper doing his duty without emotion, without remorse or pity.

Lou stood in the middle of the room and tried to get an impression of the personality that had used these walls as a canvas, a blank slate where an inner life, a deeply personal life, had found expression through art. As primitive as it seemed there was a message here, in these drawings, and Lou wanted to know what it was.

The door opened and Joey was standing there, his face pale compared to its normal ruddiness. He still held the closed cell phone in his fist.

'You almost ready? Mitch said not to touch anything.' Joey glanced at the walls in the room, trying to take it all in at once and make some sense of it. 'Mitch said something else. Thought you might like to know. The Arramingo Club is on fire. Fully involved. They're still not sure if everyone's out.'

TWENTY-FOUR

They couldn't get anywhere near it, not by car at least. A uniform cop leaned against an orange wooden barricade with Philadelphia Police stenciled in blue. He had his back turned to the growing crowd and he held a cell phone to his ear with a gloved hand, listening intently to the annoying voice at the other end of the line, his wife most likely, giving him shit for not getting home in time. Joey drove past and parked about a block away and he and Lou came back up through the alley, the dingy water from the fire scene trickling under their feet. The temperature had dropped a few more degrees and they could see the smoke from the Arramingo Club in the distance. They couldn't see flames, just curling gray smoke.

Fire trucks lined the street, their powerful spotlights aimed at the gutted nightclub. One of the trucks had its ladder fully extended and there was a fireman at the end of the ladder showering down a steady stream of water into a hole in the roof where billowing smoke rose in thick black clouds. A rainbow had appeared where the spotlight from the truck crossed the streaming water, the smoke filtering through it and disappearing into the night sky.

Mitch was standing behind one of the trucks, speaking with a fireman in a red helmet and a fireproof jacket that had Chief printed on the back in yellow letters.

'Shouldn't you be on your way to Grays Ferry?'

'Not my district. Steve Laughlin is on his way over there now. I think he can handle it.'

'Whadd'ya got here?'

'Fire marshall is calling it arson.'

'Not wasting any time.'

'He was in and out in ten minutes. You know Bedrossian. He's a hands-on kind of guy.'

'Didn't think it was an accident?'

'No such thing as accidents anymore, Lou. Your ten-year-old spills his milk at the breakfast table – that's an accident.' Mitch looked at Joey and they scowled at each other. 'Bedrossian didn't go in because he likes to play with fire, Lou. They pulled a body out of there, about ten minutes before you got here.'

'Never a shortage of dead bodies.'

Mitch turned back to Joey, who was lighting a cigarette, one foot up on the shining chrome bumper of the fire truck.

'How about one of those, Giordano?' Joey tossed him the pack. 'It was a woman. That's about all they could tell.'

'What else would it be? Seems like a lot of women think Philly is a good place to die. Don't ask me why. They're like elephants and salmon, travel hundreds of miles back home to die. It's a goddamn migration.'

'Some never leave. And by the way, Lou, salmon spawn before they die.'

'So do most of these women.'

Mitch had the cigarette going and tossed the pack back at Joey.

'It wasn't pretty. I'll tell you that. Hard to identify from the way she looked when they pulled her out. Like a French fry caught at the bottom of the fryer.'

'I wondered why you were here and not babysitting Mary Grace Flannery.'

'Laughlin will make sure I get a copy of the report from the medical examiner.'

'You're going to want to see that apartment, Mitch.'

'Oh, yeah? And how did you stumble upon it?'

'We got a lead. From one of Joey's old acquaintances.'

'I shouldn't have asked.'

'Remember Candy Bell?' Mitch rolled his eyes and took a long drag off the cigarette. His sandpaper cheeks glowed red. 'Of course you remember her. She used to work at the Arramingo Club before it got all dressed up and put a down payment on this piece of waterfront property. Mary Grace Flannery worked there around the same time.'

'You think I could care less about what an aging stripper has to say? Unless she's a fucking witness she can tell her stories to somebody else. I couldn't care less about rumors or innuendo or ancient fucking history.'

'She told us a very enlightening story, one that Mary Grace Flannery could attest to if she wasn't deceased.'

'Give me one good reason why I should listen to you, Lou. Did Franny Patterson ask you to find out who killed her brother?'

'Not exactly.'

'Then why are you telling me all this?'

'My civic duty?'

'It seems like every time you do your civic duty, old Doc Harnish has another cadaver to dissect. Do you go looking for them or do they dig themselves up?'

Lou didn't answer. He was looking at the Arramingo Club. It didn't look like the same place. He'd been there earlier in the day and now it appeared unrecognizable. He'd waded through the crowd and he'd sat at the bar and watched the girls dancing on the runway and he'd spoken candidly with Brian Haggerty and he'd left thinking that the Arramingo Club must be a pretty happening place, one of the hottest nightclubs in Philadelphia. It might not be what William Haggerty had first envisioned. It had become more of a playground for decadent children than a meeting ground for hard-working men. But it did boast its share of excitement and if that's what you were looking for it was the place to be.

Now the shimmering lights had all been shattered and the front doors hung open like a gaping wound emitting the smell of charred wood, the last of the brackish water still trickling onto the sidewalk.

The smoke was slowly subsiding and some of the firemen were already rolling up their hoses and stowing their equipment onto the idling trucks. A couple of large portable fans were positioned at the open entrance. They came on with a whir like a jet engine and began sucking the smoke out of the mouth of the Arramingo Club. Most of the ladders had been lowered and it was just the fans now left to do most of the work.

'Listen, Lou. I know you and Jimmy were old friends. And I know you feel like you owe him something, help his little sister if nothing else. But we got it. All right? We got it.'

'I just want to make sure you get the right guy.'

'We always do.'

The fireworks were over but Philly's finest still had their hands full keeping the crowd at a comfortable distance. They were lined against the barricades at both ends of the street. Lou could hear the cops telling the nameless faces before them that there was nothing more to see, that they could go home or to wherever it was they went when the bars closed. Most of them were young, only kids in Lou's eyes, who'd emptied out of the bars and had nowhere in particular to go, didn't have to be anywhere in the morning.

'When you ID that French fry I'd like to get a name.'

'You didn't hear a word I said, did you?'

'Heard every word.'

'There's a lot of pressure coming down on me from City Hall right now, Lou. They want this little crime spree wrapped up in a hurry. I need cooperation, not interference.'

'I understand the concern about the Haggertys, but what's the big deal about a few dead prostitutes? No one ever cared before.'

'It's a bit more than that.'

'How much more?'

'Police business, Lou. You know I'm not at liberty to discuss details of an ongoing investigation.'

'Cut the bullshit, Mitch.'

Mitch put his arm over Lou's shoulder and led him behind one of the fire trucks, the diesel fumes warm against the backs of their legs.

'Another body turned up. A man this time. Haven't released his name in relation to this case or any other. A big fish.'

'Too big to throw back?'

'The son of a federal judge.'

'That's big enough. A little out of your league, wouldn't you say?'

'Let's just say he was discovered in a very uncompromising position. Up in Judy Garland Park. Strictly under the radar, Lou. And we'd like to keep it that way.'

'Uncompromising position? That's a mouthful, even for you.'

'You've been a cop a long time, Lou. Use your imagination. Some guys like little girls and some like boys and some like a combination of the two. The sex trade is alive and well in your cherished City of Brotherly Love and there's some strange birds out there. Don't look any different than me or you, Lou. But if you keep stickin' your dick where it don't belong, you might just lose it.'

'Care to elaborate on that?'

'There's a bad boy out there, Lou. Someone who didn't get enough love as an egg. Someone who swings both ways, even when it comes to choosing his victims. But you didn't hear it from me.'

Lou seemed lost in thought, his eyes glued on the waves of heat and smoke still rising from the Arramingo Club. And then someone was pushing past the cops, coming toward him. It was Brian Haggerty.

'Mr Klein, please, can you tell these officers who I am?'

'He is who he says he is, Officers.' They looked at him skeptically. They looked to Mitch for some kind of confirmation. 'His name is Brian Haggerty. He owns this place. What's left of it.'

Mitch nodded and that did the trick. The cops returned to their posts, leaving Brian Haggerty straightening his jacket and staring dumbfounded at the smoking shell of his precious club. He seemed more distraught about the Arramingo Club than he was about Franny Patterson.

'What the hell happened?'

'I don't doubt that Lieutenant Mitchell might want to ask you the same question.'

Mitch didn't say a word. He knew that if he was asking the questions he'd be required to inform Haggerty of his rights and if he failed to do that, the answers would get tossed. And if Haggerty lawyered up there would be no more questions. But if Lou was asking the questions and Mitch just happened to be within earshot, that was a different story, perfectly acceptable in any court in Philadelphia.

'If you think I had something to do with this, you're wrong. You're all wrong.'

'You don't get it, do you, Brian? You keep finding yourself in the position of having to deny your involvement in all sorts of crimes but you won't come clean, won't just tell the truth.' Lou stepped in front of him, blocked his vision of the Arramingo Club. 'Tell us about Billy Sapphire.'

Haggerty shrugged his shoulders and his head seemed to fall, almost shrink like a turtle pulling his head into its shell.

'It was only a matter of time, wasn't it?'

'A matter of time before what, Brian? Before he kills more people? Before he kills Franny Patterson? Before he kills you? Before some ambitious cop pins a murder charge on him? What exactly are we talking about?'

'He's my brother. My little brother. My stepbrother, really.' Haggerty's eyes, red-rimmed and raw, rose ever so slightly and looked into Lou's. 'I hadn't seen him for a very long time. I didn't even know it was him at first. He'd changed so much. When I last saw him he was a boy, twelve years old at the most.'

'You're saying you didn't recognize your own brother?'

'I know what it sounds like. But it's the truth. Maybe I didn't want to believe it. I don't know. He walked into the Arramingo Club, spoke to one of my managers, asked him for a job. He hired him and I hadn't laid eyes on him until he'd been there a couple weeks.' Haggerty saw the cigarette in Joey's mouth and asked him for one. 'He looked familiar but I thought it had to be coincidence. I mean, how could it have been William? It just seemed impossible after all this time.'

'Why?'

'I thought he was dead.'

'Why would you think that?'

'You can probably figure out the reason for that, Mr Klein.'

'Enlighten me.'

'I only know what I heard.'

'From who?'

'My mother led me to believe William was gone forever. And knowing my mother, that meant dead.'

'But you didn't really believe that either. It was just another lie you pretended to believe because you had to, because it made life easier for your mother, because it kept so many things hidden, kept another scandal off the front page. But you knew the truth the whole time, didn't you?'

'Yes, Mr Klein. I knew that Billy Sapphire was my brother and I knew that he had problems. But I had problems of my own.'

'What kind of problems?'

'He'd run away and then one day he just didn't come home. He'd been living on the street and my mother was giving him money. He was a drug addict and a prostitute, Mr Klein. What could I do?' Haggerty took a long drag on the cigarette. 'Then I heard he was living with someone.'

'Someone special?'

'Someone who knew my father. Let's leave it at that.'

'I can leave it any way you'd like. You can read that someone's obituary in tomorrow's paper.'

'Not the first and it won't be the last.'

'Your mother's kept tabs on him?'

'My mother keeps a strict account on everyone, Mr Klein.'

'Are you willing to testify to what you know?'

'I know he killed William Haggerty and Valerie Price, if that's what you want to hear? I know he found them together and he blew their brains out with a thirty-eight-caliber pistol. I don't doubt it was my mother who gave him the gun. But that was almost ten years ago and what do you do with a twelve-year-old killer, Mr Klein? You tell me. Turn him over to the police? Lock him up? Put him on trial?' There was a tear forming in the corner of his eye but he blinked it back. 'I knew my mother had him in her plans. My mother made a lot of plans.'

'You think she might have put the idea into his head in the first place?'

'You think my mother turned him into a killer?'

'Do you?'

'No. I think she might have used him. But she wasn't the only person who pushed him over the line. He's a troubled kid, Mr Klein. He always was.'

'Not a kid anymore.'

'I guess not.'

'And now the killing has begun again. Is that part of your mother's plan, too?'

'I don't know. You'll have to ask her.'

Mitch had been listening to every word and apparently he'd heard enough. He approached Brian Haggerty, flanked on both sides by the same two officers who'd been forced to let Haggerty slide by them, both of them liking the idea of getting another shot at him. Mitch already had the cuffs out.

'Brian Haggerty, I have a warrant for your arrest.'

'You're kidding me, Lieutenant. All this time you planned on arresting me and now you decide to do it.'

'That's about it, Haggerty. Turn around and put your hands behind your back.' Brian Haggerty hesitated and the two officers were smiling at each other as if they were in on some private joke. 'You heard me, Haggerty. Don't make me say it again.'

Haggerty looked at Lou. Joey was smiling as if he was in on the joke. Mitch was already twisting Haggerty's arm and pushing him, face first, against the hood of a police car. Haggerty struggled against Mitch's tactics, pushing himself up off the car with his one free arm and trying to spin away. He heard the click of the handcuffs and felt the cold steel clamp around one wrist. Before he could fully turn the two cops had his other wrist locked behind his back and all he could feel was the steel biting into his skin. He twisted his neck almost all the way around, looking at Lou again.

'Jesus Christ. You didn't even tell me what I'm being locked up for.'

'You'll find out at the arraignment.'

Mitch led him to the police car, dropped him into the back seat and slammed the door. Mitch didn't usually make his arrest with such dramatic flair. He left that to the younger cops who still had something to prove. But that slamming door did have a ring of finality to it, Lou thought, like the sliding steel door of a prison cell banging shut. It was a sound cops wanted their prisoners to learn early and often.

'What's the warrant for, Mitch?'

'You're a piece of work, you know that? I have a job to do. I don't have to tell you anything. I don't even have to talk to you.' Mitch looked over at one of the officers, pointing at the car. 'Get him the hell out of here.'

'Is it some kind of secret?'

'What's that supposed to mean?'

'You don't want to tell Haggerty what he's charged with. You want to make him sweat. I got it. Does that mean I have to wait and read about it in the papers like everyone else?'

'Does it really matter, Lou? His mother'll get him the best lawyer in town and he'll be out in time for a lunch at Glassman's. He'll probably be home before you. The Haggertys don't worry about grand juries or district attorneys or indictments. Even if they're facing a murder charge.'

TWENTY-FIVE

Lou watched the unmarked police car take Brian Haggerty away. No lights. No sirens. Just a routine transport. Kind of like a taxi with a hard plastic seat and a plexi-glass cage and set of iron bracelets on the house. If the meter was running for Brian Haggerty, he would have one hell of a fare to pay. But like Mitch said, he'd just get a receipt and turn it over to his mother.

Lou and Joey started down the empty street, back the way they came, toward the cop on the corner that seemed to be getting aggravated with the few stragglers that refused to disperse. Most of them were just hanging around like a herd of bored protesters who'd lost their signs and had grown too cold to chant. And with their signs gone and their voices muted, they seemed to have lost their sense of purpose. They huddled around each other in the cold, small groups of baby-faced boys and girls, college students from the looks of them, laughing for no other reason than they liked the sound of it.

'I never could understand why you and Mitch didn't get along. I think I do now.'

'What d'ya think?'

'He thinks he's always right. And he'll do anything to prove it. Even if he's wrong. Even if the evidence is against him.'

'You don't know the half of it.' They continued down the
street, their shoulders touching as if they would link arms and
go strolling down some fog-drenched runway and board a plane
for sunnier places. 'You want to know the real story?'

'Don't hold back now.'

'Remember, I came on before either of you guys. If I was still
with the department, I'd be a captain right now.'

'And Mitch doesn't like the sound of that? Doesn't like the
idea that you would have been his boss?'

'That's part of it. But there's more.'

'Another history lesson.'

'You can learn a lot from history, Lou. You of all people. And
it's not the kind of history you read in a book. You can't learn
it in school. You learn it on the street.'

Joey paused for a second as a ladder truck roared past, blaring
its horn as the cop pulled the barricades apart.

'True.'

'Mitch and I were riding the Twelfth District. It was the coldest
night of the year, just before Christmas. We usually rode the
Seventeenth, like you did. But we were covering for Joe Mecca
and Johnny Zombec. They were playing cards over at Weber's
and asked us if we'd cover.'

'I get it. So what happened?'

'We're dispatched to a call at the homeless shelter at Trinity
Lutheran. They got like a hundred black guys sleeping on mats
on the floor in the basement. The smell will make your eyes
water. But it's cold outside and the shelters are packed. You can't
imagine what goes on in there once the lights go out. You fall
asleep and you got some schizo humpin' your leg and stealing
the change in your shoe.'

'Is there a moral to this story, Joey?' They'd stopped walking.
Another cop had come over and was arguing with a college-aged
girl, a first-year law school student with purple spiked hair and
a ring in her nose. She refused to leave and was quoting the
constitution as if she were practicing for a future with the public
defender's office. ''Cause I'm ready to call it quits for the day.'

'They got this guy at the shelter, young guy, maybe mid-thirties
and big. And he's freakin' out. Highed up on something or just
plain crazy. We get there and this guy's got the thousand-yard stare

going and he don't hear a word we're saying. He's in his own fucking world and they want him out of there.' Joey tapped another cigarette from the pack. 'These goddamn do-gooders drive all over the city in these white vans picking up the homeless and bringing them to these glorified shelters in nice residential neighborhoods. And when they can't deal with them they call us.'

'That's how the system works.'

'Well, there's no talkin' to this guy. So we each grab an arm and we get the guy out the door. The next thing you know, we're on the ground rolling with this fuck. And the guy's like a raging bull. The way he was throwing us around he could have killed us. And we're not small guys.'

'You're still here and so is Mitch. So I guess he didn't kill you.'

'It was the other way around.'

'You killed him?'

'Not right away. I mean, we didn't kill him. We wrestled him into a double set of handcuffs and managed to get him in the back seat. He starts headbutting the cage and trying to kick out the windows. He's going nuts back there. We're going to take him down to the crisis center at Fitzgerald Mercy. It's the only place that would take him. Try to get him some help, you know.'

'Sure.'

'Then it suddenly goes quiet back there and we can't see him anymore. We open the door. He's slumped over in the seat and he's not breathing. So we drag him out, start CPR and we're trying to get the cuffs off and we're pounding on his chest. Nothing. The guy's fucking dead.'

'You should have called the medics.'

'Yeah, we should have but we didn't.'

'OK. But you still haven't done anything wrong. It's not like you beat him to death.'

'I knew that and so did Mitch. But needless to say, we weren't happy. And for different reasons. I'm thinking of all the paper-work. It was late and I didn't want to be in front of a typewriter for the rest of the night instead of sacked out somewhere.'

'And what's Mitch worried about?'

'Mitch is more concerned about his spotless record. He's thinking this corpse could become a thorn in his side. Maybe turn into an official investigation, maybe a written reprimand, maybe a fucking civil suit. Right away, I know he's thinkin' of something. I could hear the wheels turning in his head.'

'One of the department's great thinkers. There should be a statue of him in bronze at the Rodin.'

'So, Mitch decides to get rid of the body. Just like that. We pop him in the trunk and we head back up to the Seventeenth. Back on familiar ground. Mitch is driving and he's headed for The Hole.'

'Jesus Christ. The Hole. I haven't heard that place mentioned in a long time. I used to meet up with Donny Weeks down there and we'd smoke cigars and relieve ourselves in the river. Our headlights would shine out onto the refinery across the river and then we'd turn them off and it'd be pitch black.' Lou took a cigarette from Joey and put it in his mouth. 'Did I tell you I ran into Donny at the hospital? Working a detail, watching Franny Patterson. Never knew the man to turn down an hour of overtime.'

'If you see Donny again, tell him I said hello.'

'I will.'

'Anyway, Mitch figures The Hole is a real scenic spot to dump this guy. A lot of the bums set up camp down there and it'd be no big surprise to find one dead.'

'A lot of dirty laundry got washed out down there, too.'

'That's where Glen Sickler shot Patty Passariello for fucking his wife. Actually had a duel. It was like the goddamn wild west.'

'Lucky Patty didn't die.'

'Lucky they were all cops.'

They finished their cigarettes, threw the butts down and watched them roll in the damp breeze. The street was practically deserted now. They started walking again.

'I don't like it, Joey.'

'What? The Hole? It was a good place to dump a body. Slid his ass right into the river and it just carried him away.'

'It was a bad decision.'

'Nobody knew the difference, Lou. I'll admit it bothered me for a couple days, thinking maybe somebody saw us. But the only people down there are the bums and no one's gonna believe them anyway.'

'And the cops. They're down there, too.'

'Yeah. And the cops.'

'And that's why you and Mitch don't get along?'

'I got something on him. He'll never be comfortable with that.'

'Prefers it the other way around.'

'Wouldn't you?'

Lou and Joey found themselves walking behind the group of kids that had been giving the officer a hard time. They all seemed to be congratulating the girl with the spiked hair for using her wit to make the cop seem like an idiot. But not all of them were laughing. One guy was lagging behind, didn't seem to be part of the group.

He was wearing a long wool coat to his knees. It looked like Salvation Army material or some Main Line thrift shop. It could have belonged to his grandfather; he could have found it hanging in a garment bag in his parents' attic. His head lolled forward as if there was a screw loose in his neck. He just seemed to be carried along with them like a broken branch carried by the tide. And this thin, sleepy stick-man in the oversized wool coat suddenly looked over his shoulder and tripped on the cracked sidewalk. Lou saw his face. It was Billy Sapphire.

He'd been there all the time watching the fire burn, watching the firemen struggle against the flames and the thick, black smoke. He was there to watch the crowd gaze admiringly at his work and to see this house burn. Lou should have been looking for him, should have known Billy Sapphire wasn't very far away.

Their eyes met in a momentary flash of recognition before they were both running. They ran through a parking lot, dodging the few cars parked like stray puzzle pieces on a board. Their footsteps clapped on the wet pavement. The lights in the lot were on but Beach Street was dark in the distance and that's where Billy Sapphire was headed.

Lou could still smell the smoke from the Arramingo Club but he could smell the river now too, hear it moving apathetically in the night nearby.

The initial rush of adrenaline helped Lou to keep pace with the younger man, his legs moving autonomously, all that exercise finally paying off. But Billy Sapphire was already starting to put some distance between them, taking two and three steps to Lou's one. They'd come alongside the Greyhound Bus Terminal and Lou lost sight of him in the shadows before Sapphire seemed to suddenly appear at the top of the chain link fence that surrounded the terminal. In the next second he'd dropped to the other side and was lost in a maze of buses parked side by side in four long rows the length of a city block.

Lou willed himself forward, hitting the fence at full throttle, hooking his fingers into the metal fence while his legs scrambled for a foothold. The fence swayed under his weight but he made it to the top and hoisted himself over. His grip gave way and he plummeted to the ground, landing on two feet and rolling to his side. He'd heard the pop in his left knee. He pulled himself up and limped toward the first row of buses.

The only thing Lou could hear now was the sound of his own labored breathing. It had replaced the hush of the Delaware River rushing by in the otherwise silent night. The endless drone of cars speeding down Delaware Avenue had melted away. Lou kneeled in the shadows, leaning against a dusty bus tire. The terminal was completely deserted behind him. He could smell the pitted rubber from the tire. There didn't seem to be anyone left to chase. He took a deep breath, nourishing his strained muscles with oxygen and trying to keep his mind alert. Billy Sapphire was close by. He could feel it.

He crept slowly down the length of each bus, peering cautiously around every corner. There couldn't have been more than a few feet between buses, their tall shadows making it difficult to see. There were a few spotlights shining from the top of the terminal building but their light never reached the ground. It seemed to reflect off the buses, their silver exterior glimmering like burnished armor. Creeping from bus to bus like a rat in a maze, all Lou could do was listen.

He rounded one corner and then another. It was as if Sapphire had disappeared into thin air. They could spend all morning roaming around in that bus yard, playing cat and mouse, and never lay eyes on each other. Billy Sapphire could be reclining in a seat inside one of those buses, watching Lou from behind the tinted glass as he wandered aimlessly in the dark. He could have found a way into the terminal or he could have gone straight to the other side of the lot, climbed the fence and been long gone.

At the end of each bus there was a thin, vertical mirror. Lou used them to see between the narrow rows. The images in the clouded mirrors were obscured in the dark. He caught movement and stopped dead in his tracks before realizing that it was his own reflection he'd seen. He deliberately slowed his breathing and waited for his pulse to catch up.

It was no use and he decided to try a different approach. He stood up, stepping out from behind one of the buses and yelled.

'Billy Sapphire!'

He got only his own voice coming back to him, hollow amidst the solid partitions of steel and glass.

'Billy Sapphire! Come out.'

Still nothing.

'Billy! I just want to talk. I'm not the police. I'm not going to arrest you. I'm here to help.'

The sound came from above followed by movement in the corner of his eye. Sapphire had leapt from the top of the bus, descending upon him like some kind of wild bird, feet first with his arms outstretched and the gleaming blade of a knife visible in his right hand. His face was twisted into a snarl, his eyes like black pearls. The long coat he'd worn was gone. The black skull-cap remained, covering a head shaved bald and marked with tattoos.

Lou jumped back and attempted to deflect the blade with his upper arm. He felt the point ripping through the leather jacket, puncturing skin and muscle and entering deep into his shoulder. He felt the warm blood running down his arm under the jacket. What pain there was seemed not to belong to him. It seemed to belong to someone else, someone in one of his dreams, him and at the same time not him. He'd had that feeling before, things slowly winding down, the tunnel vision exploding in his brain.

The blade came again. Lou turned his body sideways, making himself less of a target. Sapphire seemed tireless, the knife slashing again and again with the same speed and the same force, the same hyperbolic arc. Lou was bleeding. And not just from his arm.

Then, everything began to slow down again. And again he felt as if he were in one of his dreams, the seemingly translucent blade taking forever to reach him, his own hands moving with a lethargic malaise, his whole body weighed down. He began to envision himself floating, gradually losing command of every muscle in his body, a slow relaxation of physical control. And what he feared most in this dream-like struggle, this seeming pantomime of life and death was that his will to live would fail him at last, for with each stroke of the knife his blood seemed to flow more freely.

He was fending off the attack purely by instinct now, his conscious mind fighting the urge to believe that this wasn't real.

Another flash of steel streaked before his eyes and he reached for it. The edge of the blade sliced the top of his hand but he didn't pull away. His hand slid down the knife, greasy with his own blood. His fingers were cut and stinging. He grabbed hold of Sapphire's wrist with one hand and then the other. Sapphire leaned in, grabbing hold of his own wrist, his hand on top of Lou's, rotating toward him until they were face-to-face and struggling for leverage over the knife, which was now pointed at Lou's chest.

Lou could see Sapphire clearly for the first time now. His face was narrow and hairless. His teeth were small, his breath was sour and his cheeks were hollow. His head was bald under the hat, his eyes cavernous and dark. But something burned in them, a red-hot fire in a black sky. He wasn't tall but he was wiry and strong and he was pushing hard on the knife, driving it closer by inches. He spun Lou around and drove him backward against the bus, the pointed blade entering his shoulder. Lou groaned from deep in his throat, the knife piercing the soft tissue just below his collar bone, the acid and blood rising up from his stomach and oozing from his open lips.

And just as the knife penetrated his flesh, his mind losing consciousness, a shot rang out. It echoed between the buses and it was difficult to tell from what direction it came. Lou wasn't even sure he'd heard it. It could have been a tendon snapping in his shoulder, the pain reverberating in his brain. The shot was followed by another. This time the bullet ricocheted off the steel of the fence, the shots coming from the other end of the lot.

Sapphire suddenly pulled the knife from Lou's shoulder and was running again, his steps crisp and flat in the renewed silence. Lou pressed his palm hard against the open wound, closing his eyes and sucking air. He pushed his back off the bus and opened his eyes to see Joey on the other side of the fence, the spotlight

catching his silhouette. He had the gun in his hand, aiming at
Sapphire's back as he retreated into the dark.

The outline of Joey's broad shoulders and round head faded
in and out, Lou's blurred vision unable to focus, the fiery
discharge from the gun lighting Joey's face for an instant. Joey
had fired the first two shots as warnings. Now, with a clear target
to shoot at and all the justification he'd ever need, he would
shoot to kill.

Lou started to drag himself across the lot. The next shot seemed
to miss its mark by mere inches. Joey got off one more, shat-
tering the windshield of the first bus in the line before Sapphire
disappeared again, climbing the fence behind the last row of
buses and hitting the ground running.

'You OK?'

'I don't know.'

'You're cut pretty bad.'

'I don't think it's deep.'

'Want me to call an ambulance?' Joey looked at him through
the fence. 'Your boy's getting away.'

'I just need to catch my breath for a second.'

'Jesus Christ! This kid runs like a goddamn rabbit.'

'All right. I'm coming over.'

Lou hooked the fingers of his right hand into the chain link,
his left arm tight against his side. His feet scrambled against the
metal for a hold. He pulled himself painstakingly toward the top
of the fence. He hung himself over the top rail and got a glimpse
of Sapphire crossing Delaware Avenue into a freight yard filled
with containers ready to be loaded onto waiting ships docked on
the Delaware River. Lou braced himself with his good arm and
dropped to the other side.

'Lou, for God's sake. You're bleeding like a stuck pig.'

'We can still catch him.' Joey followed Lou across Delaware
Avenue. 'There's nothing over here but the ships and the river.
He's got nowhere to go.'

They split up, taking separate paths between the metal
containers. They were getting closer to the river. They could hear
it now and feel the cold breeze and the spray carrying over the
docks. They emerged simultaneously to see Sapphire climbing
onto a concrete ledge that seemed to be there for the sole purpose

of keeping the river from crawling out of its bed and stalking over the land. Joey got off a quick shot.

Sapphire ducked at the sound. Joey leveled the gun, bringing it back on target. His finger tightened over the trigger, the slow pull coming in barely perceptible increments as the hammer lifted from its seat. Lou reached him just as the gun exploded, pushing his arm down at the last minute, the shot ringing out just as Sapphire dove into the icy water.

'Are you crazy?'

'Yeah, maybe.'

They ran to the water's edge, leaning over the concrete abut- ment and staring silently across the river at all that black water. It seemed impossible that anyone could enter it and come out alive. It would never stop for anything or anyone. It had a power fed by the ocean and the wind and the moon and it was enough water to swallow them and the whole city of Philadelphia as it had just swallowed Billy Sapphire.

'Do you see him?'

'No, I don't see him. There's nothing to see. He's gone.'

'Goddamn it.'

'What the hell were you trying to prove, grabbing my arm like that? I saved your ass from getting filleted like a cold fish. We could have ended it right here.'

'I want him alive.'

'Yeah, well, I hope he can swim. Maybe he'll wash up in Jersey.'

'And maybe he'll swim back home.'

'Like those salmon you were talking about?'

'Yeah, just like the salmon.'

TWENTY-SIX

Lou lowered himself onto the concrete wall, sitting with his back to the river. A faint glow of morning light seemed to be hovering in the east, taking its good old time coming across. No reason to hurry now. The cold sunlight that washed across that river every morning was still somewhere

out over the Atlantic, just beginning to cast its gray light onto
the Jersey shore. But the water would stay cold, even through the
summer. The water would always be cold.

'You want me to call Mitch?'

'No.'

'I'm calling an ambulance. You don't look good.'

'Don't bother. It's only a flesh wound.'

'It's worse than that.'

'I'll survive.'

Lou had started to shiver. It had started as a shudder up his
spine but had quickly spread and now his hands were shaking
and his knees were knocking and his teeth were rattling in his
head. Huddled against the wind coming off the river, with his
arms tight around his body, he shivered like a half-drowned dock
rat, one of those bums that had spent the best years of his life
humping freight on the Philadelphia dockyard and drinking
whiskey until there was nothing left of them but a haggard shell.
They still sat along the waterfront, like prehistoric birds, flight-
less and half-blind and waiting to die.

'I'm taking you to the hospital.'

'Good. Maggie's over there, keeping Betty company on the
night shift. I think she wants to be a nurse when she grows up.'

'Then you'll be her first patient.'

'I think Catherine Waites might have that distinction by now.'

Joey had grabbed Lou by the arm and Lou was leaning heavily
on him.

'Want me to get the car? You can wait here.'

'I'll make it.'

It was a long, slow walk back to the car. Joey helped Lou into
the passenger seat. He got the car moving and the heat going
and Lou's head fell back against the headrest. It was the closest
thing to sleep he'd had in a couple days.

They found Maggie and Betty sipping coffee in the first-floor
visitor's lounge. Betty helped Joey with Lou, getting him into
the empty emergency room. She peeled him gingerly out of his
jacket and the doctor used a pair of scissors to cut him out of
his shirt. Lou didn't notice at first that it was the same doctor
from the night before.

'Long shift, huh, Doc?'

'You do seem to have your share of trouble, Mr Klein.'

'It's my middle name.'

'I'll note that on my report.'

'Glad you haven't lost your sense of humor. Lack of sleep will do that.'

'I'm not laughing. I told you before, you should leave police work to the cops. If you want to get yourself killed I can't stop you. I'd just hate to see you endanger someone else.'

Betty got an IV going as the doctor began to suture Lou's shoulder. He stuck Lou with a few long, ugly needles first and then he began to sew it up with what looked like a fish hook and black thread, patting away the blood with gauze pads soaked in peroxide. Maggie was holding his hand, trying to warm it in hers.

'What happened, Dad?'

'Cut myself shaving.'

'That's the official story.'

'Joey!'

'Your dad decided to chase a murder suspect down a few dark alleys. Only he forgot to ask him if he still had the murder weapon on him. A nice, dirty carving knife with a six-inch blade and a lot of other people's blood on it.'

'Hope the other guy looks worse than you do, Lou.'

'Nice try, Betty. He got away. Dived into the Delaware River after I took a few shots at him. Would have got him too if he hadn't stopped me.'

The doctor put in a last stitch and tied it off. Lou grimaced. He looked ready to throw up. Betty dressed the wound with a lot of tape and suggested Lou keep the arm immobilized in a sling for a while. The doctor wrote out a couple of prescriptions on a pad and tore them off one at a time. He suggested Lou spend the rest of the day in the hospital under observation. Joey yawned and they all walked out into the lobby together.

'Where do you think Sapphire is headed, Joey?'

'You don't think he's dead?'

'Something tells me it's going to take more than a little swim in the Delaware to kill this guy.'

'I know what you mean. Unless, of course, he has a bullet in him.'

'Which might make him even more dangerous if he thought he didn't have much more time.'

They stopped at the coffee machine, Lou digging in his pocket for loose change. Betty pulled a few coins from her purse and dropped them through the slot. There were too many buttons to choose from. She ran her hand over the various selections as if they were written in Braille. Joey reached over her shoulder and pushed the one that had **black** next to it in bold letters. The cup dropped down and a weak stream of brackish fluid filled it while they all watched.

'Where do you think he's headed?'

'Home.'

'Back to Grays Ferry.'

'Nah. Home to see Grandma.'

Lou slowly lifted the cup to his lips with his one good hand. And though it burned his fingers he was glad for the warmth. He was about to take another sip when Donny Weeks came around the corner jingling a handful of quarters in his hand. The dark circles under his eyes made it look like he'd been in a fight. Apparently he'd had the same idea as Lou – a cardboard cup out of a machine filled with scalding hot coffee that tasted like gasoline.

'Your girlfriend's up. She's asking for you.'

'I could use a smoke.'

They all walked outside. Lou's jacket was draped over his shoulder and Joey slid his hand inside one of the pockets to extract a pack of cigarettes. The men smoked while Betty warmed up her car. Joey slipped the keys to the Cadillac into Lou's jacket.

'Betty said I could catch a ride home with her, Lou. I'm going to bed. I'll make sure Maggie gets in safe. You take your time.'

Lou looked at his daughter. She looked worried.

'Hey, how's your patient?'

'If you mean Catherine Waites, she's still in a coma.'

Franny was sitting up in bed sucking ginger ale from a straw, the crushed ice crackling in the cup. Her eyes rolled upward as he came in. She was still pale but the shadow of death seemed to have passed, her face regaining some of its original color. Her eyes seemed brighter. Maybe that was because Lou was there.

And maybe she just hadn't given up yet, wasn't quite ready to follow her brother into heaven.

'I call your name and you're here. My errant knight.'

'Donny told me.'

'Told you what? That I needed a shoulder to cry on? That one of my brothers is dead and the other one blames me for it?'

'None of this was your fault, Franny.'

'You're the only one who thinks so.'

'Since when did you care what anyone else thinks?'

'You don't have to lie to me, Lou. Not now. And I promise I won't lie to you. Is it a deal?'

'It's a deal.'

She took the last few sips of soda and it sounded like rainwater trickling down the rusted gutter at his mother's house. Whenever it rained the water would roll off the roof and into the leaky gutters and then on to the driveway where it ran into the street. Around this time of year it would form a thin sheet of black ice. Philly was known for it. And more than once Lou had found himself on his ass because of it.

He refilled Franny's cup from the green can on her tray.

'I'm not going back to Brian, you know.'

'That's not what he says.'

'He says a lot of things. Most of it is bullshit so people will feel sorry for him. About how hard it is living in the shadow of William Haggerty. And his domineering mother who won't cut the apron strings. The purse strings, more like it.' She paused to catch her breath. She took another drink. Lou sat quietly watching the monitor, watching Franny Patterson's heart rate climb. 'I never met the father but the mother is enough to drive anyone crazy.'

'You talking about Brian Haggerty or Billy Sapphire?'

Franny's face reddened. The monitor above her bed kept time with her rising pulse, ticking like a clock on the wall. She slid a piece of crushed ice from the cup into her mouth and started chewing it.

'You know about Billy?'

'You told me.'

'If I did I don't remember. I must have been delirious. What did I say?'

'Not much. I was hoping you could fill in some of the missing pieces for me.'

'Do the police know?'

'Not the whole story.'

'I'll give you one piece of the story. Billy didn't kill my brother.'

Lou stood and walked to the window. It was developing into a bright morning with the sun beating down on the growing number of cars in the lot below. The glare hurt Lou's eyes. They were tired, bloodshot eyes.

'But he has hurt a lot of people, Franny. You know that. He's hurt you.'

'A lot of people. Who? Girls from Brian's stable? Some pervert in a public park?'

'You sound like Eleanor Haggerty now.'

'Don't say that. It's not true. You can't blame him for what he is. Kids like that are created, Lou. They're not born that way.'

'He's not a kid anymore. He's a grown man.'

'You don't know him like I do. He's still a kid. That same little kid on the inside. He could have been my little brother.'

'A kid that put a gun to the head of his mother and grandfather.'

'Someone put that gun in his hand, Lou. Someone poisoned his mind. Whatever he is, whatever he did, it was because of Eleanor Haggerty. God only knows what she told him. You don't know what he saw in that house.'

'What about Valerie Price? She had a role to play.'

'I don't blame Valerie.'

'You were trying to help him, weren't you? Undo the damage Eleanor had done. You were the only one.'

'I think he knew that. That's why I never felt threatened by him. I don't think he wanted to hurt me.'

'You might have been that boy's only hope, Franny. You did all you could. But you couldn't fix him no matter what you did.'

Franny pushed the button on the side of the bed and slowly reclined until she was staring up at the ceiling, at a glossy coat of fresh paint and rows of fluorescent lights. Her eyes closed for a moment.

'You're wrong, Lou. I could have done more. I could have

prevented Jimmy from being killed. It was my fault and Tony's right to blame me.'

'You need to rest, Franny. We can talk more tomorrow.'

'No, Lou. I want you to hear it. I want you to know the truth.'

She ran the point of her tongue over her dry, chapped lips. The doctor had told her that she needed to keep drinking, even with the bag of saline dripping continuously into the plastic tubing that carried it, clear and cool, to the bruised and bulging veins of her motionless left arm. She held out the plastic pitcher and asked Lou to refill it with water and ice. He returned with the pitcher and poured her a fresh cup and she seemed to recover her voice, wetting her lips with slow, lingering sips.

'I let Billy stay in the shed behind our house. He didn't have anywhere else to go. I never told Jimmy. I wanted to but I never did. I knew what he'd say, or so I thought. He'd been back there for a couple of months.'

'Jimmy and I spent a few nights in that shed ourselves. Kept our beer back there. As I recall I might have tried to get you back there a few times.'

'Don't joke, Lou. I don't want anybody to be nice to me, especially you. I don't deserve it.' She put down the cup and covered her eyes. 'I should have seen it coming. Billy seemed angrier every time I saw him. He was out of control. He overheard a conversation between me and Jimmy. We were standing on the driveway. I told him to forget about the ring. I told him to forget about Valerie Price, that once it touched her finger it was cursed. Brian got his hands on it after Valerie was killed and it ended up on my finger. I didn't want it but Jimmy liked the idea. It was kind of like the ring had come back to him. Billy must have heard everything we said.'

'About his mother? And the ring?'

'About everything.' Franny's eyes came up to meet Lou's. 'I didn't see him for a few days after that. I took some food out to him. He never touched it. I thought he was gone for good. He'd disappeared before, sometimes for months on end. Then I came home late the other night, the same day I spoke to you, and he came at me in the dark. Jimmy must have heard me scream and came out of the house with his gun. I heard a few shots before I passed out.'

'Then why do you say it wasn't Sapphire that shot Jimmy?'

'I was conscious long enough to see someone else there. It was Brian. It was his face I saw looking down at me.'

'Are you sure?'

'I'm pretty sure, Lou. I wasn't dreaming.'

'Well then, Mitch got his man. Brian was arrested earlier this morning at the Arramingo Club. After Billy Sapphire burned it down.'

The room had suddenly become much warmer with the sun climbing slowly higher in the sky and coming through the window in waves of yellow light. The flowers that had been accumulating along the window sill were beginning to droop in their fanciful bouquets as if they'd grown parched with no one to water them.

Lou filled a cup of water from the pitcher and poured it into one of the flower pots. He repeated the procedure until he'd watered them all.

Through the thick glass he could hear the birds outside, singing and diving toward the window and turning away at the last minute. They must see their own reflection, Lou thought, and their acrobatics are just showing off, a dangerous mating dance they performed only for themselves.

'Did you ever wish you could go back in time, Lou? Go back and change something, a decision that affected your entire life. Change directions. Did you ever wish you could just go back and change everything?'

'I'm tired, Franny. If I could sleep for a solid week, I'd feel ten years younger.'

'There isn't anything you'd like to change?'

'There's a lot I'd change, Franny. I just don't know, given the chance, that I'd be able to change anything.'

'You could try.'

'I could.'

Lou pulled open the door and hung in the doorway, his eyes searching the ground, never very good at saying goodbye.

'Lou, tomorrow is Jimmy's funeral. I was hoping you'd come with me. I think Jimmy would like that.'

'Me, too.'

'Don't be gone too long, Lou. Please.'

TWENTY-SEVEN

Lou didn't remember much about the ride to Torresdale. He'd lost track of time, the world around him moving in flashes; people and cars, laundromats and nail salons, pizza shops and used car lots, funeral homes, a karate studio, a beauty parlor, a gas station, an insurance office. And bars. Too many bars. They went by in a blur, an urban landscape seared into his exhausted unconscious. He pulled in front of the Haggertys' house, thinking of the many secrets concealed behind those brick walls and curtained windows, the ones he knew and the ones he'd never know.

Eleanor Haggerty had seemed content to keep her secrets hidden. If Billy Sapphire was here he wasn't coming out and Lou wasn't getting in.

He pressed the lighted button on the door and listened to the chimes tolling inside, eight congruent notes, evenly spaced as if they'd originated with some vociferous child at the piano, repeating the first four notes he'd ever learned, performing the same basic passage over and over again on his grandmother's baby grand until she'd finally come down the stairs and ordered him to stop.

Now he waited, his arm throbbing in the sling. The flat thwack of the deadbolt sliding back sounded like a shot.

Eleanor Haggerty opened the door about a foot and peered at him through her thick gold-framed glasses. She was wearing the same light blue quilted housecoat. It was zipped up to her neck where she held it fast. She wore the same padded slippers and was pushing the blue-gray hair back on one side of her head and adjusting her hearing aid, its petulant whine ebbing reluctantly. She removed her hand from her ear, unable to conceal her irritation.

'Most people call first, Mr Klein. They don't just drop by unannounced.'

'I'm looking for Billy Sapphire. Is he here?'

'What happened to your arm? You look injured.'

'Is he here?'

'I have no idea what you're talking about. Is this a police matter? You go around acting like a cop, but you're not.'

'You like to keep reminding me of that. What difference does it make?'

'Well, someone needs to remind you. You have no right to take the law into your own hands. You can't stick your nose in where it's not wanted. Last time I heard, it takes a warrant for that. As a matter of fact, I think I'll give the chief a call and maybe he'll send a couple of his men over to visit you. See how you like it.'

'As long as they call first.'

'You think you're smart, don't you?'

'Smart enough to see through the lies of a very mean, selfish and greedy old woman.'

'I am very old. I thought maybe you'd forgotten that.'

'And smart enough to know when I'm being deceived as well.'

'You don't know anything. What gives you the right? Because you were a cop? That makes you nothing but a cheap public servant. Name calling is all you know.'

'No more games, Mrs Haggerty. Where is he?'

'Is that what you do? Go around looking for missing persons? And what if they don't want to be found? Do you bring them in dead or alive? And don't you have to be hired by someone? I can't believe anyone is actually paying you to be such a nuisance.'

'Jimmy Patterson hired me.'

'Jimmy Patterson is dead.' The wind whistled through the open doorway and Eleanor Haggerty pulled her housecoat tighter around her wrinkled neck. 'For your information, I've been instructed by my attorney not to speak with you. You're familiar with Warren Armstrong; I'm sure you boys have tangled in the past.' She coughed roughly, the wind taking her breath away for a second. 'Isn't that the way you'd put it?'

'Warren Armstrong won't be able to protect you.'

'What makes you think I need protection?'

'Billy Sapphire will turn on you. Mark my words. You're the meddling nose he'll need to cut off to spite his face. I'm surprised it hasn't happened already.'

'Is that why you're here, then? To save me from my grandson.'

'Is that what he is?'

'I think you better go, Mr Klein.'

'Did you know that even the best-trained police dogs have been known to bite their masters? It usually comes after repeated stress. It's their nature. They can't help it.'

'Well, whatever bit you on the shoulder seems to have sunk his teeth in pretty deep. It looks like you're bleeding.'

Lou looked down and saw that the blood had indeed begun leaking through the bandage, turning the white gauze to a dull rust. He only noticed now that he was shivering again. His cell phone began vibrating in his pocket. He'd almost forgotten it was there and had a little difficulty fishing it out. It was Mitch.

'Where you at?'

'Haggerty's, if you must know.'

'Well, Haggerty got bailed out a little while ago. But he didn't make it very far.'

'What's that supposed to mean?'

'We're at Fifteenth and Lombard. Not far from City Hall. So there's quite an audience.'

'We?'

'Half the fucking Philadelphia Police Department. Got ourselves a little standoff. You know all the players. I figure your presence might come in handy. Looks like this is going to be the final act, Lou.'

'I'm on my way.'

'Hey, Lou. Step on it.'

A command post had been set up on Lombard Avenue about a half block from the scene. All police activity would be coordinated from there. They'd run the show from inside a large rectangular van filled with radios, transmitters, riot gear and a fully equipped arsenal. There was a satellite dish on the roof and a row of spot-lights that could light the street like it was Veterans Stadium. Lou thought it looked like the bread truck that delivered hoagie rolls to Carlino's every morning on Brookline Boulevard.

Cops had positioned themselves behind parked cars and in the vestibules of buildings and began moving along both sides of the street. Their guns were drawn as they moved past a dark green Ford sedan angled awkwardly in the middle of the road. It appeared to have been in a collision with a blue Corvette. A news chopper hovered overhead. There were two bodies, a male and female, sprawled on the ground. They looked dead.

Lou spotted Mitch following behind the squadron of police. They were headed toward Judy Garland Park.

'Glad you could make it. Hey, what the hell happened to you?'

'Rotator cuff.'

'How'd you get that?'

'Wiping my ass.'

'Looks like you'll just have to use your other hand.'

'What I miss?'

'That's your friend Brian Haggerty out there bleeding all over my nice clean street. Not sure who the woman next to him is. We're thinking one of the girls from the club. This thing came in as a traffic accident. Then shots fired. Witnesses report seeing a woman in a red dress, a tall blonde running toward the park. Had a gun in her hand. Could be some kind of lover's triangle.'

'Is that your assumption?'

'You got a better idea?'

'How long you going to wait it out?'

'I ain't callin' the shots on this one, Lou. I'm sure Captain Linker is sitting in that van right now sipping a hot coffee and scratching his balls. He'll pull the plug as soon as he gets tired of paying all these guys overtime.'

'Witnesses see anything else?'

'They all say the same thing. This Ford comes out of nowhere and cuts off the Corvette. A blonde jumps out and she's got a gun in her hand. One guy says she looks like a high-priced call girl: short red dress, sequins, high heels, lots of pearls around her neck, a lot of blonde hair all done up, make-up, the works. Pumps about six slugs into Haggerty and does the same to his girlfriend. She gets back in her car and the thing won't start. She just sits there for a while, puts on a fresh coat of lipstick and makes for the park.'

'You sure it's Haggerty?'

'Tags on both cars come back to Haggerty, William Haggerty. The media had it as fast as we did and they're already running with it. The Arramingo Club burns and Haggerty gets iced. Not bad, huh?'

It was closing in on lunch time, late morning of a fairly sunny day in Philadelphia that brought a great many suits and skirts out from behind their concrete enclosures and mirrored glass windows and computer screens. They hit the street hoping to blow the dust off and instead found out just how cold it still was even with the sun shining in their faces. From Lou's vantage point, they all looked the same, clad in the same dark sunglasses, talking into cell phones, all of them annoyed that they'd been detoured by another inner-city crime scene. Annoyed at the cops for telling them what side of the street to walk on. It was for their own personal safety, they'd said. Yeah, right.

'You calling in a negotiator?'

'Not a hostage situation, Lou. You can't take yourself hostage.'

'You going to try talking to her?'

'Yeah. When we find her, we'll tell her to come out with her hands up. She either comes out on her own or we go in and get her.'

Lou looked at the disabled Ford and the demolished Corvette, its front end crushed, and the double yellow lines down the middle of Lombard Avenue that seemed to bisect them both. Haggerty was face down in the street. He tried to get a look at him and his girlfriend, who he assumed was Angel Divine, collapsed on top of him. He could see her blonde hair with its fiery splashes of red. He could see her blood-stained jeans. She was wearing silver cowboy boots. Looked like good leather and expensive stitching, Lou thought. She probably wanted to be buried in them.

He looked back down the street toward City Hall only a few blocks away, where the face on the statue of William Penn looked bored by all this petty human drama, his gaze cast westward as if he were more interested in the Penn Relays at Franklin Field than what was playing out just below him. What did he care? What did anyone care if the city's founding father refused to look down from his pedestal? He'd managed to remain unscathed by the sun and the wind and the cold for all these years; naturally he'd be indifferent to the actions of one wasted nightclub owner and the women that wanted to fuck him and those that wanted to kill him. He cared even less what the cops had to say about it.

The circle of armed officers seemed to tighten around the park. Onlookers had pointed them toward the wall where the crumbling trellis still sat and the crawling vines had supplanted what was left of the roses, leaving only a tangled bed of pickers and wild, unruly bushes with thick, succulent leaves, oily with poison. They'd seen a woman run behind it. They'd seen the gun.

Some of the cops were wearing flak jackets. Others had on helmets. Most of them had either rifles or shotguns aimed at the ready. They jockeyed for position, waiting for the word from command to make their move. The snipers were sighting in their scopes, adjusting for wind and distance.

'Let me give it a try.'

'Give what a try?'

'Talking.'

'You expect me to let you go walking in the park all alone? Have a little chat with Miss Annie Oakley in the red cocktail dress? Are you crazy?'

'Why not? You want the police assassinating a woman on the six o'clock news? What do you have to lose?'

'I don't want to lose any cops. And even though you're the biggest fool I've ever known, I don't want to lose you either.'

'You brought me here for a reason, Mitch. It wasn't to be a spectator.'

'Do you know the person in the park, Lou?'

'I might.'

'Do you think you can talk her out without getting yourself killed?'

'It's worth a shot.'

It was eerily quiet in Judy Garland Park considering it was the middle of the day. There was no traffic noise, no wind. The birds were silent in the trees. There was very little sound at all. Even the crowds forming at both ends of Lombard Avenue seemed to be holding their collective breath. And then, as if on cue, she appeared: the woman in the red dress, stepping gracefully from behind the battered wall.

It really was a very grand entrance, one spiked heel at a time coming across the stone walk, her legs smooth and muscular under the flesh-colored stockings. The dress was short and red, a liquid, candy-apple red that seemed to flow from her breasts to her hips as if she'd been dipped in a vat of red paint. The moment she was on her feet, she'd smoothed the wrinkles out of the thin material, her movements slow and sensual, running her hand over the glowing red dress until it was flat against her skin and then teasing a lock of blonde hair. The other hand held a large black automatic pistol.

They all stared in amazement as a gust of wind whipped between the buildings and ran across the ground into the park. It looked as if it might tear the dress right off her and she held it down with a hand between her thighs, her face hidden behind an expressionless mask of heavy make-up, red lipstick and rouge.

Her blonde hair hung in long spiral curves, the wind pushing it off her shoulders and over her face. And now that she was out in the sun, it shimmered in the cold light, appearing almost crystalline as if it had been frozen in place by a lot of spray and suddenly exposed to the wind, it was ready to crack.

'Lights, camera, action.'

'Mitch, let me talk to her.'

Mitch reached through the window of the police car, grabbed the mic and keyed it up, turning the knob on the transmitter until the public address system crackled and squealed.

'Drop the gun!' His voice boomed and every officer seemed to come to attention, gripping their guns a little tighter. 'You're surrounded! Drop the gun! Now!' The officers had begun moving, a converging army of blue still behind cover but getting closer. 'Drop the gun and get down on the ground!'

She didn't seem to hear him. The way she looked around it seemed as if she wasn't sure where she was. She gazed up at the sky, at the sun burning through layers of white clouds as they rushed by overhead, trying to catch a lift on the jet stream. She followed them longingly with her eyes as if she'd awakened on some remote island, surveying the vast ocean spreading out on all sides and realizing for the first time that she might never leave.

Lou was able to see her face now. Her make-up had begun to wrinkle and crack. Lou imagined her putting it on in front of a mirror until she'd been unrecognizable even to herself. And now it was falling apart. Lou recognized the face as he stared at her from no more than thirty yards away, the face beginning to look as much like a man as a woman.

He came up along the opposite side of the wall and let her see him. He was asking for the gun, his hand out as if there would be some exchange, as if he had something to negotiate with, something to trade, some way he could strike a bargain they could both agree to. Whatever he had to offer, it didn't seem like much.

'Give me the gun.' A few more steps and repeating. 'Give me the gun. Please.'

'I know you.'

'You almost killed me.'

'And now you want me to finish the job.'

'It's not worth it.'

'Oh, no? Well, I'm done now anyway. I'm tired. I just want to go to sleep.'

'I know. Put the gun down, Billy, and it'll all be over.'

'I don't think so. I don't have to listen to you. You're not my father. You're just a nobody.'

'Franny sent me. She needs you.'

'Franny's dead. They're all dead.'

'No, she's not. She's getting better. She's in the hospital. She'll be out tomorrow. You can see her.'

'She tried to help me.'

'I know.'

'She knows what it's like. She's the only one who understood.'

'I understand, Billy.'

'No you don't.'

'Billy!'

He raised the gun in his trembling hand, not pointing it but simply raising his arm in the same orchestrated movement in which he'd stepped from behind the wall, self-conscious and self-possessed and vaguely predatory, a Hollywood starlet on the red carpet, playing the only role she knew to the bitter end.

Lou wasn't sure where the first shot had come from, a line of trees at the park's edge maybe, one of those snipers putting a round right through Billy Sapphire and he wouldn't know it until the initial burn brought the blood to his throat and his legs went weak. Lou was yelling for them to stop, yelling so loudly he was sure the whole world must have heard. And his only answer was the great volley of gunfire that seemed to come down from the heavens like a sudden hail storm on a clear day.

That first shot had only brought more. Every cop on the street took their turn, aiming at this woman in the red dress waving a gun around, her body twitching spasmodically, the red dress now riddled with bullet holes and saturated with her life's blood.

Lou hadn't taken more than a few steps from the time the gunfire started to the time it ended though time itself had seemed to stand still. Now, in the brief silence, he stood over the mangled corpse, staring into a set of lifeless eyes.

Mitch came up alongside him. The officers stormed the scene, pushing forward with their guns still smoking, some of them reloading as they came as if the blood-soaked body at their feet might spring up and lunge at them with its last dying breath.

None of them touched her and Lou couldn't help thinking how unreal it had all seemed, like one of his dreams again, wondering if he would wake up and it would all disappear, wondering too if Sapphire had planned it to unfold this way, as if this was the way he wanted it to end. And still, Lou felt as if he'd seen it coming and was unable to stop it.

He looked through the blood-smeared make-up and the splintered dress and the blood-stained pearls that still circled her neck. The blonde wig had been twisted around and pushed back from the force of the trauma and the heavily applied make-up had peeled away enough to reveal the face underneath. It was the face of a boy. A boy who was caught in his own dream and couldn't wake up.

Mitch kneeled and pushed the gun away from Billy Sapphire's slim hand. He saw the flash of color on his nails and thought it was blood before he realized it was polish. He picked it up and felt its weight. He popped out the magazine and racked the slide, locking it back and making it safe. He was crouching over the body, examining the gun. He stood with it in his hand and turned to Lou.

'It's empty, Lou. It was empty the whole time.'

TWENTY-EIGHT

Lou had resigned himself to the idea that funerals were a fact of life. A revelation he'd made a couple years ago at the Mass for Charlie Melvyn at St Gabe's. He'd stood outside smoking for much of the eulogy, wondering what the hell Father Kane could say about Charlie that most of his friends from the neighborhood didn't already know. When he finally went inside and took his place among the other pallbearers, the casket had been closed and there was nothing left to do but carry his old friend out.

Lou had worn his dark blue sport jacket over a light blue shirt. He was wearing the same thing today. His pants were a soft wool blend and if he had to describe the color, he would have said copper, the color of an old penny. He wore brown loafers with leather laces that seemed to come slowly untied no matter how tight he tied them, women always whispering in his ear for him to tie his shoes. He'd shaved, though, and Maggie was thankful for that.

She was on his arm in a pair of black pants with gray pinstripes, a gray shirt, a shiny black belt with a silver buckle and a matching black jacket. She wore heels, the big square ones that brought her very close to Lou's height. There were four or five guys smoking cigarettes outside St Peter's Cathedral and Lou and Maggie walked past them up the wide granite stairs. They looked like cops.

Mitch was sitting in the back row and they slid in next to him. Joey and Betty sat across the aisle. Organ music filled the church with an Irish funeral dirge saved only for cops and firemen and soldiers.

Jimmy was laid out in a charcoal-gray suit and a raspberry-red tie with a white shirt and his hair brushed back with a layer of gel, his skin a light brown as if he'd spent the day at the shore.

Mitch leaned in close and murmured grossly, 'He never looked better.'

'Franny might have something to say about that.' Franny was in the front row next to her brother, Tony. Lou couldn't see her face but even from behind she looked like she'd aged. 'Gargling with bourbon again, Mitch? I thought you were on the wagon.'

'Very expensive bourbon. Breakfast at Francesco's.'

'Is that anything like Breakfast at Tiffany's?'

'Mimi threw me out last night. Frankie's renting me a room on the second floor. We're taking it day by day.'

'After thirty years she decides to call it quits? What pushed her over the edge?'

'I don't know. The hours, the distractions. She said I don't talk to her anymore. Said I ignore her, don't respect her. Maybe she just didn't want to share me with the Philadelphia Police Department anymore. I don't know. I guess I don't blame her.'

'Hell of a thing to come home to after sweeping bodies off the street all day.'

'For now, home's a single room over a bar. Looks like I might have to get used to it.'

'Join the crowd.'

The organ music faded and Father Penn took his place on the pulpit facing the congregation. His cheeks were red and his nose was red and even his round head was red under the sparse gray hair. He must have been humbled, Lou thought, speaking to all those cops and ex-cops, the high-ranking and the low, their wives and children, all those unbelievers who assumed to know more about death than he did. He recited a few psalms and a few homilies and his words seemed to float over the congregation and get lost somewhere amidst the arched dome of stained glass. Nobody really seemed to be listening. The janitor sitting alone in the balcony, waiting to clean up, was probably listening. But he'd heard it all before.

'I have more good news.'

'Never doubted it.'

'DNA report came back on Sapphire. Just preliminary. There's a lot of shit we're trying to match him up to.'

'And . . .?'

'Billy Sapphire does not have one drop of Haggerty blood in his veins. Not a drop.'

'Don't tell me.'

'The mother, as you know, is the late, great Valerie Price. The father is our boy up there, Jimmy Patterson.'

The most reverend Father Penn concluded his eulogizing for one day and his distracted flock chanted 'Amen' in unison. Lou and Mitch stared dumbfounded at the face of Jimmy Patterson as two ushers closed the lid on the casket, turning the screws on both sides, cranking it down tight and sealing it shut. They wheeled Jimmy down the center aisle to the main doors where Lou and Mitch and Jimmy's brother and a handful of cops were waiting to carry him down the stairs and into a waiting hearse.

Franny Patterson came up behind them, watching from the top of the cathedral steps. She was thin as a rail. Standing there alone in a long black dress and no coat, with those deep-set eyes beneath a black veil, she seemed like a ghost, inured to the cold.

The procession was led by two cops on motorcycles. They cruised in tandem, staying ahead of the hearse, lights flashing red and blue. They were dressed entirely in black leather: heavy polished jackets, boots to their knees and thick gloves. Their helmets were white, though. They wore black mirrored sunglasses and from where Franny was sitting they must have seemed like a pair of knights on horseback, delivering the dead to the doorstep of heaven.

They'd close each intersection and let the cars in the funeral train glide by, their orange flags waving like banners. Most drivers didn't have a problem waiting for death to pass. They'd gape open-mouthed as the traffic signal cycled from red to green and back to red again, grateful that it was someone else this time. But the clock was ticking. That much they knew and that's why they waited.

Maggie rode with Lou. She'd been quiet thus far. She'd always been quiet in church, Lou recalled. They followed Joey's white Cadillac with Betty in the passenger seat and the traffic on Sproul Road slowing to a crawl.

'I'll never forget the night Jimmy Patterson died on our porch. Jesus. How do you deal with that?'

'You don't.'

'No wonder you have nightmares. You still having them?'

'Not as often. But I don't sleep much either.'

'Still dreaming about Catherine Waites?'

'That. And others. They're nothing, really.'

'They're not nothing.'

'They're just dreams, Maggie. They're not real. What does it matter?'

'It does matter, Dad. They mean something. You can't just ignore them.'

A high stone arch stood at the entrance to St Peter's Cemetery, tall, wrought-iron gates standing open. The procession weaved along a narrow path and stopped beside an open grave with a large mound of rich black dirt ready to cover it over. The line of cars pulled onto the grass and parked. The pall-bearers, including Lou and Mitch and Joey, went immediately to the back of the hearse while the rest gathered around in a half-circle.

The air was biting, a cold rain falling. It seemed to be getting colder, the rain beginning to mix with frozen crystals, fine particles of ice that tapped against the top of the casket as they maneuvered it into position.

Franny looked frail on her brother's arm as Father Penn recited a final prayer for the dead and she watched her brother's casket descend into the ground. It disappeared into the blackness, seeming to take a very long time until it reached bottom, resting finally in the earth beyond their sight. Joey crossed himself. He and Betty moved back up onto the narrow road and lit cigarettes. Maggie went with them. Betty had her umbrella open and Maggie hunched under it. Others followed suit, walking back to their cars, their faces hidden under black umbrellas.

Lou moved up beside the open grave and stood next to Franny. He took her hand. When he let go she had the ring. He'd passed it to her wordlessly and she looked down at the diamond in her open palm. It wasn't big, not much more than a couple carats. But it sparkled where the rain hit it, making it look larger and brighter than it was.

'I thought you might have had it.'

'I got it from Jimmy. He had it when he died.'

'Remember I said we wouldn't lie to each other anymore? And now you're here, still waiting for me to tell you the truth.'

'I can wait.'

'You shouldn't have to.'

'Secrets rarely stay secrets for very long, Franny. The truth comes out. It has a will all of its own. You don't owe me any explanations.'

'Still, you should hear it from me, Lou.' Lou took her arm and together they inched to the edge of the open grave. 'It was Jimmy's ring all along. He gave it to Valerie Price.' She held the ring out in front of her and stared through the circle of white gold. 'And you know what she did? She laughed. She put the ring on her finger and laughed at him, laughed at him for thinking she'd marry a cop when she could have anyone she wanted, pregnant or not. She paraded around saying Brian Haggerty gave it to her. Said it was his baby inside her and he was going to make her an honest woman.'

'I don't know what to say, Franny.'

'Jimmy told me everything that day, the day he died. He even asked me to forgive him. He never thought any harm would come to me. He thought he could protect me. He was a good man, Lou. He made mistakes. But he was a good man.'

'I know.'

She dropped the ring into the grave. They listened but it never made a sound and Lou imagined it falling forever, a bottomless pit where all of Jimmy's best laid plans inevitably fell.

Lou walked her back to the limo. He opened the rear door and felt the heat from the warm car. Franny put her arms around his neck and rested her head on his chest. His hands went to her waist and she felt light and withered under his touch, light as the air and weak as the winter sun.

'Everything got so mixed up, Lou.'

'It sure did.'

'Are you coming by the house?'

'Yeah, I'll be by.'

Franny crawled into the back seat and Lou closed the door. He watched the car drive away, he and Maggie standing there alone, the last ones left.

A sharp gust of wind revved up and blew across the abandoned cemetery, splashing over Maggie's face and blowing her dark hair into a mad tangle. They turned their backs to it, walking between the tombstones toward the car.

'Do you ever regret coming back here, Dad, getting involved in all this?'

'You asked me that once before.'

'I know. I wondered if you'd changed your mind.'

'I have a lot of regrets, Maggie. But coming back home isn't one of them.'

'Is Franny Patterson one of your regrets?'

'No.' He was shaking his head, looking down at a bunch of wilted flowers on a grave. He read the name and the dates on the stone. Max Coffey, ninety-one when he died and still someone was putting flowers on his grave. 'It's nice to think about. But no.'

They looked over the crest of the hill at the various markers and monuments that stretched out to the horizon and out of sight. The ground was still soft beneath their feet. It might not harden for another month, when winter would solidify its grip.

'Why did you come back, Dad?'

Lou slowed his pace and Maggie turned to face him.

'I had nowhere else to go.'

'That's it? You had no place to go, so you decided to come home. Just like that?'

'The house was empty. It'd been empty for a long time. That house and you were all I had left. I thought it was time to breathe some life back into it, back into the house and back into my life. At least, that's what I hoped.'

'Where were you all those years? Why'd you stay away for so long?'

Two crows caught their attention, lighting on a headstone nearby, bobbing their heads and cackling like a couple of wise guys in black suits. Lou picked a pebble out of the wet grass and tossed it at them. They leapt from the stone, both of them flapping their wings hard against the implacable wind. They drifted wistfully over the deserted graveyard, settling down on another stone to begin their laughing all over again.

'It seems like I've been holding my breath, dreading the day you'd ask that question.'

'Why?'

'I was afraid of telling you the truth.'

'That seems to be going around.'

'I wanted to protect you, Maggie. It seemed the right thing to do at the time. Your mother wanted to protect you, too. It was one of the few things we agreed on. After the divorce, we wanted to spare you any more pain. So we told you I was still a cop, that I left the police department and I was working as a detective with the district attorney and I needed some time to build a new life. You were young. It was a believable story. It didn't exactly explain my long absence, but . . .'

'But it was a lie.'

'Yeah.' They got to the car and climbed in. They just sat there looking through the windshield and listening to the frozen rain hit the glass. 'I wanted to tell you, but things were going so well between us. I didn't want to ruin it.'

'You won't ruin anything. We lost each other for a while. Now we got it back. Nothing else matters. Right?'

His hands were on the steering wheel. He thought he saw a few snowflakes swirling in front of him. The freezing rain had first turned to sleet and now it was snowing.

'I was in prison, Maggie.'

They sat in silence. Lou started the car and tried to get a little heat going and then they were pulling away.

'For how long?'

'Almost five years.'

'Five years.' Lou could see her calculating the time in her head. It was a quarter of her life. Back then it would have been half. 'For what you did to that man? The man that molested Catherine Waites?'

'Yeah. At first he was just paralyzed. The charges were dropped and he sued the city. He was paid off and I resigned and that was supposed to be the end of it. All he cared about was the money. But he got some kind of infection. He went back into the hospital and twelve days later he was dead. His family claimed his death was a direct result of the beating he took. The one I gave him. The medical examiner agreed and the district attorney charged me.'

They were rolling slowly down the narrow drive, exiting the cemetery, passing back through the stone archway and the wrought-iron gate.

'I pled guilty to involuntary manslaughter.'

'You pled guilty?'

'A long trial would have made things worse. It just would

have dragged things out and I didn't want that. I wasn't afraid
to go to jail. I'm sorry, Maggie. I never wanted to lie to you. I
didn't know what else to do.'
    She reached across the seat and took his hand.
    'It's OK. You did what you thought was right. You always did.'

TWENTY-NINE

Maggie wasn't comfortable going to the Pattersons'. She
wasn't in the mood for coffee and cake and didn't feel
like spending the rest of the day listening to a bunch
of cops talk about Jimmy Patterson as if he was sitting there in
his favorite chair, matching them beer for beer. She pictured her
father with Joey and Mitch and Jimmy's brother, Tony, and Donny
Weeks, all of them getting drunk together around the kitchen
table. It would probably end up in a fist fight. Lou wasn't surprised
when she told him she'd promised to meet Betty at the hospital.
    Betty's shift would be starting soon. She'd been working
twelve-hour shifts round the clock for weeks now as a result of
the nursing shortage. They'd work all night and sleep all day or
vice versa. They'd cover for each other if need be, a lifestyle not
much different than that of a cop, working and sleeping and
trying to find a way to stay human. Maggie had decided to pursue
nursing as a career and Betty was getting her an internship at
the hospital. Lou wondered if she had any idea what she was
getting herself into.
    'It's long hours. And hard work. There's death, up close and
personal. You got to go in with your eyes open.'
    'I know all about it. Not everybody could do it. I think I could.'
    'My little angel of mercy.'
    'What's wrong with that?'
    'You'll never be out of work. That's for sure.'
    'What're you afraid of? You think I'll meet some cop in the
emergency room and want to marry him?'
    'I was hoping it'd be a doctor.'

*   *   *

They drove in silence for a while. And he was reminded that he still saw something beautiful in this city. There was the physical beauty, rivers running through it like arteries through a beating heart. And there was its age-old architecture, the old churches and the monuments and the cobblestone streets. But it was more than just its physical beauty. It was deeper than that. It was the soul of Philadelphia that drew him to her.

He'd been to other cities. He'd spent time in Baltimore and had actually been accepted to their police department. It was a time when he thought about leaving Philly for good. And yet it had been like a game he'd played with himself. He knew he'd only end up coming back, working for the Philadelphia Police Department and following in his father's footsteps.

There were still so many things he needed to tell Maggie, things about himself that he'd never told anyone, stories from his childhood, things they had in common, the most defining moments of his life. He hoped she would begin to know him for who he really was. The first story he would tell her would be about a time he'd been sitting at his bedroom window, as was his custom in those days, and had seen a bird falling from the old maple tree in his front yard.

He'd followed it with his eyes, its wings beating wildly as it descended, fluttering between the branches and wet leaves as it fell with no sound at all, disappearing and then appearing again on the soft grass. He'd watched from the window and looked at the bird lying motionless for quite a while before he decided to go down. He wasn't sure what to do. He was just a boy, no more than twelve. He thought it was dead, wondering if this was what death really looked like, until it opened its wide, unblinking eyes. Its head twisted around as if something had come loose in its neck and only needed to be tightened.

Lou had cupped his hands gently around the crippled bird and carried it onto the porch. He trapped it under one of his mother's milk crates and set one of his mother's bricks on top of it. He'd been suddenly pleased with himself. His bird was alive and safe in his care, his first rescue attempt a success. He remembered how anxious he was to show his father.

He'd retrieved a box from the basement, one of those five-sided boxes where his mother stored her hats. She'd kept them on a dusty wooden shelf in the basement and Lou didn't think she'd mind if he used one for his precious bird. He'd pulled the box off the shelf and removed the lid. It was dark in the basement and the black, fur-lined hat looked like a raccoon, curled up and asleep. He reached in and removed the hat, placing it back on the dusty shelf.

He ran up the stairs with the box and down the narrow driveway to the front porch. He got there in time to see the milk crate overturned and a shining black cat leaping from the porch with the baby bird clamped in its teeth. The cat paused as Lou turned the corner, and then it was gone, racing toward the bushes at the back of the yard, the bird still alive in its jaws.

Lou had watched in horror, powerless. He'd given chase, albeit briefly. Then he fell to his knees in the backyard, letting his head sink into his hands. He swore he'd never come down from his window again. He'd stay in his room and ignore the world outside. And he swore if he ever saw that cat again, he'd kill it. These were promises he'd made to himself, vows he'd made as a boy, on his knees under a summer sun. But they were promises he hadn't kept.

He'd never told his father what happened just as he'd never told anyone about his dreams. He was afraid of what they'd think. He felt he knew now what his father would have said. He'd say, 'get used to it.' He'd tell Lou these were facts of life destined to repeat themselves, imminent events that occur at times of their own choosing. The dreams that follow stay with you forever. They could remain dormant for years and then surface when you least expect. You keep reliving it until you get it right or you die trying. For Lou's father, it had been the latter.

He'd been killed on the job, answering a domestic dispute up in Logan. It had been the same day Lou had decided to become a cop himself. He'd told him that morning before he left for work and by nightfall his father was dead.

They pulled up in front of the hospital and stopped in the cafeteria before going up to Betty's floor. Lou ordered a black coffee. Maggie got hot chocolate. They rode the elevator to the third floor, looking at themselves in the mirrored walls. The second they stepped out they saw Betty coming down the corridor. She was almost running toward them.

'You guys are just in time.'

'Why?'

Betty was smiling. She had a nice smile, Lou thought, as if he'd forgotten what a smile was supposed to look like.

'Catherine Waites is awake.'

'You're kidding. When?'

'Just a little while ago. I was updating the chart in her room. Next thing I know she's asking me for a drink of water.'

'Can we see her?'

'You can but it's not all good news. After the accident we knew she had a brain injury but it was difficult to assess the extent of the damage. We think now that her brain had suffered some oxygen deprivation.'

'What does that mean?'

'She can't remember anything, not a thing. She doesn't even know her own name, doesn't recognize anyone. She's got no recollection of the accident. The doctors said some of her memory might return. Otherwise, she'll have to relearn everything, her whole life.'

'Why don't you go in and see her, Dad?'

'I don't know. What would I say?'

'She doesn't have anyone else. She's all alone in there. You know her. Say anything.'

Lou pushed the door open a few inches and looked in. His arm was still in a sling and his chest felt heavy. He went in and the door closed behind him. Catherine Waites stared up at him. Her eyes were bloodshot and her face was still yellowish and swollen. There were stitches visible along the left side of her head. The respirator was gone. She didn't say a word as Lou came to the side of the bed and sat down. He placed his hand over hers.

'Hello, Catherine. I'm Lou Klein. An old friend.'